D0031455

Relative Danger

Relative
Danger

Charles Benoit

Poisoned Pen Press

Poisoned
Pen
Press

Copyright © 2004 by Charles Benoit

First Edition 2004

10 9 8 7 6 5 4 3 2 1

Library of Congress Catalog Card Number: 2003114178

ISBN: 1-59058-091-5 Hardcover

Poisoned Pen Press
6962 E. First Ave., Ste. 103
Scottsdale, AZ 85251
www.poisonedpenpress.com
info@poisonedpenpress.com

Printed in the United States of America

To Rose.
All my love, always and all ways.

Chapter 1

The first shot went through the oriental patterned upholstery and lodged in the wood frame of the chair. Later, Singapore police were able to match this bullet to the 7.62 Russian TT-33 Tokarev pistol with the initials CH engraved along the back of the grip that they found under the stairwell behind the New Phoenix Hotel.

Originally known as the Peacock Hotel, the current building was gutted by a suspicious fire in the 1930s and when rebuilt was renamed, naturally, the Phoenix Hotel. Gutted again during the Japanese occupation, the owners rebuilt one more time and, to ensure that their target market—AWOL sailors, prostitutes and opium smokers—would recognize a name they had come to trust, they called it the New Phoenix Hotel.

The second shot passed through the open window of the New Phoenix Hotel and was not recovered.

The third shot struck Russell Pearce in the throat, severing both his jugular vein and his windpipe. There was an amazing amount of blood, but it pooled in the center of the room, under the body. The shots did not attract attention—it took much more than a few gunshots to attract attention in this section of Singapore—but the manager was eventually forced to check the room when Danny Wu, a permanent resident of the hotel, complained that there was blood dripping on his ceiling fan, spraying his flat with a fine, red mist.

The body matched the U.S. passport authorities found in the coat pocket. The passport stated that Russell Pearce was twenty-eight years old, which he was, and a professional athlete, which he was not. Given his passport photo Pearce could have claimed to be an Arrow Shirt model, which would have been closer to the truth, but the blood-covered face was starting to swell in the midday heat, and while it was definitely Pearce, it was no longer photogenic.

The room was not registered in Pearce's name, nor was he a resident of the hotel. The scrawl in the guest book, like most of the signatures in the New Phoenix guest book, was illegible and fictitious. The man who worked the front desk, a Kashmir Sikh who also served as the hotel's pimp, stated that he had no recollection of who rented the room and that he did not see Pearce enter the hotel, nor did he hear anything unusual since gunshots were not all that unusual at the Phoenix. He had his own reasons for not cooperating with the police but he also had three twenty-pound notes in his wallet that ensured his lack of cooperation.

For the past month, Pearce had been staying at Raffles, the once spectacular colonial hotel that served as a second home for many of the region's expatriates and the handful of tourists that were trickling back to the island. He had a modest single room and his freshly laundered clothes hung in his closet. The staff and guests remembered him as friendly and carefree, typically American in that he was just too loud most of the time. He drank, no more so than everyone else, at the hotel's Long Bar, but avoided the fruity gin slings for which the hotel was famous.

His conversation centered on sports and he nightly lectured on the superiority of American baseball over sports he did not understand. He proved willing to build an impressive bar tab and therefore he was mourned and missed for almost two days.

To assist in paying this bar tab and outstanding hotel bill, his possessions were claimed by the hotel and sold to a used clothing store in the Islamic quarter. His sunglasses were donated to the chief porter, and, in case he was indeed a professional athlete, his baseball glove and ball were placed in the hotel's already overcrowded trophy case. A handwritten card identified the tattered objects.

Russell Pearce had mentioned, often, that he was waiting for his friend Charley Hodge to arrive. He said his friend was "a firecracker" and that they would paint the town red when Charley got there. Since the authorities already had the CH engraved murder weapon, everyone assumed that while Charley had arrived, the reunion did not go as Pearce had planned. Charley Hodge was never found.

For the two days that the murder was a topic at the Long Bar, patrons joked that while Russ and Charley had not painted the town red, they did a fine job painting Danny Wu's room.

Chapter 2

Twenty kilometers outside of Toronto, Douglas Pearce reflected on his first visit to a foreign country.

Three hours earlier he had crossed the Rainbow Bridge in Niagara Falls and passed through the security check without the guard so much as asking him if he was an escaped felon or weapons smuggler. No passport, no visas, no "papers, please"—just "have a nice visit." Not that he was an escaped felon or a weapons smuggler, but he was disappointed they didn't even ask.

Douglas Pearce had left his home outside Pottsville, Pennsylvania; earlier that morning and, other than having to ask for directions three times, he had had little trouble. So far this international travel thing was all right by Doug.

There was that confusion about the speed limit, and it took him a frantic ten minutes to figure out that "Speed Limit 100" meant 100 *kilometers* an hour. He managed to get his Ford pickup to a truck-shaking ninety before he realized his mistake. Still, the Canadians seemed to treat the speed limit as a mere suggestion and, even at ninety miles an hour, he was passed on both sides.

From what he could tell, Canada seemed a lot like the U.S. True, he had only traveled through a small part of it, but then he hadn't seen much of the U.S. either. He knew a fair piece of central Pennsylvania, bits of western New York State, and most of the area around the Massaweipi Boy Scout Camp in West

Virginia; where he had spent six days when he was a kid. Most everything he had ever seen looked a lot like central Pennsylvania, just sometimes not as hilly.

He worked at the Odenbach Brewery in Pottsville, or he had until four weeks ago when, for no reason he could figure, he was laid off. Sure, he'd been late now and then, and he took home an occasional six-pack, but so did everyone else. He wasn't the worst employee they had, in fact he was probably better than most. But old man Odenbach had called him in, told him foreign investors were phasing out his position, and gave him a check for a thousand bucks. In the eighteen years he had worked there it was only the third time the old man had talked to him—one of those times he had mistaken Doug for someone else. And the grand surprised him, too. The Odenbach family was not noted for giving their employees any more than they deserved, and Doug couldn't figure out any reason why he'd deserved it. Doug had replayed his meeting with the old man dozens of times and it still didn't make sense.

Really, he thought, nothing in my life has made sense since I got that letter.

"Dear Mr. Pearce," it read. "You don't know me but I was a friend of your Uncle Russell."

Uncle Russ. Crazy Uncle Russ. Wild Uncle Russ. Dead Uncle Russ.

No one in the family talked about him, none of the adults who knew him anyway. The only time Doug even heard his name was when he was listening in on late-night whispered conversations in the kitchen. And all he knew about Uncle Russ was what he could piece together from his own screw-ups. When he was caught cheating on an algebra exam, and when the cops busted him for drinking beer in the park, his father warned that if he didn't straighten up he'd end up "just like my lousy brother." Caught smoking cigarettes, "that's how Russell started out." Totaled his first car, "you're no better than he was." A black eye from a barfly, "God, how can there be two in one family?"

Thanks to these comparisons, exaggerated and obscure, Doug was able to determine that Uncle Russ drank whiskey from a hip flask, smoked unfiltered Camels, caught the clap from a prostitute in Philadelphia, was busted out of an unnamed branch of the service, was a reckless driver, and would cheat at cards if he thought he could get away with it. He never wrote, he never visited, and he died in Singapore.

For much of Doug's life it was a simple formula: Fuck up and learn about Uncle Russ.

But there were times, usually in early fall, when his father would get sentimental and make comments that told him more about his uncle. When Doug helped turn a triple play in a county-wide semi-final, his father, over the first beer he had ever bought his son, mumbled that he "looked a lot like Russell out there." And when he nailed thirty skeet in a row, he overheard his father say, "His uncle once got a hundred." Slowly Doug uncovered that, along with being responsible for most of the crimes in central Pennsylvania, Uncle Russ could have made it to the majors, was a decent horseman, taught himself to play the guitar, and would never turn his back on a friend. There were times that Doug felt his father looking at him out of the corner of his eye and he knew that something he had just done sparked a memory his father had thought he'd long forgotten.

Uncle Russ had died fifty years ago in Singapore—end of story. Doug learned never to push for details, not from his father or from his aunts or from his mother's two brothers, who seemed to know more than anyone else, at least they said they did. "He wasn't so bad," Uncle Carl would say, "your dad just never forgave him for running off the way he did. And five years later, when your folks got married, I think he hoped Russ would be there, do the Best Man thing, but of course that didn't happen. That's what your dad remembers." When Doug's father died three years ago, Doug felt that they would tell him more about Uncle Russ, but it was as if his father's last wish were that no one mention his brother again. And no one ever did.

And now someone he didn't know from a foreign country he'd never been to was writing to tell him about an old friend, his uncle. And it was a woman.

"I knew your uncle for about ten years and I have a lot of great memories courtesy of Russell," the letter continued. "I also have a box of his things and I thought you may want them. If you're interested...."

He called the woman, Edna Bowers, in Toronto and made plans to come up that week. He had no place to be on Monday morning, unless sitting on the couch, flicking continuously through the same sixty-two cable channels, was a place to be. At first it was great to be home watching TV all day, but after two weeks of it Doug found the magic was wearing thin. He had added "hanging out at the mall" to his daily itinerary and that made things better, but even that was starting to seem sort of dull. And now the chance to take a few days off before he filed for unemployment and pretended to look for a job looked more interesting than staying home.

Mrs. Bowers sounded like a nice old lady—if she knew his Uncle Russ she had to at least be in her seventies—and of course there was that hope that he'd learn something new about the Pearce family Official Black Sheep.

Doug missed the turnoff, missed the exit, missed the right-hand turn and the second left, and had to drive up and down the street three times before he found the address, an ivy-covered brick building in the Rosedale area, just outside of downtown Toronto. A small brass nameplate by the door held the hand-printed names Mr. and Mrs. Frank Bowers.

When the door opened, Doug figured he had the wrong address. Dressed in the kind of suit he'd seen on network news women, and wearing her tin-colored hair in a short, almost boyish style, this women looked more like a flattering "where are they now?" shot of some Fifties movie starlet than anybody's grandmother. He was ready to apologize and leave when she opened the door further.

"You must be Douglas," she said. "I'm Edna Bowers. I hope you were able to find the place alright, I can't say I've ever given directions from Pottsville before."

"No, I found the place without a problem," he lied and followed her up the stairs and into a brightly lit townhouse. He'd seen places like this, but not in Pottsville. They were the kind you found on the covers of home remodeling magazines and in sitcoms set in wealthy, big-city neighborhoods. Everything, he was sure, was part of a plan created by some high-priced interior designer. He was just as sure that nothing Edna Bowers owned came from K-Mart. Everything matched, everything fit, everything except the large painting on the wall that just did not go with the couch.

The misfit painting was flanked by bookcases, fifteen feet tall, which wrapped around the room. Light poured in from the skylight and the glass doors leading to the patio. He had never been in a home like this before. No television, though. And that probably meant no cable. Rough.

"I can't thank you enough for calling me and agreeing to come up. It had been years since I thought about Russ and, from the way he talked, I assumed that no one in the family would want to hear from me."

She pointed to a leather chair as she took a seat on the couch across from him. "Did your parents tell you much about Russ?" she asked.

"No, I'm afraid not, Mrs. Bowers, and I can't say that I know a lot about him either. You were right, my family wasn't too fond of my uncle."

"First, there's no Mr. Bowers," she said, "I just put that on the door to scare off trouble. And please, call me Edna."

"Well, uh, Edna," he said, "I didn't know him—my uncle that is—but I guess you did. And you're the only one talking."

She laughed as she stood up. "That's funny," she said, "there was a time when *everybody* talked about Russ. I was just about to have some wine, care for some?" He said yes, although he would have preferred a beer. Nobody he hung out with drank wine except at Christmas. That gay guy in the brewery's accounting department drank wine. At least he looked like he'd drink wine, and he looked gay. Here's the first thing I won't tell the guys back home, he thought.

While she got the drinks he took a look around the room. The books were a mix of biographies and fiction, but nothing like the stuff the women at the brewery read. No thick romances with busty women with piles of hair hanging on half-dressed men with even more hair. Some of the books were in what he assumed was French and he wondered if she could actually read them or if she had them only for looks, like his copy of *The Stand*. There were some seashells, some small wooden carvings, and a lot of old black and white photos in silver frames. He picked up one, a group shot of men and women sitting in a park, smoking cigars and holding up bottles of beer. In the far background, to the left, he could make out the Eiffel Tower. His eyes locked onto a stunning, dark-haired woman in the front row. She sat on the ground, her head tilted a bit to the left, a half drunk look in her eyes, a look Doug found sexy. She wore baggy khakis and a man's shirt, but he could still tell she had an athlete's body—firm and well maintained. He looked at her face again. She was amazing, like an actress or a model, but at the same time she looked so approachable. She was holding a cigar, too. Then it hit him. Same-shaped face, same eyes, younger than now, of course, but it was her. Edna Bowers, the old woman getting the drinks. He put the photo down.

"I hope you like cabernet," Edna said as she returned to the room, handing Doug both the bottle and an empty glass. "I wasn't sure so I didn't pour. Some people find my taste in wines a bit overpowering, especially this early in the day."

Doug looked at the label like he knew what he was looking for. "Don't worry," she said, "it's not a Canadian wine. I might be a poor host, but I'm not a cruel one."

Doug laughed, but he wasn't sure why. He was already feeling like some pervert—the way he had ogled the dark-haired Edna in the photo. Now he began to feel ignorant as well.

"Did you notice the photo of Russ?" she said, crossing over to the bookcases. She picked up the group photo Doug had looked at and he wondered if she had seen him staring. "Back in Paris, just after the war, a group of us used to spend too much time being crazy. We had this nickname for our group…a policeman actually gave it to us…he called us *les suspects habituals.*" She smiled so Doug smiled, not about to ask. "That's Russ with his arm around my roommate."

Doug had only seen one picture of his uncle, many years before. His father had left his gun cabinet unlocked once and, taped inside the door, Doug had found a faded picture of his father standing next to Uncle Russ—it had to be him, the family resemblance was too strong. They were teenagers, Doug's age when he saw it, and they were standing on his grandfather's front porch. And they were laughing. His father never left the case unlocked again, never asked about the missing "photography magazines" Doug had found on the shelf. When his father died three years ago he looked in the cabinet before his Uncle Carl loaded it on his truck, but the photo was gone.

The face in Edna's group photo startled Doug. The man looked so much older than the image he had created of his uncle. He needed a shave, had a fighter's build, and looked a hell of a lot tougher than his brother. His eyes, even when he was laughing, looked hard. He had the same firm jaw line as most of the Pearce men, the same small ears, the same charcoal-colored hair that, if he had lived, would have turned more gray than black. But there was something about the man in the photo, something none of his uncles seemed to have, an edge maybe, a sense of danger that just didn't fit with the genes he knew. So this was the terror of the Pearce clan, the token rebel, this twenty-four-year-old with Dillinger's eyes? Actually, it wasn't hard to imagine.

"Russell had the best stories," Edna said, breaking the silence. "You never knew if they were true or not and I suppose we didn't care. His gift was keeping us all entertained with tales right out of Conrad, full of jungles, gunfights, jailbreaks, beautiful women and jealous husbands. Just when you were certain he was making the whole thing up, that it was just too much, he'd say something like 'and that's where I got this…' and he'd pull out some souvenir—a glass eye, a shark's tooth on a chain, an opium pipe with a bullet lodged in the bowl, a fresh scar. They were never proof, and he never convinced *me* the stories were real, but it was fun listening and pretending. We all pretended a bit too much then, I suppose. It was a different time. But," she said, motioning with her wine glass, "I guess everything I have I owe to your Uncle Russell."

Doug followed the wine glass and took in the room. "He must have left you a fortune."

Edna laughed and sipped more of her wine. "The only things Russ left me with were memories," she said and laughed again. "But, yes, I guess it was a fortune because I wouldn't trade those memories for the world. What I meant was that the things I learned from your uncle allowed me to earn my keep. His expertise was smuggling and you couldn't spend as much time with Russ as I did and not master a few skills. Later, when I returned to Canada, I put those skills to use."

"You were smuggling things into Canada?"

"Out mostly, and mostly south. But only until I put together enough money to apply my skills in a legitimate import/export business. I scraped along, built the business up and sold the whole thing to a wonderful gentleman from Hong Kong back in the mid-Eighties. Since then I've kept busy investing in small businesses overseas. It pays the bills."

Doug looked around the room again. "You must have big bills."

Edna refilled her glass, topped off Doug's and motioned him to take a seat on the couch. "This is what I called you about—all that's left of Russ' earthly goods." From a shelf below the photo she took out a cardboard box, about the same size as a twelve-pack of Odenbach cans, and set it on the glass-topped table in front of the couch.

"This was forwarded to me not so very long ago when an old friend passed on. I had forgotten all about her, in a way, until I got this. The poor dear had so little yet she held on to this. Well, that was Russ—women just couldn't resist him."

The box was made of thick cardboard, like an old suitcase, a neat leather strap holding it shut. It had a few stickers pasted on the side—Tusker Beer "It's Tusker, Buster!" Pacific Rail Lines Baggage Claim #109. Madame Tussaud's Wax Museum. U.S.N. Montana/visitor—and Doug was trying to guess if the box was his uncle's or the late poor dear's.

Doug unpacked the box, setting each item down on the table. There were some folded *National Geographic* maps with seemingly random locations circled in red or black, bills of lading from a dozen different shipping companies, a penciled-in Pirates-Phillies scorecard from May 2nd, 1948, stacks of addresses, TELEX numbers, and cryptic cables with now-meaningless strings of numbers and letters, overdue bills, an owner's manual for a Norton motorcycle, two pairs of Ray Ban sunglasses, a handful of notes written in what looked to him like Chinese, Arabic, and Russian, an ashtray from Pan Am's Pacific Clipper Air Service…the mementos of a well traveled—if pointless—life. Edna pulled things out at random, explaining the more obscure items, sometimes adding a short anecdote, sometimes a laugh, sometimes a puzzled "I have no idea what this is."

There were two photos, one of Edna looking much as she did in the Paris shot, but this time wearing not much more than a towel. A small towel. "I'll take that if you don't mind, Douglas. I'm afraid I'm not very photogenic."

The second photo must have been taken the same day as the one he had seen in his father's gun cabinet, but it was only of Doug's father, arm cocked like he was ready to toss a baseball to whoever was taking the picture. "My dad," Douglas said, holding up the picture.

"Russ's younger brother, right?"

"Right," he said, hoping this mystery woman would add something like "your uncle talked about him all the time," but she didn't.

"That's it, that's all that's here," Doug said as he started putting things back in the box—last things out, first things back in, like inventory at the brewery.

"There are other things," Edna said. "Postcards and letters. Mostly to me but also to other people we knew. I appear to be the unofficial custodian of the Russell Pearce correspondence collection. Your uncle and I were close and as the people we knew died off, they'd send me their letters and photos. People commit the strangest things to writing. Especially young women. Photos, too."

"I guess they figure that you'd want to enjoy the memories," he said, but she laughed as he said it.

"*My* memories of Russell are quite different, and I was never *that* naive. No, I think they send them to me because they know that I've always had an interest in Russell's death."

"That's funny. I've always had an interest in his life and nobody tells me anything."

"These wouldn't tell you much. You'd learn more about the people who wrote them—or posed for them—than you would about your uncle. But to me each adds something to the puzzle, although I'm not sure what exactly. You see I've had this plan in mind for the longest time—I should have done something about it years ago when I was younger but, well, I didn't. Besides, the letters and things didn't start arriving until a few years ago. I wanted to use this collection of ephemera as a bank of clues and reference material. I thought with that, and a little on-site investigating, we could solve everything."

"What do you mean solve everything?"

"Well your uncle's murder, for starters."

Douglas stared at the woman. "Murder? Uncle Russ was murdered?" He tried to say more but nothing came out.

"Oh my gosh, yes. You didn't know? No one told you?" Edna Bowers set down her glass and leaned forward, gently placing her hand on top of Doug's knee. "Of course I thought you knew. I'm so sorry."

Doug shook his head, "Oh no, it's okay. Like I said, I really didn't know the guy and hey, he's been dead for years. Really, it's alright, I'm just surprised." He sighed, finished his glass of wine and held out the empty glass for more.

"I suppose you want the details? Well, he was shot in a hotel room in Singapore. The police suspected his friend Charley Hodge. I heard they found a gun, but they never made an arrest and I know Charley couldn't have done it anyway. Whoever did it—killed Russell—did it for the jewels. Russ had enemies—my God did he have enemies—but not in that part of the world. It was a robbery and Russ must have tried something silly and that's it. He bled to death on a hotel room floor." Edna stood up and grabbed the empty wine bottle. "I hope this does not sound rude, but I'm having some more. Care to join me?"

◇◇◇

Two hours later, Douglas decided that he liked wine. He liked Edna Bowers, too. He liked Fritz and Toni and Carmen and Hani and Shorty and everyone else in the silver-framed photo. He liked Paris, he liked Madrid, he liked that little place in, where was that? Andorra? Well, he liked it wherever it was.

Edna had lots of stories and lots of wine and they went well together. She did most of the talking, which was good because he had no interesting stories to tell. What could he match against her tale about the bullfight and the one-legged barber—his story about sneaking five people into the drive-in? Or her adventures with the barnstorming troupe? Or the fire at the circus, the German landmine, Bobo the gorilla, the Greek pornographer, sailing on the Nile or camping out in the Taj Mahal? He started to tell her about trying to make a still in his garage but that reminded her of the time she and Russ were stuck in Afghanistan with fifty cases of Russian vodka and no truck. She had had the life, he thought. Him? What kind of life do you get when you live in Pottsville?

It's not as if he didn't want an exciting life. He did. He had his James Bond daydreams, his Indiana Jones fantasies. And he had his Walter Mitty life. In high school a teacher had made the class write letters to themselves that she would mail back in ten years, and, true to her word, ten years later he got the letter. After an opening paragraph about how stupid of an assignment this was, he listed twenty things he said he wanted to do by the time he got this letter: "Number One, sleep with fifty HOT women, Number Two, skydive, Number Three, bag a twelve pointer, Number Four, win at Indy, Number Five, see Kiss live …." Ten years later he had accomplished none of them, with the possible exception of the last one: "Number Twenty, be a bum."

But how do you have an exciting life these days? You can't just run off and sign on some tramp steamer. He had obligations, bills, a truck loan. You have to be responsible, not like the old days. The world wasn't like it used to be, at least that's the impression he got when he watched the Discovery Channel.

"…so I figure," she was saying, "if you're interested I'd pay all the bills and…."

"I'm sorry," Doug said, snapping back, "I phased out there a second. What's this about bills?"

"I was saying that if you wanted to travel around the world a bit, I'd pay the bill."

"Whoa, I really tuned out. Can you go over it one more time from the top?" Doug was focused now, drink down, elbows resting on his knees, his hands propping up his chin.

Edna set her drink down too. "Like I said, I think we can use the information in your uncle's letters to solve his murder and clear Charley's name. You don't realize how much that means to me. And you could recover the jewels. I've read all these letters dozens of times and I think I can retrace his route pretty closely. I recognize a lot of the names and places and …."

"And you want me to go?" Doug interrupted. "How come? I mean that's nice of you, but why don't you go?" That sounded rude, he thought, so he added, "I mean if you know the places and all, it could be like a vacation, you could clear your friend's name, an adventure, like old times."

"Old times are just that, Douglas. Old. I have no trouble getting around here in Toronto or in London, but I'd have to go to Singapore and places a lot less developed. Don't get me wrong, I'd love to see them again, but I'm afraid I'm really a bit too old this time. Besides, I've seen it all—wouldn't you like a chance to see it yourself?"

She's reading my mind, he thought. And where is Singapore, anyway?

"I figure that you could visit all the places in a couple of months and the costs wouldn't be as great as you think. Besides, I'd be paying for it all. And you do have some time now that you're out of work."

Doug looked up.

"Oh don't look at me like that Doug, you told me yourself not thirty minutes ago. And it's nothing to be ashamed of. Not going on this paid vacation, now that would be a shame."

He picked up his glass again and took another large sip. "It sure sounds inviting, but I've never been anywhere. Hell, I got lost coming here. How would I ever get around overseas?"

"I've got that all worked out," she said. "I know people who would check up on you, names of hotels, places to visit. It's not like traveling in the Fifties, you know. It's all five-star hotels and McDonald's now—not that you'll be spending time at either—but it is so much simpler than you'd imagine."

"Oh," Doug said, surprised at how disappointed he felt. "So I guess there's no adventure in it, just picking up some information and stuff?"

She smiled as she took a last sip of wine. "There'll be adventure, Douglas. I guarantee that."

Chapter 3

For the fourth time that morning, Doug stopped himself whistling the opening bars of "As Time Goes By."

"Casablanca. I'm in freaking Casablanca," he said out loud as he looked over his balcony at the Sea Port Hotel, across the palm-lined street from the last remaining shops and alleys of the old quarter. He had arrived the night before and, just as Edna promised, it had all gone smoothly. The flight from Kennedy, economy, was smooth and he didn't know what all those comedians had been talking about, the food was great. He had a window seat but there was nothing to see. The airport in Casablanca was better than the one in Scranton, and there was a driver from the hotel with his name on a card, just like the movies. There was cold beer in the fridge in the room and a basket of fruit on the table. He had a passport with an exotic-looking Arabic/French stamp in it and a black folder with his instructions was waiting for him at the front desk. This was definitely cool.

He picked up the folder that contained the paperwork Edna said he'd need for this part of the trip. There was a map of the city with a few key addresses highlighted, photocopies of pages from travel magazines, a list of contacts and phone numbers, and the first set of instructions, neatly typed out. It was still early—the breakfast buffet did not open for another hour—so he pulled a chair out onto the balcony, grabbed a beer and the folder. It was already warm, but comfortable, and the smell of fresh bread—of all the smells he had expected in Morocco, fresh bread was not one of them—floated up from the bakery next to the hotel.

"The information I have that pertains to the last weeks of your uncle's life starts here in Casablanca. According to the papers I have, he arrived on June 16, 1948. He signed off the *Belle Noctche* and received four hundred and twelve dollars in back pay. Apparently, he had gotten into a fight with a shipmate over some missing hashish and the shipmate's younger sister and the captain sided with the other man. There were also some rumors about how he had conspired with Jesus to cheat his shipmates out of money."

Doug reread the last line, but it didn't make sense. The next line, however, cleared it up.

"Jesus Alverez was the radio operator on the *Belle Noctche* and, according to Charley, they would delay the results of sporting events. It's a common Spanish name and an old confidence trick," she added.

"According to information I have here from Charley," the note continued, "the two of them—and a third person Charley never met—were involved in a complex operation involving some merchandise that was being re-routed from its original destination to Palermo, Sicily. Charley was supposed to finalize the deal but became romantically involved with the wife of the port agent and the deal fell through. This is what led them to getting involved with the jewels."

It's all how you say things, Doug thought. The way she wrote it you'd hardly think criminal activity was involved.

"The third man, the one Charley knew only as Sasha, arranged for Russell to meet Omar Sabagh, a Syrian involved in the black market. These two, then, worked out the plans for the theft. Charley was indisposed at the time."

He tried the term out to see how well it would work. Indispose you. Indispose off. It was indisposingly great. We indisposed all night. Nope. It didn't work.

"Attached are the addresses of some people I want you to look up and I've marked them on the map as well. I want you to talk to them before I send you more details about the actual theft. That way you are not influenced by the things I say and are able to listen clearly to their accounts."

This was her plan? It sure sounded a lot more planned when he was half-drunk in Toronto. What was he supposed to hear and why would any of these people talk to him? It didn't make sense, but she was paying for it. Maybe it would fall together as he went. Relax and enjoy it, he thought.

He put the packet back in the folder and picked up a few postcards he bought in the hotel lobby. "Hey Guys," he wrote, "You'll never guess where I am."

◇◇◇

Thanks to the map and the saint-like patience of a young police officer eager to practice his English, it took Doug only forty minutes to find the first address on the list, a small restaurant less than a half mile from the hotel. Casablanca was not at all as he pictured it, but he realized that his picture was based more on a California movie set than anything else. There were wide streets radiating out from central hubs along which small cars of some Euro-design jockeyed for position at each stoplight. The buildings looked like four- or five-story wedding cakes with the ornate facades, rooflines, and window frames resembling intricate frosting patterns. The corners curved gently, blending into the next wedding cake building, and every floor had a balcony and every balcony had the same wrought iron rail, painted the same flat white. Up close, however, the dusting of built-up carbon from the unleaded and diesel fuel turned the frosting into ordinary cement. There was no sand, no open market bazaar, no camels, no Rick's.

At every rounded corner there were outdoor cafés, a remnant of French rule the photocopy said, but rather than chic Parisian women sipping espresso, the tables were filled with men—and only men—drinking pot after pot of a sickeningly sweet mint tea, smoking French cigarettes, and eating pastries. With every building and every street corner looking the same, it was by chance that Doug stumbled upon the right street corner and Le Café du Desert. He cleared his throat and took a deep breath. Time to start the investigation.

"Good morning, I am looking for a Mr. Ahmed. Is he in?"

"Tea?" asked a short man in a red vest and bow tie.

"No, just can I talk to Mr. Ahmed?"

"No tea? Coffee?"

"I'm looking for Mr. Ahmed," Doug said, trying not to raise his voice, but knowing that he was. "I need to talk to Mr. Ahmed. I have a message for him from America."

"Oh," the short man said. "A message from America for Mr. Ahmed. I am Mr. Ahmed. Please sit, I will bring you tea." His English was excellent, but there was a strong, and to Doug, unidentifiable, accent.

Doug had a seat outside, next to the door, and Mr. Ahmed soon returned with a small, steaming pot and two glasses. He poured the tea, raising the pot up over his head as he poured, a thin stream of mint tea filling the glass from the center.

"If you're Mr. Ahmed, how come you didn't say so?" Doug said as he sipped the tea, trying not to drop the scalding-hot glass.

"No one in Moroc calls me Mr. Ahmed. Here I am Fahad. I have not been Mr. Ahmed since before you were born. I did not know that anyone who knew Mr. Ahmed was still alive." He sipped his tea, drawing a finger along the bottom of his white moustache to remove any drops. He'd only be Edna's age, thought Doug. He must have had a harder life.

"Did you know a Russell Pearce, Mr. Ahmed? I have a message for you from him."

"He's still alive?" the man said with sudden interest. "I can't believe he'd still be alive, he was so reckless. We met not far from here, a long, long time ago. He bought me my first real hat. Brought it with him from New York City." Mr. Ahmed poured some more tea, this time without the flourish reserved for tourists. "Are you from New York City?"

"Ah, no, I'm from Pottsville."

"Is Pottsville near New York City?"

"No, it's in Pennsylvania." He tried not to sound apologetic but did anyway.

"Oh that is close. Have you been to New York City?" the old man said, sipping his boiling tea.

"Ah, no," and now he was apologizing, "I haven't."

"You come all the way to Morocco to sit at my café and yet you don't go to New York City? I would rather go to New York City than Morocco, and I'm an old man."

"I'll get there someday, but right now…."

"Somedays don't always come," he said, wagging his finger at Doug. "*Carpe diem*. Do you know Latin?"

"Afraid not. Look, what I need is…."

"*Parlez-vous français?*"

"No. I just was wondering…."

"*Wash kt'aref Arabia?*"

"Huh?"

"You seem quite unprepared for life outside of Pottsville," Mr. Ahmed laughed. "But here you are!"

Should I be embarrassed or insulted, Doug thought, looking at the hunks of tea leaves that congealed at the bottom of his glass. And who drinks tea out of a glass anyway? "Yup. Here I am," he said.

"So, you have a message for me?"

Doug decided not to tell him about his uncle; there were too many questions he did not have the answers to yet. And this was it, his first contact and his first clue to the mystery. He found himself leaning forward and talking in a softer voice. "I'm supposed to tell you that I've taken up the hunt for the eye and that you could help me find Sasha."

The old man looked at him for a moment. "What does this mean?"

"What do you mean, What does this mean? I'm doing the hunt thing now and you're supposed to have me meet Sasha."

"Who?"

"I don't know, you're supposed to know that," Doug said. He took a deep breath and tried again. "Look, you know Russell, right? Well he sent me here to find you and I did. Now I'm supposed to tell you that I'm on the hunt...."

"What hunt?"

"The hunt for the eye, that's what I'm supposed to say."

"What eye?" the man asked, still looking at Doug with his head tilted to the right, squinting.

"The eye. That's the code word I'm supposed to use. He said you'd know what it meant."

"Someone has lost an eye and I know where it is? How is this possible?"

"No, that's not it."

"Oh I see, I see," Mr. Ahmed said. "It is a metaphor. Is that the word? Someone has gone blind, no?"

Another deep breath. "No, no, no, it's not a *real* eye, it's not an eye at all. It's a code word for something else."

"For what?"

"I can't say."

"Why not?"

"Because it's a code," Doug said, leaning so far forward his nose almost touched Mr. Ahmed's forehead. "You don't tell people what the code is supposed to mean, they should know," he explained, leaning back again. "Now, let's try again. Russell told me to tell you I am on the hunt for the eye, do you understand so far?"

"Yes, I understand, you are on the hunt for the eye."

"Right."

"And I'm supposed to help you see Sasha?"

"Yes, exactly."

"Alright, but there is something I must know first."

Don't say it, Doug thought, please don't say it.

"What is the eye and who is Sasha?"

Doug leaned his back against the chair and allowed his head to arch back, his eyes closing as his face was warmed by the mid-morning sun. He sat like this for several minutes, not moving and barely breathing. The old man sat patiently across from him, mumbling instructions to other waiters and waving for another pot of tea. Doug tried to clear his mind and relax. Day one, person one, and I'm lost. He heard the old man sip his tea again and clear his throat.

"Are you looking for a jewel?"

Doug opened his eyes and stared into the bright Moroccan sky.

"I would think Russell would be looking for that jewel he helped steal, not some fake eye."

Doug leaned forward again. "Yes, it's a jewel, but we're not supposed to call it a jewel, we're supposed to use the code word."

"Oh that's silly," the old man said, happy now that he knew what they were supposed to be talking about. "Why would you need to talk in a code?"

"So people don't know what we're talking about," Doug explained.

"Well, it certainly worked," Mr. Ahmed said, draining his fifth cup of tea. "I had no idea what you meant."

"Not us, but others. We don't want people to know we are looking for the jewel."

The old man smiled and shook his head. "My friend, *everyone* looks for that jewel. Everyone talks about it, everyone knows about it, well everyone who is my age and who was here after the war, that is, so maybe it is not everyone, but it is everyone that I consider worth talking to. You see, when that jewel was stolen the authorities looked everywhere for it. They said it caused quite an international problem. Some people claim it was one of the crown jewels from Buckingham Palace, others said that the Nazis hid it here during the war. I don't know what it is, and I have never seen it, but I do know your friend helped steal it and that someone was killed and that it was never recovered. For a while we assumed that it was still here in Casablanca since we had heard from Russell's friend, Charley, that Russell did not have it anymore."

"You knew Charley as well?"

"Everyone knew those two. You seen one, you seen them both."

"Did they come here, to this café?"

"Of course, of course," Mr. Ahmed said as he waved his hand, implying that the answer was obvious. "It may not look it now but there was a time when this was the, um, what is it? Ah, the 'hot spot,' yes, it was the hot spot in Casa. There were tables lined up halfway down this block and each one filled till curfew. Russell and Charley were here whenever they were in Morocco. Usually chasing after the same French skirt. They were here when they planned the heist, at least that is what the others say."

"The others?"

"The people who were interested in making as much money as quickly as possible. Obviously," Mr. Ahmed said as he smiled and pointed with his chin to the rest of the café, "I was not interested in getting rich quickly. And it does not appear I am interested in getting rich slowly, either."

Douglas took another sip of his tea, all mint and sugar. Uncle Russell might have sat right here, he thought, sipping the same kind of tea, and from the looks of it, out of the same glass. The sun glinting off the fresh paint on the balustrade and the slowly rotating ceiling fan blades casting intermittent shadows over the tables inside—it might have looked just like that in 1948, he thought, but the neon Diet Coke sign and the hum of the ink-jet printer feeding out another computer-generated lunch receipt made it hard to completely capture the mood.

Two waiters came over to the table, speaking in rapid bursts of either French or Arabic, Doug couldn't tell, but it was clear that there was some sort of problem. Mr. Ahmed spoke to them both and then turned to Doug. "I must see to business, I'm afraid. And I did not even get your name. Douglas? Well, Douglas, I do hope you can stop back and perhaps we can talk some more. Tomorrow? Excellent. Till then, *Ma'Salama*."

Doug was halfway down the block before he remembered to ask the old man about Sasha.

He hailed a cab and handed the driver the address that Edna had sent as contact number two. It was written in Edna's neat, tight script in English, Arabic, and French. The driver nodded as he pulled away from the curb, popping in an Arabic music tape which he played loud enough to shake the windows. Douglas Pearce leaned back and decided to enjoy the moment, the taste of the sweet tea still fresh in his mouth, the shops and traffic of Casablanca racing by the window. Although he could not hear himself, he softly sang along, the words not matching the music. "You must remember this, a kiss is still a kiss…."

◇◇◇

The cab pulled up in front of yet another white French Colonial building, but instead of a café this building's rounded corner housed a shop offering what it claimed were authentic antiques, Moroccan carpets, and curios. Slipped in accidentally between three-month-old "antique Berber chests" and overpriced carpets of dubious quality were indeed a handful of authentic antiques, but the owner could no longer tell the real from the fake even in his own shop.

Abdullah Zubaid had never wanted to live in Morocco. When his father left Syria in 1935, Abdullah had little choice but to go with him, his mother and sisters dead from an unnamed epidemic that swept through Aleppo the winter before. And Abdullah had never wanted to own this shop but when his father had a stroke in the early Seventies, he had little choice again. And when his father died eight years later Abdullah had sons of his own to worry about and no skills other than an ability to predict what the tourists would pay too much for. An excellent location, the building in his name since his father's death, and no ambition all combined to keep Abdullah unhappily employed.

When the American entered the shop—only an American would wear blue jeans on a day that would reach ninety—it was still before noon, too early to expect a big sale from the tourist trade. Abdullah put on his best I-don't-speak-English face in case the man wanted directions to a different shop in the neighborhood. He picked up a pen and started writing nonsense in

Arabic to look busy. After fifty years in this business he knew a no-sale when he saw one.

"Excuse me, are you the owner?" Doug asked.

Abdullah looked up over the top of his glasses. It was a look that made tourists uncomfortable and he noticed the shuffling of the feet that signaled it had worked again.

"I'm looking for the owner. I have a message for the owner from America."

Abdullah said nothing, his face concealing his sudden interest in this American.

"Do you speak English? I'm looking for the owner. Owner? You? This shop you?" Doug said pointing to the man and then around the shop, trying to get the man to understand.

"Yes, this shop me," Abdullah said without moving his eyes off the American. "I'm the owner and the proprietor, the head sales associate, and chief executive officer for Abdullah bin Abdullah Antiquities and Exports, Limited. How may I be of assistance?"

"Oh," Doug said, "I didn't think you spoke English, you just looked like you didn't understand."

"Yes, that was obvious." He was not making this easy for the American and he still wore the expression that he knew made even his friends uncomfortable. "Now, what was this you said about a message from America?"

"The message is from Russell Pearce. I'm to tell you that I've taken up the hunt for the eye."

"I do not know a Russell Pearce and I know nothing about an eye. I wish you luck on your hunt, however." Abdullah Zubaid looked back down to the nonsense he had scribbled as if it was an important message.

"I've been told that everyone who lived in Casablanca in the late 1940s knew Russell Pearce. He had a friend named Charley Hodge. They were American, does that help?"

"No it does not, I'm afraid. I lived right above this shop most of my life and I assure you I did not know either of your Americans." The shop owner looked up from his paper and removed his glasses. "Is there anything else I can do for you, sir?"

Doug shifted his weight from foot to foot like he did when a supervisor at the brewery had to talk to him about his work. "Look, I'm not really looking for an eye, I'm looking for a jewel that was stolen here in Morocco in 1948. Russell Pearce and Charley Hodge stole it and everyone has been looking for it ever since."

"How interesting," Abdullah Zubaid said without emotion. "Now why would a jewel thief whom I did not know want to tell me that you are now on the hunt for his ill-gotten gains?"

"I don't really know myself," Doug admitted, "I was simply told to tell you and that you would help me out. Are you sure none of this rings a bell with you? I've come a long way and I was told you would know about it and could help me."

"I'm sorry that you have been inconvenienced but that does not change anything. I did not know this Mr. Pearce or his friend and I can't see how I can help you, unless of course you wish to purchase a fine, handmade Moroccan carpet?" Abdullah Zubaid managed to smile for the first time, but this did not make him seem any friendlier.

"Look, I'm sorry I bothered you," Doug said as he reached in his pocket, pulling out a business card from the Sea Port Hotel.

"This is where I'm staying. If you think of anything or talk to someone who remembers Russell Pearce, please call me." He wrote his name on the back of the card before handing it to the shop owner.

Abdullah Zubaid looked at the card and back up at Doug. "A relation, Mr. Pearce? I will call if I hear anything but I sincerely doubt that I will." He slid his glasses back on and watched the American weave his way out of the shop. He watched Doug until he hailed a cab and pulled away into the rapidly warming morning.

Abdullah leaned back in his swivel chair and sat silently for a few moments, contemplating what to do. Finally he opened the top desk drawer and began setting its contents on the top of the desk. Folders, papers, invoices, and handfuls of paperclips soon covered the worn green blotter. He pulled the drawer out of the desk and carefully tapped the stray erasers, bits of pencil lead and rubber bands into a wastebasket next to his chair. He then turned the drawer over and set it on the papers on his desk. Tacked to the bottom of the drawer was an envelope. Using a letter opener, he pried off the tacks.

He had put the envelope there back in 1982 when Casablanca's phone system was updated and many of the old numbers had changed. His father had shown him the original envelope when he was still a teenager, but that envelope and the phone number it contained were thrown out when the messenger who brought him the money each month told him that the contact procedure had changed. The money was not much—for the past six years it was ten U.S. dollars—but it was consistent and it cost him nothing to take it. The money would stop now, of course, but Abdullah Zubaid assumed there would be some sort of bonus involved. The instructions were clear but neither the shopkeeper nor his father ever planned to have to follow them. The gulf that separated him from that strange day when his father first showed him the envelope seemed small.

He dialed the numbers not knowing what to expect. The instructions said he should call every hour and let it ring many times so he was surprised when the receiver picked up on the fifth ring. "There has been a man asking questions," he said to the silence at the other end, "about Russell Pearce and the jewel."

Chapter 4

Douglas Pearce sat at the end of his bed, his heart still racing, trying to figure out how he slept through it the morning before.

The final refrains of the call to prayer reverberated through the walls of the hotel. The mosque's minaret was less than five feet from the bedroom window, and its six stadium-sized, tinny-sounding speakers blasted out a thousand watts of reminder to all believers: *Al-salatu khayr min al-nawm*—prayer is better than sleep. With the first *Allahu Akbar,* Douglas shot out of the bed, stumbling over a chair and his backpack in the predawn grayness. Every mosque in Casablanca, in Morocco, in any place where a mosque waited as the sun created a false dawn sky, echoed the call.

Religion was one of those subjects, like sex with a buddy's sister or financial investments, that Douglas was never comfortable talking about. He was raised a Methodist but had no idea what that really meant. He'd been dragged to church, literally, as a kid but it always seemed to Doug that it was more of an ordeal for his parents than it was to him. His father wore the same suit each week along with the same bored and angry look. His mother was a better dresser but no better at hiding her lack of interest, although she did enjoy the singing. They never went to church socials, never volunteered for any of the endless committees Reverend Mitchell announced each week and usually ducked out before the service was over, "to beat the traffic home." Doug could not imagine anyone taking religion so seriously that they would pray five times a day, especially when it started this early in the morning.

He showered and dressed—"Why didn't I bring any lighter pants?" he thought—and reviewed the game plan he wrote out last night in the hotel's two-stool bar. He made four stops the day before; the first was promising and the last three were dead ends. Today he'd head back to Le Café du Desert to talk to Mr. Ahmed some more, try the last name on the list, and call Edna Bowers to bring her up to date.

It was a short plan.

In the movies the hero always knew where to go, who to talk to, and how to follow a lead. It amazed him how James Bond could be playing baccarat in Monaco and stumble onto a plot to take over the world before the opening credits. Here he was in Casablanca, with only a small possible lead, one more name to check and then…what? And what was he supposed to tell Edna? So far he had spent well over a thousand of her dollars and what did he have to show for it? He looked at his plan again as he went downstairs for breakfast, hoping that something more would have magically appeared on the list.

There was one other guest in the small café setting, an older gentleman in a tan linen suit sipping mint tea and breaking apart a fresh pastry. Douglas sat at a table near the window and drained a tall glass of orange juice—another one of Morocco's pleasant surprises—and ate a fruit-filled pastry. He stared out the window wondering if anyone he knew actually cared that he was here.

"Do you remember that perfect rejoinder Rick Blaine supplied the Nazis as to why he was here?"

The question startled Doug out of his daydream. He looked around to the well-dressed gentleman, the only other person in the room. "I'm sorry," Doug said. "What was that?"

"*Casablanca*. The movie. Humphrey Bogart's character is asked why he came to this Allah-forsaken city." The man stirred even more sugar into his mint tea as he talked. His voice was smooth and comforting, like a voice-over in a nature documentary, a European documentary by the accent. "'I came for the waters,' he tells Major Strasa. 'But there are no waters in Casablanca, Mr. Blaine.' And then, with perfect timing, Bogart says 'I was misinformed.' Every time I come to Casablanca I am reminded of that scene. I was misinformed. That sums up nicely my experiences with this city."

"Yeah." Doug added, "Great flick. Too bad the real Casablanca isn't still like that."

"It never was, I'm afraid," he said as he brushed some flakes of pastry out of his close-cropped white goatee. "I've been in and out of here since the Forties and this is about as exotic as it ever got. It still has the red light district, but the old quarter—the medina—is all but gone and they still don't have a single decent museum in this city, although there are a few interesting mosques and that monstrosity they are building by the coast, the Mosque of Hasan II. Have you seen it? No? I had heard it was breathtaking but again, I was misinformed. They say it will be the second largest mosque in the world, it being bad form to go one larger than Mecca, and it will prove to the world that, while we can surpass the Blue Mosque in size, we have fallen woefully behind in style."

They have a red light district here? thought Doug.

"No, if exotic locale is why you came to Morocco, I suggest you get out of here, bypass Rabat and get straight to Fez. Better yet," the man said as he sipped his tea, "go south to Marrakech. But they are more religiously inclined there. It's easy to forget that Morocco is an Islamic country if all you see is Casablanca."

Doug had never paid for sex before and was deciding if he had any strong moral code that prevented him from starting now.

"Was it tourism that brought you here?" the gentleman asked.

"Sort of. I'm doing a favor for a friend."

"Well your friend should consider himself extremely lucky to have a friend like you. Personally I'd be afraid to ask any of my friends to come to Casablanca for any reason. I just couldn't stand hearing them scramble to make up excuses."

"I had some time on my hands and figured, what the hell, right?" Doug said, trying to sound as if jetting off to obscure international locations was something he did regularly for his fabulously interesting cosmopolitan friends.

"Yes," the man said as he smiled, "what the hell. What have you seen so far?"

"Nothing, really, just a few shops and a café."

"Did you get to La Petite Roche for dinner? Le Mer? Le Cabestan?"

"No, it was Le McDonald's I'm afraid."

"Now that is just not fair. Any man who would be such a good friend deserves at least one good night in Casablanca. You'll probably find this quite forward—my friends are always telling me I lack propriety when I meet new people—but are you free for dinner this evening? The woman I had planned to dine with decided quite late last night to return to Paris. Most unexpected. I would be honored if you could join me. Perhaps I could pick up a few tips on cultivating better friends."

But there's a red light district in Casablanca, Doug thought.

"Sure, I'm not doing much I guess, nothing I can't do tomorrow." Damn, damn, damn, he thought.

"Excellent," the man said. "Let's say that we'll meet here at nine? Despite all I have said I will admit that there are some splendid little restaurants here." He motioned for the waiter and signed for the meal.

"My name is Sergei Nikolaisen," he said as he stood up, and Doug was surprised since the man had seemed taller when they had been sitting. He looked fit and trim, and his tan suit was tailored and exaggerated his height by highlighting his narrow hips.

"Doug Pearce," he said extending his hand. Sergei had a strong grip for such soft hands.

"Douglas Pearce, it is a pleasure, but…." Sergei Nikolaisen stood still for a moment, glancing slowly to his left and right.

He waited for the waiter to leave and leaned forward, motioning to Doug to do the same. "I must warn you," he said in a hushed voice, "you are in great danger."

Doug felt his eyes widen and breathing stop.

"What?"

"You are in great danger and I'm afraid it is too late to help you."

"Danger? Me?"

"Oh yes," he said, "you. You have foolishly accepted the dinner invitation of a world class old bore and if the Moroccan wine does not kill you my endless stories and obscure anecdotes will surely do the trick."

Doug couldn't help but smile.

"Till tonight then. Do try to enjoy your day and," again he dropped his voice to a stage whisper, "beware of foreign strangers."

◇◇◇

Nothing had magically appeared on Doug's list. It still had the one name, Hammad Al-Kady, and the note about seeing Mr. Fahad/Ahmed. He could add on the dinner invitation but that meant mentally crossing off the red light district.

What's a red light district like, he thought as he left the hotel. It was already blindingly bright outside, the shine amplified by the uniform white buildings, and Doug found he even squinted with his sunglasses on.

Would there be actual red lights? Would it be like all the Hollywood images he'd amassed in his fantasies with micro-skirted, spiked heeled, big titted babes leaning in car windows, or would that prove to be as disappointingly inaccurate as his whole image of this city? Jay, the guy who worked in the keg filling section of the Odenbach Brewery, used to live with a girl who, he said, was a hooker in Pittsburgh, a scrawny, foul-mouthed chain smoker with a Joan Jett haircut who, all the guys agreed, wore the sexiest smelling perfume. Despite the smell, Doug could never imagine paying her for sex. Not her, anyway. What would the prostitutes in Morocco look like? Would they be

French or Moroccan and would he be able to tell the difference? How much would it cost? Would they overcharge him just like every cab driver and souvenir vendor? And would they guess he was an American and rip him off or stick a knife in his ribs or have their pimp—or are pimps only an American thing?—beat the crap out of him? And what about diseases? Would he even be able to find a condom here? The more he thought about it the less upset he got about his new dinner plans.

He had left the hotel and had decided to walk the few blocks to Le Café du Desert, confident he could find the right block of white buildings. He took a seat among the older men who were sipping their tea or smoking the elaborate water pipes, the aromatic fruit-flavored tobacco creating small clouds around the heads of the smokers. When he asked for Fahad, the name Mr. Ahmed said he went by these days, the waiter's face changed expression. He bit his lower lip and looked toward the small group of waiters passing time by the cash register. "Wait a moment, please," the waiter said and walked over to the other waiters. They talked a few moments in Arabic and glanced over to Doug. He watched as one of the waiters took a deep breath, set down his tray and walked over to his table.

It took the waiter five minutes to get around to the sentence "Mr. Fahad is dead," and another five for the details to be made as plain as possible considering his heavy Moroccan French accent.

"It was an accident. He was walking home, up on the sidewalk. It was dark and the car came in quickly. It did not even stop when it hit him."

Doug Pearce felt a sharp chill deep in his chest despite the climbing temperature. Dead. The man lived in Casablanca all his life and less than a day after talking to Doug about a past he had almost forgotten, he was killed when a car jumped the curb, a high curb at that, and ran him down from behind as he walked home from a place he had walked home from every night for fifty years. Mr. Ahmed was his link to Russell and Charley, to the missing jewels, to the Casablanca of the past, and now he was dead. His only link.

It could just be a coincidence, Doug said to himself. People have accidents all the time. And considering how they drove, they probably have more than their share of accidents at that. It probably had nothing to do with him and his one question. It wasn't his fault.

If he said it enough times he figured he'd eventually start to believe it.

Doug Pearce sat at the café for over an hour, the nervous waiters replacing his empty teapots with fresh ones. He tried to figure out what to do next but his mind kept wandering off into the strangest directions—names of old schoolteachers, the new batting order for the Pirates, the break room at the brewery. He remembered what his high school math teacher once told him, that he had a mind like a rudder-less speedboat. So he thought about boats for a while, too. After discovering that the bathroom was just a hole in the floor, he took out his list of things to do and a pen.

At the top of the page he wrote "jewels stolen" and at the bottom he wrote, "jewels recovered" and then, after looking at the list, added a question mark after "recovered." About a quarter of the way down the page he wrote "Uncle Russ killed." He stared at this for another fifteen minutes. On the other side of the paper there was one name and an address. This was it, he decided. If he didn't get a decent lead, a strong idea about what the hell he was doing from one Mr. Hammad Al-Kady, he'd call Edna that night and tell her he was coming back.

Chapter 5

As he sat with Mr. Hammad Al-Kady, holding onto yet another cup of tea, Doug Pearce was hoping that Mr. Al-Kady had not just died. His head had drooped to his chest and his labored breathing had become imperceptible. The top of a real fez was all that Doug could see of the man.

That's it, Doug thought, I quit.

The old man sat like this for five minutes before jerking his head back up, the tassel of his fez stuck to the corner of his mouth by dried spit. He chewed noisily on air, cleared his throat and said for the third time, "Who are you?"

Doug took a deep breath and was ready to apologize and leave when he heard someone approaching through the living area of the house. It was an impressive house, new, but designed in the Moroccan tradition, with elaborate tile work on the white plaster walls and, in an open air courtyard in the middle of the house, a lap pool ringed with the same tile pattern. Doug turned towards the sound and couldn't believe what he saw.

Her thick, black hair hung loose on her shoulders, contrasting with her white tee shirt, which was pulled taut by a chest that Doug found spectacular. She had the kind of body built for tight, black jeans and Doug found that spectacular, too. She had a face, but he hadn't noticed that yet. When he did, he saw that it matched the body—almond shaped eyes and deep honey-colored skin with a designer smile.

"Hi. You must be Doug. The maid told me you had called to speak to my grandfather. Maybe I can help you." She extended a well-manicured hand as she walked towards the two men. "I'm Aisha Al-Kady."

"Doug Pearce." Doug kept it simple. He knew he tended to get stupid around beautiful women and could feel his IQ dropping as she sat in a chair next to him. She looked over at the silent figure in the stripped garabella, the traditional Moroccan costume.

"My grandfather used to be so active. I would race him up the driveway of our old home and, until recently, he usually beat me. About four years ago he had a stroke and, well…." Aisha Al-Kady let the words trail off. She had a slight accent, part French, part Arabic. Doug decided that it fit her well.

"So anyway," she continued, "down to business. First, let me tell you that no one makes it harder, or longer lasting, than Al-Kady."

"Excuse me?" Doug said.

"Concrete? The family business? I assumed you're the contractor that called about concrete."

"No, not really," Doug said, trying unsuccessfully to disprove the family slogan as he pictured her naked, gliding through the pool. "This is going to sound really weird but I got your grandfather's name from a woman in Toronto. I'm trying to track down some of her old friends and she thought Mr. Al-Kady could help."

"Oh, *that's* not so weird," she said as she smiled, as if she knew some things that were.

The old man snorted and shifted in his chair, looked up, mumbled something, and put his head back down.

"That's okay," Aisha said, "he gets like this. You can talk. Even if he hears you he won't have any idea what you're talking about."

"Oh great."

"At times it's convenient…."

"No, what I meant was that I had hoped to ask him some questions and, well, I guess now I won't be able to."

"Well," she said sitting forward and smiling again, "you can always try me." She said something else after this, something about tea, but Doug didn't hear it. He could, however, hear the water drip off her sculpted arms as she paddled her naked self across the pool. She had refilled Doug's cup and was pouring one for herself before he snapped back. Jesus, he thought, it's not like you never talked to a beautiful woman before.

"So what would you have asked my grandfather?" she said.

"Let's see. Have you ever heard him talk about a couple of guys named Russell and Charley?"

"Russell Pearce and Charley Hodge. Oh yes, many times. And the jewel heist and Russell's murder and how Charley got blamed and how the jewel was smuggled out of Casablanca and it went to Nasser Ashkanani in Cairo then on to Singapore. It was one of his favorite stories to tell, that and the stories about the resistance movement and the Nazis. What do you want to know?"

It's about time, thought Doug.

"Russell Pearce was my uncle. I'm trying to find out more about him and to see if I can find the jewel."

"Well," she said with a laugh, "you came to the wrong place. If that jewel were in West Africa my grandfather would have had it years ago. But I thought you said you were doing this for some woman in Toledo?"

"Toronto. Yes, a Ms. Edna Bowers. She knew Russ and Charley, too, and she's helping."

"Don't know the name, sorry," Aisha said, sipping her tea. They fell into an uncomfortable silence, interrupted by the old man's chewing sounds.

Now what, Doug thought. In the movies the guy would steer the conversation around to her and before you could be back with the popcorn, they'd be having NC-17 sex. Do I talk about Uncle Russ? Do I bring up my exciting life in Pottsville? Do I sneak out now before I say something stupid?

"I suppose you want to know more about the jewels and the theft then?"

"Yes, that's it. I mean I'd like to know more, sure."

Aisha glanced over at her grandfather, who was mumbling something unintelligible as he lifted his head and rubbed his eyes. "This is not very comfortable after all," she said standing up. "Do you mind if we talk somewhere else?"

She assumed he'd agree and led the way back into the house and up a flight of stairs, through a door that led to a private sitting room. It was decorated in the same Moroccan style but with more modern touches, like the abstract painting above the leather chair and the elaborate computer system on the glass-topped desk by the window. Aisha tossed herself into one of the overstuffed couches and at the same time tossed her hair back, out of her face. "Get comfortable," she said. "I'm going to tell you a story."

Doug wanted to sit on the couch, right next to her, but opted instead for one of the matching loveseats. Focus, he thought. Pay attention. Be professional.

"Since it was your uncle I assume you know something about him, right?"

"All I know is that he drifted from place to place and was involved in a lot of interesting things."

"'Interesting things.' Well that's one way of putting it."

"Okay," Doug said, "he was a thief." Where did that come from, he thought.

"Better. But I'd prefer to call them all adventurers. You see at that time, right after the war, the line between good guy and bad guy was not so clear and if your uncle and my grandfather ever ripped someone off you can bet that that person was a bigger thief than they were. From what I've heard they did a lot of harmless smuggling, some drug dealing, and the occasional burglary. My grandfather liked to tell of the time—this before the war, I think—that he and some friend from France stole and sold, and re-stole and resold the same antique carpet six times.

I'm sure the things your uncle was involved with were similar. But of course, the jewel was different."

"You mean jewels, right?" Doug said.

"There were jewels, yes, but it was one jewel in particular that they were after."

"The eye?" Doug guessed.

"The eye?" Aisha said, squinting a bit as she said it. "Oh I get it. That's cute. It wasn't 'the eye,' although I bet that's what your uncle and Charley called it. No, it was *Al Ainab,* the grape. It was a red diamond about this big." She held up her hand, making a circle with her index finger and her thumb.

"Diamonds come in red?"

"Diamonds can come in several colors, actually. Of course colorless diamonds are the norm, but if other elements are found in the diamond structure you can end up with colors. Golden-yellow is the most common, and there is also a brownish colored diamond, but the two really rare colors are blue and red. We used to think the red color came from manganese impurities, but the latest gemological research seems to indicate that the red color is the result of a sub-atomic deformation in the carbon structure. Colored diamonds are worth far, far more than flawless clear diamonds, and blue and red are worth the most. You know the Hope diamond? That's a blue diamond. *Al Ainab* is supposed to be the largest red diamond in the world. It didn't hurt that it has an interesting history either. How much do you know about eleventh century Iran?"

Absolutely nothing, he thought. "Just the basics," he said.

"Well then," she continued, "you probably recall that Seljuks took over the Samanid Dynasty around 1040. The Seljuks were from what is now, roughly, Afghanistan—raiders but surprisingly decent rulers, as far as absolute monarchies go. Within twenty years they captured Baghdad and were the power in what we call the Middle East. They ruled for about a hundred years."

She stood up and walked over to one of the many bookcases in the room and took out a thick leather-bound file. The papers were arranged with different color tabs separating the sections.

She walked back across the room and sat down next to Doug. She smelled of warm vanilla and he felt the blood rushing from his head when she slid her hips against his.

She flipped through the pages saying something about having samples of the arts of the era.

"Did you study this stuff in college?" Doug asked. "I mean, do you have a Ph.D. or something in history?"

"I wish," Aisha Al-Kady said, pulling a stack of papers from the folder. "My undergrad degree was in archeology and I've completed most of my Master's work. There are a lot of history courses in the program so that's where I picked up what I know. The diamond is a hobby, I guess. More like an obsession, really."

"Did you go to school in the states?"

"Of course. My family's rich and I'm spoiled. Here it is," she said, focusing on her notes. "*Al Ainab* was owned by the Seljuk sultan Tughril. At this time, the so-called Middle Ages, diamonds were valuable as talismans—good luck charms. It was believed that diamonds in general made you invincible in battle or protected you against poisons or scurvy or arthritis. And if a plain old, colorless diamond helped, imagine what a rare, red diamond would do. Tughril was supposed to have carried our diamond with him when he took Baghdad. There's a manuscript in Malta that states that a crusader from an obscure branch of French nobles saw it when he was held prisoner by Salah al-Din around 1188. I have the transcription but I'm afraid it's in Latin."

"Darn," he said. It was like having someone give him directions in a city he had never been to; the words sounded vaguely familiar but he had no real idea what she was talking about. But she smelled so good and was sitting so close he was willing to listen.

"After that," Aisha continued, "the jewel disappears for a bit. There's a mention of it in an official dispatch to Rome from a Jesuit emissary at Akbar's court in Fatehpur-Sikri in 1575, and he says that it was mounted on a short ceremonial staff. It may have been re-cut soon after. I have an old college friend who lives in Beijing who tells me some department of antiquities has a detailed description of what may be the jewel—along with an illustration—dating from the early 1700s, but I don't know how carefully she has checked it out. Richard Burton claims to have seen it…."

"The British actor?" Doug said.

"The Scottish explorer. He made some wild claims in the 1850s, all sorts of fantastic discoveries along the upper Nile, most of which turned out to be true by the way, but this might have been an embellishment to spice up one of his stories, something he did as well. It's so hard to do any research on it because so many myths have been made up and it's been connected, somehow, to just about every important person in world history. I seriously doubt if ninety percent of what I've read about it is true."

"So maybe it doesn't exist at all," Doug said. "And even if it did once exist it may have been lost. How do you know it's still around?"

Aisha smiled. "I'd agree with you, Doug, if it wasn't for this." She flipped through the file and pulled out a manila envelope. "My grandfather saw it around 1921 in Paris. He was working for a jeweler who specialized in buying stolen goods."

"A fence."

"Exactly," she said. "My grandfather didn't know much about jewels then but he did know how to work a camera." She opened the metal clasp and removed a black and white photograph from the envelope. It was a close-up of a jewel lying on a cloth; next to it a French coin provided a sense of scale. It was almost round in shape with several large facets ringing the center of the stone. Even without color Doug had to admit it was beautiful.

"Amazing, isn't it?" Aisha said.

"How big is it?" Doug Pearce asked.

"Straight size wise, it's about this big," she said, again making a ring with her thumb and index finger. "About one and a half inches in diameter."

"How many carats is that?" Doug said, mimicking the shape she made with his fingers.

"Carats don't tell you size, they tell you weight, but of course the larger the size the more carats you have. Your grape is eighty-three point six carats."

"My God, that's huge," and he thought of how proud Ted the bartender was when he showed off the one-carat ring he bought for his fiancée. When she left him for the UPS guy, he heard she sold it for three grand.

"Like I said, it may be the biggest red diamond ever. The next largest red diamond, the Moussaieff Red, is just over five carats."

"And? You know I gotta ask."

"Who knows what it's worth. What would someone pay for the Hope Diamond? Or the Kohinoor? Or the Star of Yakutia? When you have a diamond this large the question is not how much it costs but how are you going to find a buyer. It would be a steal at eight million and easily worth twice, three times that, but how many people have that kind of money to spend on one diamond? You know the most common use of gold in the U.S.?" she asked as she riffled through the leather folder.

Oh great, time to look stupid, Doug thought. "Maybe gold deposits at Fort Knox? An industrial use for a lot of gold?"

"High school rings. Yes, really, those class rings everyone buys and gives to their sweetheart and never sees again. And that's not a lot of gold per ring. So what do you think the market is for diamonds of this quality?"

Doug looked at the back of his left hand as he held up the picture. "It would make one impressive engagement ring."

"It's too big for a ring, really, but you're right, it would be impressive."

"So what would your grandfather do with it if he had it?"

Aisha shrugged her shoulders. "Knowing my grandfather? He'd keep it in a desk drawer and look at it about once a year."

"Is that what you'd do, stick it in a desk drawer?" he asked.

"I'm a bad person to ask. It's beautiful, but that's not what interests me. Really, it's the history. Someday I'd like to publish the definitive biography on that stone. I think it's just fascinating. So what would I do with it?" She re-filed the photo and straightened the papers in the folder. Doug stared at her hands and then past her hands, past the folder, to her legs, wrapped in those tight, black jeans. She bounced her knees slightly as she slid the pages back in place. Doug's gaze wandered off her knees and up her thighs.

"What would you do with it if you got your hands on it?" she asked.

"Hands on what?"

"Hello!…the diamond. What would you do with it if you had it?"

Doug thought about it for a moment and then sighed. "I really don't know. I mean, yeah, I'd sell it, but like you said, to who? I don't know any fences and I doubt that the local jeweler would be interested. I'm assuming that if you split the diamond up…."

"Cut the diamond," she corrected him. "You cut a diamond, and pray to God you don't split it."

"Whatever. I assume it would lose much of its value."

"One hundred percent of its historical value, that's for sure," Aisha said. "You'd probably end up making more money, though. Like I said, who can afford it but sultans and emperors? Not a lot of those left. You'd still have to find someone who could cut this rock without damaging it. But, yes, smaller, one carat diamonds are much easier to sell. You'd make a couple of million quite easily."

"I could deal with a couple million," Doug Pearce said.

"And I could do with a couple more," Aisha said as she stood up to replace the folder. Doug watched her walk back to the bookshelf. Did she sense him watching or did she always move her ass like that, he wondered.

"Assuming you got a hold of the diamond," she said over her shoulder, "you'd still have a little problem with the rightful owner."

"Come on, he couldn't still have a claim to it, after all these years, could he?"

"His estate—he died in the Thirties—has a very active claim on the diamond. In many cases, international art theft, as you probably know...."

No I don't, he thought.

"...has no statute of limitations. The rightful owner has claim to it in perpetuity." She replaced the notebook and walked over to the computer. Doug couldn't see what she was doing but the hidden speakers started playing some soft, Arabic sounding music. "If you found the diamond you'd either have to sell it on the black market to someone who would keep the purchase quiet, meaning you'd have to sell it for a fraction of what it's worth. A tiny fraction. Or," she said, adjusting the volume on the screen, "you'd have to have an excellent diamond cutter—who'd be willing to work illegally, of course—cut the stone so it couldn't be traced. But then there goes the diamond's real value."

"So no matter what I do," Doug said, "I'm going to lose a fortune. I'll try to keep that in mind when I find the diamond."

Aisha smiled as she looked over at Doug, the soft blue light of the computer screen tinting her white tee shirt. "Ah, the truth comes out. You're after *Al Ainab*."

"I guess," Doug said, "but I'm just as interested in what happened to my uncle."

Aisha walked back to the couch and stood, leaning one knee on the coffee table, her hands on her hips. "*Just* as interested? Millions of dollars interested?"

"Alright. The more I know about the jewel the more interested I become. But realistically," he said, looking up at her as she posed—and it was definitely a pose—"what am I more likely to find? The solution to a fifty-year-old murder or a million-dollar grape?"

"Is neither an option?" Aisha said, tilting her head to the side as she said it.

"Neither is a possibility. More likely a probability." Most likely, he thought, a certainty.

"Enough diamond talk for now. You get me started on that topic and I'll never let you go. So, is this an all-business trip or can you squeeze in some tourist activities?"

"I definitely have time for that." Choose your words carefully now Dougie, he thought. "Do you know anyone who could show me around?"

"Come on," she said, reaching for a purse on the back of the leather chair, "I'll give you a lift back to the city. It'll give me a chance to tell you all about my special 'First Time to Casablanca' package tour."

Chapter 6

"I hope you are no judge of wines," Sergei Nikolaisen said as one of the swarm of waiters filled their glasses. "With Moroccan wines it's best to be ignorant. Less painful."

"Well then this will be quite painless." Doug sipped the wine. As he predicted, it tasted fine to him.

"The wine industry here is not so young as you'd expect but even the French cannot beg a decent vintage from this soil. I can order a bottle of French wine if you'd prefer? No? Fine then, we'll go native. And, if you don't mind," he motioned for the maitre d', "I'll have the chef put together something special for us."

A relay of waiters spent ten minutes arranging various plates, bowls, and covered dishes with the unstated goal of filling every open space on the table with some food item. Sergei explained what each dish contained and warned Doug which spices to avoid. Sergei kept the conversation light as they ate, and it wasn't until after the train of waiters had cleared away their display and they were sipping the French port forced on them by the owner that he asked Doug about his trip.

"Like I said, it's a favor for a friend. She wants me to look up some of her old friends and pick up a couple of gifts. Nothing important."

"Well don't let the touts hear you say that. They'll have you off to their 'uncle's shop' pricing second rate carpets before you know what hit you," Sergei said. "I'd offer to help but I doubt that your friends and mine run in the same circles. I'm not a jet-setter like yourself."

Doug smiled. "I have to admit this is only my second international trip. I'm not as jet-set as you think."

Sergei Nikolaisen nodded his head. "You pull it off admirably, young man." It was a compliment and an exaggeration and Doug knew it.

"And you? I'd guess it's not tourism that brings you here."

"You'd guess correctly. I was recently retired from the Berlin Art Museum. Of course they called it a well-earned respite from a lifetime of service," he said, holding up his glass in mock salute, "and instead of the gold watch gave me a title. *Curator emeritus.* The end result was the same, I suppose—put out to the proverbial pasture. And I'd like to think many years before my time. Anyway," he said, his hand making a slight wave in front of his face as if to blow away a bad smell, "I had traveled here and there scouting interesting little items for their collections and, as sort of a farewell tour, the trustees decided to send me to a few places I still had living contacts. They gave me a modest budget and an even more modest honorarium and told me to bring back some treasures. Considering the size of the budget I hope they will be happy with souvenir tee shirts."

"So who do you know in Casablanca?" Doug asked. "Maybe you'd know some of the people I'm looking for."

Sergei Nikolaisen laughed as he leaned back in his chair. "Douglas, my friends are all gray and dusty. Museum officials and collectors. Even I find them an insufferable lot. They are certainly not the type of people to arouse the interest of old friends across the seas."

"But you're here, aren't you?"

"Yes," he said, still laughing, "and doesn't that say something sad about me?"

Doug poured himself another glass of port. Port, he decided, was a lot like whiskey and that was all right by him. "In all your travels did you ever hear much about jewels?"

"But of course. Would you?" he said, holding out his glass. "While the museum trade is mostly in historical artifacts and the occasional gold coin, we did get offers now and then for gems and the like."

"Ever hear of *Al Ainab*, the Grape?"

Sergei Nikolaisen pursed his lips and looked up at the ceiling. "No," he said, drawing the word out, as if waiting for the memory to rush back and cut him off, "I don't think I have. Is it a ruby then?"

"I was told it was a very famous red diamond."

"A red diamond? Are you sure? There are few of those, you know. Could it have been a red sapphire?"

"No, it was a diamond. I was told it was stolen here in Casablanca back in 1948."

"Oh *that* diamond! Of course I heard of that," Sergei said, leaning back in his chair. "But what did you call it? The grape? How did you come up with that name?"

"I was told it was an old treasure from some king in Baghdad and Akbar had it and it may have been in China, too, and Africa. What's so funny?"

"Oh Douglas, please don't think me rude, but someone has been pulling your leg." Sergei put his hand up to cover his smile, yet he continued to chuckle into his palm.

"You mean there is no red diamond?"

"There is definitely a red diamond, Douglas, but I'm afraid it does not have the colorful history of your grape. The diamond you are referring to was discovered in a wadi, a dry riverbed, in South Africa around 1910. It was called, simply, the Jagersfontien Diamond, after the closest town, and maybe that's not such a simple name but it wasn't called anything so," he paused, looking for the right word, "so *romantic*. But it was big, something like eighty carats, if I recall."

Doug ran his tongue across the back of his teeth. The port and the wine were making his upper lip feel numb. He was thinking about Aisha and the file.

"And indeed it was stolen here in Casablanca," Sergei Niko-laisen continued. "It was a bloody affair, a real mess. Three, four people killed rather brutally. Butchered, really. One of my old friends here in Casablanca is a retired police captain. He worked that case. He said that there was so much blood...." He paused and looked up at Doug. "Anyway, it was a rather unpleasant affair."

Doug sighed. He drained his glass and was debating whether it would be rude to polish off the bottle. He decided to be rude and poured another. "I suppose," he finally said, "that they never caught the thieves?"

"From what I recall you are correct. I'm afraid I don't know much more than what I've told you.... There was a problem with the insurance claim, some nonsense about Nazi soldiers hiding in the Atlas Mountains, and of course the story of how it went on to Egypt—another bloody tale." Sergei looked across the table at Doug. He waited an uncomfortable minute before he said, "The thieves were not good people, Douglas. I do hope that they are not in any way related to your friend."

So do I, thought Doug.

◇◇◇

Three cups of Turkish coffee—tiny little things with a black sandy sludge on the bottom—counterbalanced the alcohol so Doug was awake when Edna's call was forwarded to his room. "I'm sorry if I'm calling too late, it's eleven p.m. here so it's, what, two there? I just haven't heard a word from you and I was nervous."

"Yeah, I should have called," and he knew he should have, too, "but I just wanted to wait until I could tell you something besides a weather report. I'm sorry, I mean you're paying for all of this and the least I could have done was call."

"Don't worry about the money, that's not important, I thought I made that clear. As long as you're safe...." Her voice trailed off and Douglas thought for a moment he was talking to his mother.

"I've made some progress. There was a large red diamond stolen here back in forty-eight. I'm getting different stories from my sources and I'm not sure yet which source is most reliable, but I'm going to do some background work tomorrow, try to get to the truth." Doug was aware that he was sounding like a movie detective, but how was he supposed to report? Tell her everything, down to the way Aisha looked in the white tee shirt and black jeans, not sweating in the ninety-degree heat of the shade? No, follow the role models, even if it did sound strange coming from him.

"Were my notes of any help? Did you find everything?"

"It's interesting reading. I could have sworn, though, that you said you had a plan."

"What do you mean? Of course I have a plan."

"All you sent me was a list of names and a general idea of what my uncle and Charley were doing at the time."

"Well what did you expect, Douglas, a step-by-step map? Follow your leads, ask some questions, and we'll see what turns up."

"I'm not a detective."

"Oh that's obvious," she said. Doug thought he heard her laugh.

"I just don't want you to get your hopes up. I'll ask around, maybe somebody will know something, but I can't promise anything."

"Of course not, Douglas. But you're a bright man, I'm sure you could piece things together as well as a detective."

"Do you actually know any detectives, Edna?"

"I've run into a few over the years and I wasn't impressed with what I saw. Any idiot could do their jobs. You should have no trouble."

"Thanks, I think."

"Just snoop around and we'll see what you turn up. So," she said, "about those notes I sent you."

"I can see why my family avoided the guy."

"They just didn't know him. He was a real sweetheart."

"Sweetheart? Let's see, he stole from his friends, smuggled drugs, was involved in a crime where someone was killed...."

"True. But he was also a lot of fun."

"And his friend Charley? Quite the ladies' man."

"I wouldn't put it quite like that," Edna said, "but yes, Charley did chase the women back then."

"They were quite a pair, I guess."

"Yes, quite a pair," she said. "Now, what did you find so far? Did you visit the places I suggested?"

"Yeah, at first. Some were helpful. Listen, do you remember the guy named Mr. Ahmed?"

"Of course, he was the first name I gave you, a real dear. Did you find him at the café? How's he holding up? Oh, I wish I could have seen the look on his face."

Doug drew in a deep breath. "Look, Edna, I don't know how to say this but Mr. Ahmed is dead. He was hit by a car the day I spoke with him. I'm sorry."

There was a long pause before Edna said, "I see. Thank you." There was another, longer, pause before she continued. "Did he remember Russ and Charley?"

"He did, but we didn't get a chance to talk. We were going to meet at the café today."

"Oh Lord," she said into the phone. "Do you think your visit and his death are related? No, never mind, that's a silly question, of course they're related. Douglas, are you sure you're all right? I mean if you want to come back, I understand."

Yes, book me a flight home, get me the hell outta here, I want to sleep through a night without the prayer call blasting me out of bed, I want to hear English, drink a Odenbach beer, hang out with the guys, get my job back, eat food I can pronounce, avoid homicidal drivers, and quit chasing the killer of a lousy bastard who probably deserved it anyway. "No, I'm fine, really. Things are going well here and I feel like I'm making progress. I'm meeting again tomorrow with my main source and I should know better then where this is going. It appears the jewel left here for Cairo. If my leads indicate that's what happened, do you want me to go there and have a look around?"

"Douglas, you are amazing. That's exactly where Russ and Charley went after Casablanca. I didn't say anything to you because I didn't want to influence your investigation."

My *investigation*, he thought.

"Yes, yes of course that's what I'd like you to do," she continued. "If you want to. If I don't hear from you tomorrow I'll call back to the concierge of the hotel. I'll take care of everything. If you need anything, just ask him. And Douglas?" She paused. "Thank you."

Chapter 7

"What do you want to drink?" Aisha asked as they settled into their seats at the outdoor café that looked out across the beach and the Atlantic. She had picked him up at the hotel for lunch and, as promised, showed him the sights of the city. It took all of two hours.

The sights of the city—the sites Aisha felt were worth seeing—were limited to a few older buildings, which she consented to slow down in front of as they raced by, and dozens of shops and boutiques that ringed the city.

"Everyone should have a Great Quest in life," she had announced as she cut around a speeding Fiat, her BMW convertible just missing the Fiat's back bumper. "Being me, I have two. You know about *Al Ainab*. My other great quest in life," she said, "is to find the perfect LBD."

"LBD? Large Big Diamond?"

"Little Black Dress. Every woman should have at least one perfect LBD in her wardrobe. I own, well, a lot of them, but I still have not found the perfect one.

"It's not just the fit," she continued, "it's the fabric, the cut, the color…."

"What color? It's black."

She raised her eyebrows as she looked at him, amazed at his level of ignorance. "Some blacks," she said with authority, "are blacker than others."

Most of the important sites in Casablanca were potential LBD sites. Aisha tried on different outfits, twirling around a few times in front of the mirror, adjusting straps or raising up on her toes to simulate high heels. She'd sigh, complain that she was too fat for this one or too small breasted for that one, too old to be seen in this style, too young to be wearing that. No one believed her. The salesgirls and other shoppers stared openly at her and even Doug, with his undeveloped sense of fashion, knew she looked perfect. She stopped asking Doug's opinion after the tenth outfit since all he said was that it looked great. Like a Midas of fashion, she made every dress, every skirt, every blouse look stunning.

"What would you like to see me wearing?" she had asked, "This? This? Or none of these?" Doug could only smile.

"So what do you want to drink?" she asked again. She was 'Absolutely Exhausted' from sightseeing and had power-slid her car into the parking lot of the seaside café three minutes ago.

"Anything but tea."

Aisha ordered two Budweisers and they sat sipping the warm beer as the locals tried to keep cool in the ocean breezes. The beach was littered from one end to the other with fast food wrappers, empty water bottles, and things that looked like car parts. The ocean rolled up the sand, depositing some debris and pulling some back out to sea. The air smelled of salt water and gasoline. It could have been a beautiful place, Doug thought.

"I'm sorry they wouldn't let you in the mosque. It really is quite impressive. It was probably because they knew you weren't a Muslim. You have to be a Muslim to go into the mosques here."

"You think it was because of *me?*" Doug said as he laughed.

"You don't think that the way you are dressed influenced their decision?" She was wearing white shorts, no doubt to highlight her perfectly tanned and sculpted legs, and a man's button-down oxford with the sleeves rolled up past her elbows. Her's, Doug thought, or a yet unmentioned boyfriend's? After seeing her in all those short, wonderfully short, LBDs Doug couldn't decide if she looked better in black or white. In any case she looked just like she wanted to look—like a model at the beach.

"What is wrong with what I have on?" she said, looking over the top of her sunglasses.

"Honestly, nothing." And he meant it, too.

"So where were you last night? I called around eleven to see if you wanted to get together but the desk said you were out?"

Holy shit, he thought, she called me. "I had dinner with a guy I met at my hotel, this older guy from Germany, I think. He used to be a museum curator. We were talking about artifacts and things like that. It was interesting, he seemed to know so much." Doug took a long pull on his beer before he continued. "It's funny, he recalls the diamond theft but his details are quite different from your research."

"Oh," Aisha said as she adjusted the thin paper napkin under her glass. "How strange. The story is well known."

"Oh yeah, it's well known, but he seems to believe that it was only discovered this century, someplace in South Africa." He watched as she continued to re-adjust the napkin.

"Hmmm," she said as she finished with the napkin and moved on to removing the label with a thumbnail. "He must not have been a very good museum person if he'd get the basic facts of the story all wrong. He must be thinking of a different diamond."

"Maybe," Doug said, "but he sounded like he knew exactly what he was talking about."

"So I guess he showed you all of his research? The eight years of notes put together in dark library reading rooms form Kiev to New York? The accounts he translated *himself?* From Old French on fucking thirteenth century vellum manuscripts?"

"Ah, no, he…."

"Did he tell you how he spent a whole summer in Agra, paying western wages to Indian grad students to transcribe reams of documents, only to find two obscure references to the diamond?"

"No, but…."

"And did he tell you how rather than vacationing in Aspen he spent every spring break going from one archive library to the next? Or how he once had to sleep with a Yugoslavian antiquities official just to look at some papers that turned out to be worthless anyway?"

"Look, Aisha, I'm not doubting you...."

"It sure the hell sounds like it to me," she said, looking up from her now naked beer bottle. "What did you do, run out right away to check up on me?"

"No, no, no. Honest, Aisha, I was just out to dinner with this guy when we got to talking about why I was here and I told him the basics and he just added the information about the diamond. I trust your research and I trust you. I just have to figure out why the guy would have a totally different story, that's all. Maybe he is confused, I don't know. Maybe he's senile or been in the sun too long." Although she had focused back on her napkin this made her smile. "Aisha," he said, getting her to look up, "I do believe you, you know."

"It's just that when you doubt the story you doubt all my work—*my work*—and you make my grandfather out to be a liar. And like I said," she was looking at him again, her voice steady, but softer, "it was his favorite story and it's all I really have of him anymore."

"Don't forget," Doug said, "you're also a rich, spoiled brat. You owe him that too."

"Cute, considering that I'm still pissed at you. Want another?" she said holding up the empty bottle.

"What I don't get," she said when the beers arrived, as warm as the last two, "is how you got involved in this. Why look for it now? What's the sudden interest?"

"Good question. I've been thinking about it a lot lately. I just wanted to learn something about my uncle. The woman who's funding this little expedition was a friend of my uncle and she has all these old letters about him and I get to read the parts she decides to send me. And I had the summer off. I don't do this all the time, you know."

"Do what? Have a beer at a beach?" she said, starting in on the new label.

"A beer, yes. The beach, maybe. Morocco, no."

"As you can see," she said, motioning around with her hand, "you haven't missed all that much."

"Not much to you," he said, "but more than I've ever done. You've been everywhere…."

"Hardly."

"Close enough. But me? Aisha, this is my Big Adventure. I've never been anywhere before, I'm not rich like you, I work in a fucking brewery. No, I *used* to work in a fucking brewery. I don't even have that career anymore. So when this woman offered me a chance to actually do something besides sit in a rut, I jumped on it. She thinks I'm doing a great job and I don't know what I'm doing. Everything I tell her she already knew and she's all happy."

"Hey, sounds good to me. She's happy, you get a trip. What are you complaining about?"

"I don't know, it all seems so weird. Things like this don't happen to me."

"Well they do now. And you get to learn all about your uncle." She drained her beer and looked around for the waiter.

Doug laughed. "You know, I don't know if I want to. It turns out that my dear, sweet, departed uncle was a big dick. I'm glad I never met him and I see why my father never talked about him."

"Well? Is it genetic?" she said, standing up.

"What? His attitude?"

"No, his anatomy. I've got to hit the ladies room, order me another, will you?"

Holy shit, Doug thought. Holy shit.

So now what, he wondered? Invite her back to his hotel, to a room the size of her car? Ask to go to the Al-Kady mansion, with the old man wheezing by the pool? Doug quickly ordered the two beers when he spotted her weaving through the crowd, back to their table. Damn, he thought, what should I do?

"After we finish these beers, I'm afraid I'll have to drop you off at your hotel. I have some family business to take care of, arranging for some deliveries to be made. I'd take you along but you'd cramp my negotiating style."

Damn, he thought again.

"How long will you be in town?" she asked, taking a long pull on her beer. This woman, this amazing woman, could suck back the beers.

"Good question. I have to sit down and figure out what the hell I'm doing next." He didn't want to sound like he was clueless but that was what he was. But incompetence, he had found, seldom aroused a woman's passion, and he was halfway there with his brewery story. "I've already let Edna know that I'd probably be heading to Cairo next. You said that you knew who ended up with it in Cairo?"

"Yes, a man named Nasser Ashkanani. My uncle. He owns a shop or two in the Khan al-Khalili. That's the big bazaar in Cairo's old quarter. When my grandfather and your uncle and his friend got hold of the jewels they had to get out of Casablanca quickly. I mean *everybody* assumed they did it, your uncle and his friend, that is. My grandfather was never connected to the theft at all."

"The home field advantage. Was your Uncle Nasser in on the original idea?"

"I don't think so," Aisha said, "but I do know that it was my grandfather's idea to hook up with him. Our families have been involved in one business deal or another for a hundred years, still are, in fact. But why go to Cairo? Wasn't your uncle killed in Singapore? I'd think it'd make sense to start there."

"You'd think so, but this woman in Toronto...."

"Ah, the mystery woman!"

"...she wants me to go to Cairo first. She might have some contacts there she wants me to look up. Maybe a real live clue."

"I know some people in Cairo, too," she said. "Maybe I'll hook you up."

"What about this Nasser guy? He still alive?" Doug asked.

"Oh very much so. I visited his shop in the Khan just last month. He'd be the person to talk with about the jewel. I'll make sure to draw you a good map. I can still get lost in the Khan now and then, but I'm usually pretty buzzed when that happens. You almost ready to go?" she said, checking her watch.

Doug drained the rest of the beer and put a hundred dirhem note on the table, which made Aisha laugh. "You buying drinks for the house? Give him five and he'll call himself lucky." They headed towards the car and she slipped her arm through his, ignoring the stares from the old women with their heads covered with black scarves.

"If you've known this ash can guy...."

Aisha laughed, gripping his arm. "Ashkanani."

"Whatever. If you've known this guy for years why didn't you ask him about the jewel? Or your grandfather? I mean, we're talking millions here, right?"

"Right, definitely right. I have asked Uncle Nasser but he always tells me to stick to concrete. As for my grandfather, once Nasser passed on the diamond and sent him a small finder's fee he lost interest in it. He thought my fascination with *Al Ainab* was a waste of time, but he still loved to talk about it."

They reached her car, a silver BMW convertible that she had parked, Doug noticed, as recklessly as any other Moroccan. "I'd really like to see you again before you go, Doug. Can you fit me in somehow?"

"Let's see," Doug said rubbing his chin, "there's dinner with the King, and then that little gathering at the British Embassy.... I *might* be able to squeeze you in."

Aisha laughed that light, honest laugh that Doug loved to hear. He hadn't blown it. Yet.

"I'll give you my number," she said as she raced the car backwards out of the tight space, "you can give me a call later. But you have to promise to spend a long evening with me before you leave."

Doug raised his right hand and looked to the broad Atlantic sky. "I swear," he said.

Chapter 8

There were days when Tarek Taksha felt he had the best job in all of Morocco.

Today was one of those days.

Not that being the manager of a former, and rapidly deteriorating, premier hotel was an important job, but it was a definite step up from trying to hustle decades-old postcards along the cornice. The Sea Port had lost its four-star rating in the early Seventies and another star in the mid-Eighties, but that did not concern the owner, who had a fifth star painted on the red awning in ninety-five. Tarek had started as a bellboy when he was fourteen, working for tips and a share of what people left behind in their rooms. There were enough guests back then to warrant two bellboys. It was old-fashioned hard work and intense sucking up that allowed Tarek to keep his job when the guests dwindled to a trickle.

When the Sea Port was self-upgraded to a five-star hotel, Tarek became the concierge/bellhop, partially because his English was better than anyone else's at the hotel, but primarily because he would do the job for the least amount of money. It took a few weeks to find out what it was that a concierge actually did, but once he figured it out, he dedicated himself to being the best damn concierge in a bogus five-star hotel in all of the old area of Casablanca east of the Rue Centrate.

That dedication paid off when, thanks to obviously doctored books, the last manager was fired for embezzling from the already struggling hotel and Tarek was made manager of the Sea Port. Due to the economic difficulties at the Sea Port, he maintained his concierge and bellhop titles as well, and without complaint worked for less than the last manager. This was the opportunity he had worked so hard for and he wasn't about to let it slip away with petty complaints. He worked even harder, sucked up even more obsequiously, and he made sure that the books would never show his embezzling.

Lately things had picked up at the Sea Port and, for the first time in years, they had over half the rooms rented. The last week had been especially good, with the American bringing so much traffic to the hotel. True, the people who asked questions about the American didn't rent rooms, but they tipped well when Tarek allowed them to read his dark blue passport. And, for more than it would have cost to rent it, they paid to poke around in the American's room. He drew the line, however, at removing objects, but saw no harm in letting them read his papers or take photographs.

And there were the phone calls, strange phone calls—"No, sir, I'm afraid I don't know how tall he is," "I believe he was wearing a blue shirt, sir," "Can I arrange it? Of *course* madam, but it is *quite* unusual, and these things, well, it would cost…. Excuse me? Oh *yes* madam, I'm *sure* we can take care of it." No, it wouldn't last forever, but it was nice having the American at the hotel.

So it was with a genuine smile that Tarek greeted the American when he stepped out of a silver BMW that disappeared down the crowded street. Good afternoon, sir. Yes, a woman did call from overseas. Of course I can take care of all of your travel arrangements, sir. Everything will be aligned for your speedy departure in the a.m. two days hence. No sir, that's not necessary. Well if you insist, sir, thank you, sir, you are *most* generous.

Yes, it was nice having the American at the hotel.

◇◇◇

It was still mid-afternoon and despite the heat Doug decided to investigate the area around the hotel. He grabbed the *Lonely*

Planet guide he had picked up at JFK and the tenth-generation photocopy of a mimeographed map, circa 1972, that the man in his concierge role insisted he take with him. He had tried to read up on Morocco on the flight over, but the guidebook droned on and on about Berbers and Almoravids and people with names he could not remember from one sentence to the next. He picked up enough to know that the place was old, that there had been a lot of fighting over the years, that the Nazis had been here—but he knew that from the prologue to *Casablanca*—and that they were independent with a king. He had skipped whole sections entitled Economic Outlook, Relations With Israel, and Sunnis and Shiites, Saints and Mystics. The guidebook had warned him about starting conversations with women—"given the sexual mores of the culture"—but the authors had obviously never met Aisha.

He oriented himself with the map of central Casablanca. His hotel was on Boulevard Houphouet Boigny—Humphrey Bogart?—across the street from what the guide book said was a "smallish version of a typical Berber style souk; bright and affable, it meanders serendipitously around several architectural gems." On the hotel's map it just said shops. By the time he had walked past five shops he had twenty offers to come in, look around, have some tea, no charge to look, because, they all assured him, he was their special friend. One by one the touts that Sergei had warned him about introduced themselves, swore that they just wanted to practice their English, and really, *really* wanted him to come and meet their uncle who owned a shop near by. They were "bright and affable" all right, and a pain in the ass.

Most tourist shops were filled with the same tourist crap that they sold at the rest stops off the Pennsylvania Turnpike. Glue anything—a dried lizard, a vial of sand, a rock with eyeballs painted on it—to a piece of driftwood, write a town name underneath it, and some tourist will always buy it. How else could you explain the quantities of the stuff? Doug was offered "real" Rolexes for what worked out to ten bucks. The Rolex he eventually bought, talking the man down from an outrageous fifteen dollars, worked for most of the rest of the afternoon. And this, Doug decided, was why they designed the marketplace like a maze, with every shop looking just like the last. They could rip you off with confidence, knowing you could never find your way back and that if you did, you could never be sure you'd find the right thief.

Despite the watch, despite the touts, despite the fear that he'd get his wallet snatched even with it stuffed in his front pocket, Doug had to admit it was wonderful. There were vegetable carts loaded with fresh produce he'd never seen before, shops with carpets spread out onto what passed for a sidewalk, crammed with so many brass coffee pots and glass water pipes that the shop owner seemed trapped inside, the overpowering smell of the leather shops where craftsmen worked traditional patterns with wood handled punches and tiny hammers, the pastry and bread shops, with their room-sized brick ovens encased with the same white cement that seemed to encase every building in the souk, every building in the city. Small kids, baskets filled with the hot pastry, raced past him and up the narrow staircases that clung to the sides of the alleyway. And everywhere the teashops with their sickeningly sweet tea that Doug had grudgingly started to like. After several hours of touring modern Casablanca, with its Pizza Huts and Gaps, its mobile phones and rap music, its familiar franchise look, the souk reminded him that he wasn't in Pottsville. It was like nothing he had experienced before, a real adventure in an exotic location, just like Edna had promised. He knew that he was walking around with that big, shit-eating grin he associated with rubes in the big city, but he didn't care.

When he got back to the hotel there was a note from Sergei Nikolaisen—was he available for an early dinner? Sure, Doug thought, why not. He wanted to call Aisha but didn't want to sound as desperate as he was. As instructed in the note, he left word with the desk that, yes, he'd be in the lobby at eight. Doug showered and started to read more about Casablanca. He finished two whole paragraphs before he nodded off.

Chapter 9

He was a cop. He had to be. He had that bull neck, that close-cropped hair, and that look that always seems to say I can fuck with you all I want and you can't do squat. Not all cops had the look, just the few who got off on harassing guys like Doug for petty shit like open beer in a car or a loud party in the middle of nowhere. He was a cop but fortunately he was Sergei's friend. Unfortunately, Doug was struggling not to laugh at him.

"Yehia here was the police captain I was telling you about," Sergei said as he waved off the waiter with the wine list. "Since you had a common interest I thought it would be helpful if you met."

Doug didn't know if it was Sergei's accent or if it was the way it was supposed to be pronounced, but the burly ex-cop's name sounded like "Ya-ya." It was hard for Doug to look at a man he'd just met and call him Ya-ya. Especially a man like Yehia. Doug chose to call him sir, which the power-deprived ex-cop liked.

Yehia was leaning back into his chair, his bulky body—once impressive, now just fat—lapped over the arms of the chair like a candle melting in the North African sun. Dark stubble covered the acreage of his chins and somewhere under those eyebrows, two black eyes stared out, still trying to intimidate guys like Doug. "I was captain here in Casa for twenty-eight years. I saw many things." He flipped his hands over as if to say it was nothing, routine for a man like me.

"So when did you retire?" Doug asked, but Sergei leaned forward, cutting off Yehia's answer and Doug's apparently stupid questions.

"Yehia was an excellent officer and the way they treated him…well it was all politics, and personally I think that it should have been the government's barrister who was forced out of office. Criminal, really."

"If there was corruption it certainly wasn't in my department," Yehia said offhandedly, either tired of defending himself or no longer believing his own protests. "And as for the money, well they never found it at my home and do you see me living like a rich man? And besides, those who insulted me the loudest were too busy to show up for court. Yes. Politics indeed."

"Yehia and I were reminiscing about the post-war years and I reminded him of the robbery of the red diamond you mentioned," Sergei said. Doug wasn't sure what to say so he just smiled and nodded and thanked the waiter for the whiskey and soda that Sergei had ordered for them all.

"I don't know what your esteemed friend here told you," Yehia said, motioning his glass towards Sergei, "but Casa was not as lawless as your movies make it out to be. Those of us who found it necessary to work for the Germans when they were here were able to keep our positions after they left. Of course it was not easy but…." Again that offhanded shrug. "No, it was quite civilized here then. If you had problems with someone—an opium dealer, say, or a sex maniac—you didn't have to wait for the courts to get around finally to do their duty. They were always delaying things, pushing things back and making our jobs complicated. And for what? They might as well have put the handcuffs on us for all the good they accomplished. A quick ride out of town and pop," he made a gun shape out of his first two fingers and his thumb, "just like a dog. No, the streets were quite safe."

Except from the police, Doug thought. He swirled his drink around in the glass and wondered if the restaurant used bottled water to make the ice.

"Of course I remember the red diamond case. It had a strange name, German I think."

"The Jagersfontien Diamond," Sergei said. "South African."

"Yes, South African. But then South Africa after the war was where you went to find Germans," Yehia said, chuckling to himself.

Sergei smiled. "There were many Germans there indeed, but the diamond was actually found before the war if you recall."

"Whatever," Yehia said and waved for the waiter to bring him another drink. "While we were questioning a well-known thief he mentioned that there was going to be an attempt to steal the diamond. I don't remember who owned it."

"A gentleman with the misfortune of having one of those absolutely unpronounceable Afrikaner names. I'll admit that German names are bad enough, but that so-called language, well it sounds just too comical when two Boers get together on the *stoep* for a *braai* to talk about life on the *karral*. We used to call them ropes. Thick and twisted."

"Yes, well," Yehia said, dismissing the interruption, "the man we were questioning said that a couple of Americans and a Moroccan planned on ambushing the rightful owner—your South African—somewhere here in the city but he knew little else so…."

So you put a bullet in his forehead, thought Doug. He remembered something Aisha said about post-war Casablanca, about there being a gray area between the good guys and the bad guys. So far Doug hadn't seen much of a difference.

"Late one night," Yehia continued, "we get a call about some bodies in the wharf area which, of course, was not unusual. What was unusual was who made the call. It seemed that this was different, he didn't want his people accused of this one. I didn't understand what he meant until I got there myself. Sergei, I must say that this is damn good whiskey you ordered." Yehia looked at his half full glass and Sergei understood the not so subtle hint and motioned for the waiter to bring and leave the bottle.

"Have you ever seen a dead body, Mr. Pearce?" Yehia asked as he topped off his glass.

"Yes, many times I'm afraid," Doug said. And it was true. There was his grandmother's funeral, his father's, his uncle Pete's, the security guard's from the brewery whom Doug sort of knew. In Pottsville every funeral was an open casket funeral. There wasn't much excitement in Pottsville, the joke went, so you might as well entertain your friends on your way out.

"In my line of work it is almost everyday. I have seen men strung up with piano wire, a woman whose head was cut off and baked into a cake. And when the Gestapo was here, well, let us say they worked hard to earn their reputation."

Didn't you say you worked for them? Doug thought.

"What I saw that night, it stays with me still. It was a ware-house, an older place, dark, of course, and deserted. Most of the honest companies had moved to the newer docks. There were five or six bare bulbs hanging from the rafters. I was a new lieutenant and I wanted to make a good investigation. I entered the crime scene slowly, just like I had been taught, trying to see the whole scene. At first I thought there were small stacks of sand bags here and there. When I came closer I saw they were men...bodies...curled up on their sides like infants in a cradle. My men were afraid to touch them, there was far more blood than normal and my men were simple men, easily spooked by such things." Yehia sipped his drink and paused for effect.

"I rolled the first man over with my foot." He pushed his leg out to demonstrate, as if the body lay on the floor under the table. Doug pulled his own legs up under his chair. "His body was still soft. He had been dead less than an hour. When he flopped onto his back I saw why there was so much blood. They had been gut shot, two or three times, with a big bore handgun. Their intestines were squeezing out of the holes and you could tell that they were a long time in dying, trying to hold their insides in with their own hands. It was the same with each of the bodies. Whoever shot them had meant them to die slowly."

"How can you tell?" Doug asked.

"With a gun that size, one shot to the chest and they would die instantly, or at least quickly. No, whoever shot them knew exactly what he was doing. No vital organs, but no hope of surviving. Just a long, slow and painful death. I have shot a few men myself, I'll admit, but never in the stomach. In the back of the head and they die painlessly, they don't even know what it was. A man who shoots another man in the gut is an animal."

Was Yehia telling the truth? Doug couldn't tell. There was that show that comes with being the kind of cop he was, but something about his manner changed while he was describing the scene. Was he truly remembering what he saw or was he trying to create the scene the way he felt it should have looked? Was he exaggerating for effect or minimizing to be polite?

"We never caught them. We found one in an alley not far away, his face shot off. We still were able to identify him, a local man, petty thief. We found two more bodies later, but we often found bodies. As far as the crime, we don't even know that the red diamond was involved...."

"But the South African insisted that it was there," Sergei said. "His claim, as I recall now, insisted that the men who were killed worked for him and that they were transporting the diamond, along with some lesser jewels."

"But the insurance companies disagreed, my friend."

"Of course. Who wants to pay off on a claim that size?"

"In any case, the jewel left Casablanca within a day and with it went the killers and my connection to this case."

"Weren't you interested in catching whoever did it?" Doug said. "I mean, you are clearly a professional and a famous police officer. It must have bothered you."

Yehia smiled, enjoying the compliment and the attention the story had bought. "Of course, of course. Naturally I wanted justice and to find who was responsible. And we did search around here, made a few arrests...."

"Rounded up the usual suspects, I suppose?" Doug said.

"Yes, that, and some unusual ones, too. But my friend, I had by then learned that if I was to grow old wearing that uniform, I had to develop a certain attitude. *C'est la vie*, this is the life; you do what you can but learn to walk away and trust in Allah."

"And Douglas," Sergei said across the table, "that might be the best advice when it comes to your friend. Do what you can for her but don't get too involved."

"When did this robbery happen? Forty-eight? That's over fifty years ago. I doubt that bloodthirsty killers are still lurking around, trying to get their hands on this diamond."

"Fifty years is not that long ago, Douglas. I was twenty-two then and I'd like to think I'm still able to get about. But perhaps my years of lurking are behind me," Sergei said, darting his eyes from side to side theatrically, like a silent movie version of the villain.

"Don't underestimate men our age," Yehia said. "Time may have made us patient, but it has also made us desperate."

"Douglas," Sergei said, dropping the stage voice and looking Doug steady in the eye, "I'm not suggesting that the original killers are out there…."

"They may be. I never found them," Yehia said and added a burp.

"Correct, but what I mean is that this diamond, well, it's not that I believe in curses, but it has brought out the worst in people. And that can span generations, passed on just as surely as a genetic trait."

"So you suggesting I should go home? That I'm not up to it?"

"Not at all Douglas. I don't doubt your tenacity. I just want you to remain as safe as possible—don't take any risks that you don't have to. There was a local connection, here in Casa you know."

"If it makes you feel better I'll be leaving Morocco soon, so don't worry about the local connection."

"To Cairo? That's where the jewel went, isn't it Douglas, to Cairo?" Sergei said, his eyes fixed on Doug's. Doug nodded and drained the rest of his first drink. Sergei sighed and fell back into his chair. "Your Canadian friend doesn't know how lucky she is, you know that?"

"Oh I don't know if she's all that lucky to have me working for her," Doug said.

"Lucky?" Yehia shouted, startling people several tables away. "Lucky is what the other guy has to be. Real men don't need luck, they have their skills."

"Well then, gentlemen," Douglas said, raising his empty glass, "wish me luck."

◇◇◇

"Nice friend you've got there, Sergei," Doug said as the taxi zigzagged through the identical-looking streets of downtown Casablanca. "Where'd you meet him? A flogging?"

Sergei let out a sigh. "Douglas, don't tell me that you don't have a few friends who are a bit rough about the edges."

"Edges? Sergei, that guy is rough down to the center."

"Yes Douglas, I know this," Sergei said. "Captain Yehia was a crook, a bully, a sadist and possibly a murderer. But you know Douglas, if you are not part of the culture, not part of an era, it is easy to look and make judgments."

"Yes, I understand Sergei," Douglas said, "but come on, he all but told us he shot anybody who pissed him off. Doesn't that bother you?"

"Of course, what kind of man do you think I am? No, I understand, that's not what you meant and yes, I agree, Yehia is difficult at best, but when he was faced with a tough situation, when he had his finger on the trigger, he did what he felt he had to do. How many of us would know what to do in that situation?"

"I would know," Doug said. "There's no way I would just kill somebody. I'm sure of that. Bet on it."

"I'm just as sure as you that you would not," Sergei said, slapping Doug's knee. "And as you put it, I'd bet on it. You're a good man, Douglas, you can't hide it."

Doug smiled back. It was easy to feel self-righteous after a dinner with Captain Yehia.

◇◇◇

Two hours later, as Doug wandered around the red light district, he didn't feel so self-righteous.

At first he planned on a good night's rest and tried again to read the guide book, certain it would work its magic and put him under fast. But in the middle of a general description of the city was a warning to avoid the area the guidebook called "decidedly seedy." "As unlikely as this sounds," the book said, "in the area between the Boulevard Hassan Seghir and Rue Mohammed Smiha, from where they join at Avenue Zaid to the roundabout a half a kilometer away, the unwary late night visitor may find himself accosted by *Les Demoiselles d'Avignon* plying their trade."

He just came to look, he told himself as he tried to use the map in the guidebook without walking into a lamp pole. How do you *not* look around, he reasoned, he went on this trip to see the world and wasn't this part of it, a part he'd not really seen and only a fifteen-minute walk from his hotel? And with syphilis being the nicest thing he might catch—would catch—he wasn't going to go for it, no matter how good-looking they were.

He didn't know what to expect but he expected it to be better than this.

The street wasn't bright and flashy, there wasn't chest-thumping music coming from every window and there weren't any red lights. But there were women. They were not sashaying up and down the sidewalk in clingy short dresses and seven-inch heels, they were not swinging tiny silver purses as they laughed with other hookers and shouted out racy offers to the fun-loving guys driving by in convertibles. They hung in the shadows of many doorways, backs to the wall and, while not conservatively dressed, none were dressed as provocatively as Aisha had been to go shopping. And nobody was laughing.

They weren't even Arab women. They looked like the immigrants he'd seen from eastern European countries, thick necks, double chins and hairstyles out of the Fifties, their phony smiles heavy with kilos worth of steel fillings. Their hard eyes and expressionless faces, the monotone delivery of their offers, let Doug know that to them fucking was a job, like scrubbing floors or bottling beer, a monotonous, dead-end, when-will-this-goddamn-shift-end type of job and that sex with them would be as much fun as pumping gas. Get in line, stick it in, hurry up and finish. Have a nice day.

As he declined perfunctory offer after perfunctory offer, he wondered what shitty turn of events sent these women to these streets. They weren't teenaged runaways tying to make it in Hollywood. The youngest was as old as Doug and the oldest—he didn't want to think about that. Maybe they *were* teenagers, just turned old by the job, and that seemed plausible to Doug, who had watched himself age at his dead-end job.

But as sad and pathetic as they seemed, the men gliding by in their cars were worse. Young guys, old guys, good-looking guys, guys who looked like they had leprosy, drunk guys, guys in BMWs and guys in their wives' Hondas, and all of them leering without saying a word, getting some sort of secret rush out of seeing women reduced to screwing for money.

But you're here, too, Doug, he thought. Good point. Either there's other guys here, just seeing the world like me, or I'm just like them....

Doug took his first right, off the Boulevard Hassan and onto some no-name side street. He knew he might get lost, despite the guidebook in his back pocket, but he couldn't bring himself to backtrack up the boulevard, past the same women who would recognize and know just the kind of guy he was. And while the street got darker and narrower he kept walking. He tried hard to think of nothing.

He first noticed the two men when they startled a stray cat about thirty yards behind him. When they crossed over to the other side of the street when he did, he knew they were following him. Doug picked up his pace a bit and glanced back to see if they did the same. They were running.

He didn't want to panic but it was coming so naturally. He bolted down one side street and then another until he was sure he was lost. They were still behind him, closer and gaining quickly.

He took another turn and knew this was it. A metal garage door stretched from one side of the narrow street to the other and the padlock on the small entrance door was visible twenty feet away. Doug spun around and waited for the two men.

They had stopped running and came around the corner with a steady and confident gait. They knew the streets and knew he wasn't going anywhere. They were large men, for Moroccans, which made them smaller than Doug. They looked about his age but perhaps the mustaches and the dark complexions made them look older. Like the prostitutes, maybe life had made them too old too young. Their fists were clenched, which Doug was glad to see. That probably meant they didn't have weapons and it was going to be an old fashioned beating.

As they came closer Doug planted his right foot behind him and got ready. There were two things to do in Pottsville on a Friday night—get drunk and fight—and Doug did both as well as anybody he knew. And, as back in Pottsville, he would just rather run away, but that wasn't an option now.

The taller of the two men stepped in first and telegraphed a right hook that Doug ducked under easily, hitting the man hard in the stomach. As he pulled back the man aimed a kick at his crotch but Doug turned and took the kick on the thigh. The man got in a quick punch that caught Doug above his ear before Doug fired out two fast left jabs and a perfectly timed right that sent the man stumbling back. Before Doug could hit him again the second man charged from his right and wrapped his arms around Doug, trying to take him down. Doug had only a second to spin himself around to slam the attacker against the brick wall, bringing his knee up hard into the man's gut. The man tried to stand back up but Doug held his head down with his left hand and got in two solid hits before the taller man, smacked him on the side of the jaw. Doug let go of the smaller man, who dropped to one knee, then slid down to lean against the wall.

The taller man tried to rush Doug into the wall but it was an old bar fight tactic and Doug was ready. He turned sideways, grabbing the man's shirt and belt, and rammed him into the wall. Before the man could move, Doug had him by the hair and was breaking his face against the white concrete. When the man stopped struggling Doug pushed him hard to the left, trying to trip him just in case he was going to charge again, but the man fell on his own. The smaller guy was still sitting and, when he saw Doug, he cowered down, covering his head with both hands.

Doug ran out of the alley and down the road for a block or two. He wanted to run all the way back to the hotel but his pounding heart scared him into forcing himself to slow to a brisk walk. Ahead were the bright lights of a major intersection and Doug could already see the neon Coca-Cola sign he recognized from his walks near the hotel.

As he lay in bed studying the ceiling fan, a sock full of ice propped against his cheek, he tried to figure out if this trip was truly the stupidest thing he had ever done. He'd been in Morocco for three days and what had he accomplished? He'd probably caused the death of a café owner, sponged a couple of meals off a retired German, met an asshole ex-cop, bought a fake Rolex, and beat up two men. Okay, granted, meeting a hot babe made up for most of these things, but how long before the balance tipped on that one?

As far as the diamond—*Al Ainab,* or Jagersfontien, or what ever—he knew no more than what Edna Bowers had already guessed. His uncle was either an adventurous kind of rogue with the required heart of gold, or he was a psychotic killer with no soul. And in about thirty hours or so he'd be flying off to Egypt, wasting more of Edna's money, doing nothing in yet another country.

Maybe Aisha was right, if the old lady was happy with him spending her money maybe he should sit back and enjoy it, but he couldn't help thinking that the whole thing, the trips—the "investigation"—was a waste of time. He'd never find the diamond, he knew that, and he began to feel that he didn't care who killed Uncle Russ.

He needed to get back to Pottsville, find a job, put his dead uncle behind him and get on with his own life. He missed his few friends, he missed the foods he grew up with, he missed watching baseball—he hadn't even seen a box score since he left the States—he missed all of these things and it had only been three days. He was not an adventurer, not a traveler. He needed to get back, meet a girl like Aisha, and start over.

A girl like Aisha.

In Pottsville.

Right.

They think red diamonds are rare?

He mopped up the melting ice with a towel and re-adjusted his position. The tall guy had clocked him pretty good. Doug opened and closed his jaw trying to keep it from stiffening up. The four Tylenols were starting to make him feel groggy and he switched off the bedside lamp and tried to forget the run-in with the two pimps or muggers or whatever they were.

Or maybe they weren't.

Maybe it wasn't him in the wrong place at the wrong time, he thought. Maybe it was something else. Maybe word was out that some dip-shit American was asking all sorts of questions that nobody wanted asked. Maybe someone thought he knew more than he really did. Maybe next time they'd come better prepared, stop trying to save money and send some pros. Maybe he was just imagining too much.

Maybe. Maybe not.

Doug lay awake watching the fan as it fought to rotate the air-conditioned air back down to the bed. It's sad, he thought. Morocco, all this shit going on, feeling lost and confused and not knowing what was going to happen next, running from God knows who down some street in a country he had no place being, wondering if the next encounter wouldn't find him dead in an alley. It's sad, he thought, that this has been the most exciting three days of my life.

After a long hour the Tylenol kicked in and Doug slept through the pre-dawn call to prayer that shook the windows three feet from his head.

Chapter 10

"Look at me a second," Aisha said as she cut through traffic in front of the Hyatt Regency, her already dangerous driving made even more reckless. "Your face looks lopsided."

"Gee thanks, and you look gorgeous too." But she did, in a sleeveless black turtleneck, as tight as everything else she wore, a pair of oversized sunglasses, and her hair meticulously styled to look like she just woke up.

He had spent the morning doing nothing, writing a few postcards, tracking down a seven-day-old *USA Today* to read about a Pirate's game he had watched at a bar at Pottsville. He found a guidebook for Egypt, just in case he couldn't sleep on the plane, and bought his mother an ashtray that said *Casablanca!* on it, not that she smoked but she would expect something. In his concierge role, the manager went over Doug's plane tickets, point by minute point. Doug was sure Edna had already taken care of the tip but slipped the guy a few bucks anyway. Aisha called at twelve and told him that she'd pick him and his bags up around six. He reminded her his flight was not till the morning. "I know. Make sure you get a receipt when you check out, we've got plans for tonight," she said.

When he came back from a final look around the souk, the doorman informed him that the manager had signed for a letter from North America and that he could pick it up with the concierge. Doug waited while the man took off his doorman's fez, walked over to the front desk, removed the manager sign and placed the brass concierge sign in front of him before he asked for his package. Doug opened the cardboard Airborne envelope and saw a small stack of pages paperclipped together. Edna's yellow Post-it note said that he should read this before he got to Cairo. When he got to his room he packed the envelope in his carry-on bag. He'd read it on the plane. At that moment he had better things to do. Like fantasize about Aisha's plans.

The Al-Kady mansion was empty, everyone at a family dinner in Rabat. "They go every week. I go once a month," she explained. The living room was as large as the lobby of his hotel but decorated like a gaudy version of a European palace, with carved and gilded chair legs, velvety fabrics, and carpets with patterns so detailed they hurt your eyes. She walked him through the house back to the poolside patio where they first met. Set between two chairs was an elaborate water pipe like the kind he had seen in every café in the city.

"The coals are still hot," she said as she poked around in a small brazier behind the chairs, "it'll only take a few minutes." She removed the long brass neck of the pipe from the glass base. She filled the base with water from the outdoor bar, tossing in two handfuls of ice cubes before she reassembled the exotic contraption.

"I'm assuming you smoke *kif*," she said as she opened a small box on the table half filled with what looked like wet, sticky tobacco. A red-brown juice dripped from the small ball she made with her fingertips. She put this in the clay head of the water pipe and covered the opening with a piece of tin foil. She used a sharpened pencil to poke holes in the foil, the point of the pencil dyed red from many such uses.

Although he had drunk gallons of mint tea, Doug had not yet tried one of the water pipes. The smoke at the cafes smelled different than the smoke from stale cigarettes he was used to in bars back home. Tobacco, yes, but with a hint of something sweet, like smoking a strawberry.

Aisha sifted through the coals with a pair of long metal tongs until she found four pieces she liked, each half the size of her little finger. One by one she set them on top of the tin foil, carefully blowing on each till most of the coal showed fiery red. She attached the flexible hose to the brass neck, midway between the coals and the ice. The hose was wrapped in different colored cords and finished in a flourish of tassels and beads knotted around a hand-carved wooden mouthpiece.

Aisha put the wooden mouthpiece to her lips and drew in a long, deep breath. The ice tumbled in the base as it filled with a light gray smoke. She exhaled a cumulus cloud of smoke, her face hidden behind the billowing screen. She could make everything erotic, even the way she dabbed the corners of her eyes as she passed him the wooden handle.

"You've got to draw harder than that, Doug," she said, adjusting the coals. His second attempt brought a lungful of smoke down his throat, but it was smooth and definitely pleasurable. "Try not to exhale it out so forcefully, just let it slide out." Doug took another draw and did as he was instructed, handing the pipe back to Aisha.

"One of the things I missed most when I went to school in New York was sitting outside, smoking *kif*, watching the stars cross the sky. When I was younger I couldn't do it enough. As I got older I learned to appreciate the subtle pleasure of it all and now know it's one of life's great treats. You don't get it often, but that's what makes it special, like hot fudge sundaes and multiple orgasms."

Doug coughed out the smoke he was trying to pull in. "You've got a way of putting things, Aisha. You pick that up in the States?"

"There I was too conservative, here I'm too liberal. In college I was a tough date and in Egypt my uncles think I'm the Whore of Babylon. I need to find a place sort of in between. Maybe Malaysia. Bali's nice too."

Doug pictured an island beach. White sands, crystal clear water, palm trees swaying just a bit in the warm breeze, and

Aisha, wearing a grass skirt, no top, and a huge orchid in her black hair. Would she still smell like vanilla there or would it be coconut? She'd step out of her skirt, set the flower on the sand, and walk out until the waves slapped at her ass, her dark brown legs just visible beneath the surface.

"Speak up, my hearing always goes when I smoke *kif*," she said as she tapped him on the shoulder with the wooden handle.

"Oh, sorry, I was trying to figure something out. So this is *kif*. What is that, some sort of cured flavored tobacco?"

"*Kif* is what we call it here. It's grown up in the Atlas Mountains and you mix it in with some flavored molasses. The word comes from some Berber dialect, but it translates pretty easily. I think in the States the current term is weed but we called it pot at Bard."

"This is marijuana?" Doug said, rather startled. "Isn't this like major illegal over here?"

"It is in the U.S., too, I recall," she said, fishing a beer out of the small cooler under her chair.

"I mean, can't we get like killed here for this? Don't they execute drug users here?"

"None that I know. I can put it away if you'd like," she said, but her voice indicated that killing the pipe would not be what she would like.

"No, it's okay, I mean it's good, it's just that I'm just surprised is all."

"I would hope that I wouldn't run out of surprises in just a few days, Doug," she said, taking the pipe handle from him with the same hand she was handing him a beer. "I've got a whole night of surprises lined up for you. Cheers."

At dinner—an Authentic Californian Bristo the sign said—Aisha introduced him to a dozen of her friends, whose names he never caught. It seemed that everyone she knew was chic, witty, and painfully good-looking. He felt painfully average. But Aisha had a way of making everyone seem more interesting, more exotic, than they really were. She introduced Doug as a private detective, just in from New York, which, technically, was sort of true. He was transformed, suddenly mysterious and dangerous. As for good-looking, Aisha's beauty seemed to spill off onto whomever she was sitting next to. He was good-looking by association.

Doug didn't remember who did the ordering, who paid the bill, who passed around the bottle of Jack Daniels, who handed him the cigar. But it was Aisha who was rubbing his leg under the table.

Dancing at the club was a sweaty blur of Euro music that he never heard before and lights like a science fiction movie. It was well past two when Aisha pulled him close, drove her tongue down his throat and after shouted in his ear, "Let's get out of here."

In her brightly lit room, she pushed him backwards onto the bed and climbed on top, straddling his stomach with her legs, her jeans unzipped but still hanging on her hips. She kissed hard, pressing her lips against his violently. Her hair was everywhere. Her heavy breathing had no rhythm and a bead of sweat rolled off her nose onto his cheek. She threw herself back, pulling her shirt off in one motion. "Get your clothes off," was all she said.

Aisha's long legs pinned Doug down, her hands pressed hard into his shoulders. Her flawless body, one shade of honey brown, constantly moved, undulating powerfully. He was amazed that he was able to hold out for as long as he did. It certainly didn't slow down Aisha, who slid her body down to his thigh, apparently trying to grind through his flesh to hit bone. Doug watched as she rode his leg, tossing her head around, gasping for breath, shouting things in a half dozen languages. And, when she sat up suddenly, taking fingernails full of his chest with her, her wild hair framing that face, their sweat glazing her chest and tight, flat stomach, and she sucked in all that air for one final, high-pitched moan, Doug never felt happier.

An hour later, she was back on top of him again.

The third time, she just went right for his thigh.

Doug woke just before dawn when Aisha whispered in his ear, "Just lie there," and snaked her legs around his.

Chapter 11

"See?" Aisha said as they raced through the airport terminal, "I told you we'd make it."

Doug readjusted the shoulder strap of his carry-on bag and kept a vice-like grip on his passport and ticket. The grip was easy since he had had a half hour practice, gripping the dashboard of Aisha's BMW as she made NASCAR time on the Avenue Moulay Hassan I. Somehow Aisha had had the strength to get up early enough to clean, press, and repack his luggage, drag him into the shower and maneuver through the early morning rush hour traffic. If it had been up to him, they'd still be in bed. Recovering.

But no, they were at the airport and he was about to say goodbye to the most amazing woman in the world. What he should say had been troubling him since it dawned on him that he was really leaving, just after Aisha blurred past the speeding ambulance on the outskirts of the city. He thought about that airport scene in *Casablanca*. The rain, the passion, Rick and Elsa, Captain Renault, the twin-engine passenger plane revving its sputtering engines. Rick didn't get all mushy, didn't ramble on about how she was the only woman he ever loved. "We'll always have Paris"—"Here's looking at you, kid." The most perfect, romantic goodbye ever. Now it was his turn.

"Aisha," he started, "it may be too early to say this, and I don't know how you feel, but I just want you to know that the past few days...."

"Here's your gate. I'll call you in Cairo. Have fun." She grabbed him by the back of the neck, pulled him in for a quick kiss and with that, disappeared behind the stream of other last-second boarders trying to muscle past him and onto the waiting plane.

I hope there's a better movie on the plane, he thought.

◇◇◇

The Egypt Air flight was overbooked by a hundred and twenty percent, standard he assumed by the nonchalant attitude of the stewards as they pulled people out of their seats and shoved them down the aisle towards the door. A male steward checked his ticket, led him to the middle seat of the middle section, between two Arab men in suits who obviously had hoped that the seat would, by some miracle, remain open. He pulled out the envelope Edna had delivered to the hotel and placed his carry-on in the already packed overhead. The steward helped by crushing the bag into as small a ball as possible, wedging it on top of a bag marked fragile, until, with a distinct snap, his bag fit.

To maximize profits Egypt Air had done away with unnecessary frills, like leg room, air conditioning, no smoking signs, and repairs to things like tray tables, arm rests, and bathrooms. To allow everyone time to get used to the conditions aboard the plane, the pilot taxied out to the middle of the tarmac and parked for two hours. This was a non-smoking flight, so children under ten were forbidden to smoke, unless accompanied by an adult. They were, however, permitted to run up and down the aisles, screaming, as the need came upon them. Just like their parents. If it was Egypt Air's plan to calm passengers' fears about the technical ability of their fleet, Doug reasoned, it had worked. If the plane skidded off the runway on takeoff and exploded into a fireball of twisted metal and luggage, most passengers would consider it a welcome relief.

As Doug was debating whether or not he would break his neck jumping out of the emergency exit door, the plane suddenly took off down the runway and into the midday sky. Something resembling cooled air was pumped into the cabin and the smell of homicidal rage dissipated along with the blanket of smog that had settled just above the headrests.

Doug pried his arms from his side and opened Edna's letter, careful to keep the pages together since if he dropped them they were gone forever, like the stray shoe he could feel in the space allegedly meant for his feet.

The first page had directions to his hotel, The Shepheard, and a selection of restaurants in the area. The second page was a list of five names and addresses of people to contact. Number four on the list was Aisha's uncle, Mr. Nasser Ashkanani. Aisha had scribbled instructions to the Ashkanani shop in the Khan on the inside of a pack of matches she got from one of the clubs they raced through the night before. If he could decipher the minuscule script he could, in theory, find the shop.

The next twenty pages came as quite a surprise—a reduced size photocopy of the *Pottsville Standard* from last Wednesday. There wasn't anything important in it, no world-shaking news first reported in Central Pennsylvania's Largest Tri-Borough Daily. There was a story about a councilman's attempts to get the county to cover the costs of repairing an intersection near Schuykill Haven, a story about how the high school varsity baseball team lost a close one to the team from Frackville, a "news story" on how Bill Powless' Chevy Land on Route 80 was honored by Detroit for selling more vehicles than any other central Pennsylvania new-and-used auto showroom last month. The Piggly Wiggly was running a special on Odenbach lager, cherries, and Red Devil paints. The weather was humid and hot, with an expected high of eighty. Blah, blah, blah. Edna must have sent it to him to help him cope with the homesickness that never came. All it did was to remind him what a dull life he had left behind.

The rest—two pages—were Edna's notes.

Doug passed on the mutton and bread breakfast offered by the stewardess, took a cup of coffee instead, and settled in, ready to read more things that would build his overall lousy impression of Russell Pearce.

"I've gathered together the letters and the personal reminiscences that relate to that summer in 1948. Most relate directly to the acquisition of the jewel, some do not, but I include them since you may find something in them that I missed. Everyone agrees that the job was planned by Russell and another man, and I think that other man was Sasha. This probably took place on July first. Charley was not at this meeting."

Too busy getting indisposed, Doug thought.

"On July third, bribes were paid to some of the larger stevedores to ensure they would not show up to work the next night. This was taken care of by Sasha. On the night of the third, Charley was updated on the plan by Russell, and, as usual, Charley would be the driver and spent the late hours arranging for a car."

Arranging for a car, updated on the plan, acquiring a jewel. It sounded more like a business meeting than a heist. Here's the first thing you missed, Edna—these guys were bad news.

"On the night of the fourth, Russell, Sasha and three other men entered the building that housed several consignment shipping offices. There was some trouble and one of the guards shot at Russell. Even the surviving guards agreed that they had started shooting first."

"Gosh, I wonder why?" Doug said out loud. He felt the bulk of his two fellow row-mates shift as they attempted to distance themselves from this freak that talked to himself on an airplane, without, of course, giving up an inch of the armrest.

"I had a friend who later met one of the guards who survived and she said that, according to this man, no one would have gotten hurt if the guards had only done what they were told to do. In any event, things didn't go quite to plan after that."

Maybe Captain Yehia was telling the truth. He didn't mention survivors, though. He may have been mistaken. Or maybe there were no survivors and someone else was mistaken. But it was the word "survived" that said a lot to Doug.

"Charley said that the five men made it back to the car but that one of the local men was bleeding and decided to stay behind."

We found one in an alley not far away, his face shot off.

"Charley drove the others to a second car and then on to a small house where they met Hammad Al-Kady. Besides the famous diamond there were several smaller jewels and some gold items. Hammad was given the smaller items to sell and the locals were paid off."

We found two more bodies later….

"It was decided that Russell and Charley would get the jewel to Nasser Ashkanani in Cairo and that Sasha would catch up with them there. I have a note that Charley wrote describing the diamond: "It's not as big as I thought it would be but it's as big as its name." I think this is a reference to 'the eye,' the real name of the famous diamond."

Well what do you know, Doug thought, I did find something out in Morocco. He made a mental note to send her the real name of the diamond when he was in Cairo. Once he figured out which was the real name.

"Several people have contacted me over the years, each one of them claiming that Russell or Charley or Sasha secretly told them what was going to happen to the diamond next. There're a few things that most of these stories have in common. First, they were definitely not planning on having the diamond cut. I don't know if this had anything to do with the value of the whole stone or the demands of some buyer, but it seems clear that the plan was to keep the diamond in one piece. Next, a lot of the stories suggest that Nasser Ashkanani had buyers arranged in Istanbul or Ceylon."

Doug had no idea where Ceylon was. A footnote informed him, however, that Ceylon was now known as Sri Lanka. Doug had no idea where Sri Lanka was.

"The stories seem to indicate something else as well. There appears to have been some sort of fallout among the partners. The exact cause of the trouble is unclear and a lot depends on who you talk to. Most of the people who have written to me over the years say that it was all Charley's fault. Apparently there was a young Egyptian woman involved, the daughter of a well-connected pasha, and Charley was blamed for exciting too much attention. I feel this is unfair to Charley—there were other issues that put more strain on the relationship than one ill-advised friendship."

Friendship. She had a way with words.

"There were other rumors, but there often are in that line of work. I can only confirm one: Charley was planning on running off with the diamond but had a change of heart once they arrived in Cairo. This may have been the cause of the bad blood arising among the partners."

Doug blew the steam off his boiling coffee and thought about the kinds of things that would lead to bad blood in partnerships. He decided that a double-crossing bastard would be one of them.

"The last thing really has nothing to do with the diamond. When they were sailing from Morocco to Alexandria, before Charley's alternative plan came to light, Russell talked a lot about his life in Pennsylvania. This often happened when he smoked hashish. He used to like to stand on the aft deck, throwing lumps of coal at seagulls. One afternoon, close to sunset, he told Charley that his favorite memory of his whole life was playing baseball in his senior year of high school, just before he left home. Charley remembered it clearly since this was the only time Russell ever talked about his family. Russell's team was playing against a rival team late in the season. It was apparently important that they win this particular game, but I don't recall exactly why. Russell made several key plays and made a final throw that won the game. He was very proud of that throw and the poor seagulls along the North African coast probably suffered every time he told that story. What he was most proud of, however, was the fact that his parents and his brother Eddie were in the stands to see him make the play. This was one of the few times, I gathered, that his family took an interest in his sports activities. He left home soon after this. He said it was the best thing he could do for Eddie, to leave him with a good memory of his brother, and he liked to pretend that this is why he chose to leave at that particular time. But he also liked to tell how he was caught that night having French sex with a sophomore named Caroline and her father threatened to kill him. That was Russell, an angelic side he seldom showed and a devilish side that everyone knew."

Doug had never heard those Uncle Russ stories before. And he never heard anyone refer to his father as Eddie. Must be an older brother's prerogative, Doug thought, since everyone else called his father Ed. But everyone, it seemed, had always called his mother Caroline.

"Sitting on that aft deck one night, Russell wrote a long letter to his family. He put it in an empty gin bottle and dropped it overboard. 'I write,' he told Charley, 'but they never write back.'"

Doug reread the entry. He thought about all the times he had asked his parents about Uncle Russ. No wonder his father had felt the way he did, no wonder his mother always looked away whenever his name was mentioned.

So this is the gang that stole one of the most famous jewels in history. And that was the uncle he had grown up idolizing. Doug watched as his still scalding instant coffee was snatched up by the flight attendant. Breakfast, apparently, was over. He tried to slide the papers back into the envelope without waking his sleeping neighbor, who had settled comfortably onto his shoulder, but he woke up nonetheless and glared at Doug for his unbelievably inconsiderate behavior. The only seat in the airplane that fully reclined was directly in front of Doug and, after a few minutes of hopeless squirming to find a position that didn't cut off blood to his legs, Doug leaned his head back and prayed for sleep. After twenty minutes of begging, it finally came.

◇◇◇

"Surprise," a voice whispered in his ear as a hand patted his knee. He had been dreaming of Aisha. She was naked, of course, smoking that big water pipe as she sat on his chest, her crotch inching forward, and for a moment the word and the patting blended seamlessly into his dream. But that wasn't her voice.

And that certainly wasn't her hand. Doug spun as quickly as he could in his seat. "Sergei," he said, almost shouting, "what are you doing here?"

Sergei gave Doug's knee one last sharp slap. "Like I said, surprise." Sergei smiled. "Oh, Douglas, you should see the look on your face."

"Well, I can imagine. What the hell are you doing here, I thought you were staying in Casablanca for a few more weeks."

"One of the great things about being my age is that you are allowed to suddenly change your plans without looking immature." He looked around the seat vacated by Doug's neighbor and his smile withered into a polite grimace. He put one finger on the seat back in front of him, feebly trying to keep it from reclining any further. "You should have flown First Class."

"It's hard to see how First Class can be much better."

"It's not. On Egyptian Air, First Class simply means they let you off the plane before the mobs," he said, holding up a tangled and broken headset that he pulled from behind the small of his back.

"Why are you here? I mean, on this plane?"

The smile returned to Sergei's face, his tightly trimmed goatee framing his even, white teeth. "I'm following you, Douglas, isn't that obvious?"

"Pardon?"

"Following you. Trailing you. Staying in your back pocket. Keeping close tabs on you. Shadowing you. Ummm…" he said as he tapped his finger against his chin. "Those are the terms that come to my mind. Know any others?"

"But why?"

"Because Douglas, I like you. I had more fun in Casablanca when I was with you than I had had in years. You said it yourself, my old friends are quite strange, and, I assure you, quite dull. Captain Yehia is the most interesting and cultured of the lot. When you told me you were leaving for Cairo, just like that, I was impressed. I haven't been around men like you in a long time and it brought back a lot of memories when I was more like you than, well, like me."

"That still doesn't explain why you're following me."

Sergei laughed. "Douglas, that's really just a figure of speech. What I am doing, what I *hope* to do, is see Cairo through the eyes of a new friend who has never seen the ancient temples, the medieval mosques or the quite modern watering holes. I know Cairo better than I know New York or London or Beijing. If you don't mind the company of an old man, I could show you a good time."

"That's great for me, but what do you get out of it?" Doug said. He noticed his sleepy Arab seatmate weaving through the throng of people crowding the aisles like a department store on Christmas Eve, the flight attendants having long ago retreated to the aft kitchen to smoke and drink the flight away.

"What do I get? Ah, Douglas, you'd have to be my age to understand, really. I get the vicarious joy of experiencing this old city with fresh eyes. I get the pleasure of sharing with you the years and years of knowledge I have cultivated, the small teashops, the exotic nightclubs, and the perfect spots to take that once in a lifetime photo of a sunrise at the pyramids. And," he added in the stage whisper he liked to use, "I get to spend more of the museum's money."

The large Arab man hovered above Sergei. "*Afwan, sadeeq,*" he said placing a heavy hand on Sergei's shoulder.

"*Tafadul, ya sadeeqakee,*" Sergei said to the man as he stood up, and then to Douglas "I'll see you in the airport. It's the most chaotic madhouse of a place so brace yourself for your first taste of third-world bureaucracy at its most refined. We'll both be in the need for a drink afterwards. Where are you staying?"

"The Shepheard. Know it?"

"Of course. The old Shepheard was much more interesting, but they burned that down during the Suez affair. It's on the Nile, or close to it. Good part of town. We can share a cab. I'll be just down the road at the Sheraton," he said as Doug's seatmate wedged himself between the armrests. Doug noticed how happy

Sergei looked, beaming like a schoolteacher on a long awaited field trip. "This will be so much fun, Douglas. I know you have work to do too, but I just know you can spare some time."

"Definitely, Sergei. I'm glad you're here," Douglas said as Sergei weaved back through the crowd. And he meant it. There was something about Sergei that made Doug comfortable and confident. He was a gentleman all right, the most sophisticated man Doug had ever met. And yet he was so easy to talk to, not like the phony "gentlemen" in Pottsville like that manager at the bank or that guy who taught at the community college.

As the man continued to settle into his seat, holding up his broken headset and casting a suspicious look at him, Doug thought about what he would do in Cairo. Edna seemed pleased with his progress so far, even if he didn't see any, and, like Aisha had said, as long as she was happy, enjoy the ride. He had a short list of people to talk to and an eager tour guide in Sergei. And who knows, he thought, maybe Aisha will show up. A month ago he had never been on a plane, now he was an hour out of Egypt. It wasn't over yet, but Doug was sure this would be the best summer of his life.

Chapter 12

Sergei was wrong about the airport. The government ministry in charge of updating the airport would have to make a lot of changes before it would be as organized and logical as a madhouse. There were "lines" that looked like the crush at the door of a Who concert, smoke from a thousand cigarettes, the smell of sweaty, unwashed bodies with breaths made toxic from strange foods, and stone-faced clerks who pounded their official stamps on the blank pages of his passport. Above it all, the mind-numbing din of everyone shouting to the person three feet away, the crackling PA announcing, in an impatient voice, messages intended only for those who understood Arabic, and the whole building acoustically designed to amplify it all and echo it back again and again. And then, when the mind could not absorb another sound, the call to prayer, filling the dingy terminal with ear-shattering reminders of piety, delivered in that same impatient tone.

And that was before he got to the baggage claim.

The airport's one conveyer belt ran just thirty feet and every male passenger who had arrived at the airport in the past four hours was crowding in front of it, staring at the small door through which the battered collection of identical-looking boxes and suitcases circled endlessly. The female passengers stood towards the back, shouting encouragement and instructions to husbands and porters. Occasionally a body would force its way through the crowd and scramble for a piece of luggage that would stay just out of reach, disappearing through the door at the end of the belt, never to reappear. Overhead flowed a constant stream of suitcases as people in the front lines passed back what they thought looked somewhat familiar. On the fringes passengers opened and inspected contents, only to pass them back to the front when they decided that, no, they did not own that type of underwear.

After forty minutes of bobbing in the crowd, Doug noticed that some of the passengers from his flight were plowing their way through with their luggage, or someone's luggage. He was taller than most so when his bag burst through the door, he was able to watch it glide along as he charted an intercept course. With his carry-on balanced on top, he held his bag above his head and swam upstream till he found a small clearing in front of the customs desks.

"American?" The customs man looked like everyone else he had seen so far in Egypt. Same bulky build, same three-pound eyebrows, same swarthy complexion, same five o'clock shadow, same Saddam Hussein mustache. In his rumpled uniform, with its dark sweat marks under the arms and the tightly knotted, crooked tie, he blended in with the porters, taxi drivers, and airline booking agents that swarmed around the baggage claim area. It was the large pistol and the oversized badge that made people obey him.

"Yes, American," Doug said as he handed the man his passport; setting his carry-on bag on the counter.

The man flipped through the near-empty passport, pausing to reread Doug's name several times. He handed Doug back the passport and pointed. "Not here. There. That man." By a glass door stood one of the custom man's many twin brothers. He read the first page of the passport, looking up at Doug several times as he did, and pointed to the door. Inside, a long table, with reams of forms stacked on one end, crowded the narrow office. Stale cigarette smoke hung from the ceiling along with a humming fluorescent light. Brothers number three and four sat motionless on metal chairs.

"Hi. The men outside told me to come in here," Doug said.

The men stared at him, silent, the hum of the lights drowning out the chaos of baggage claim.

"I was told to come here," Doug repeated in case they had been hypnotized by the drone. "I'm an American."

One man held out his hand and Doug reached over to shake it. "Passport," the man spat out, moving his hand to avoid touching Doug's.

"Oh yeah, sorry. Here you go."

The man took it and flipped through the same way his brothers had, reading his name several times. He said something to the other man in Arabic, who reached over to a clipboard thick with wrinkled papers. "Where are you arriving from?"

"Morocco. On the Egypt Air flight."

The two men looked at each other, then at Doug. "Put your bags here," the second man said as his partner came around the desk, still flipping through the passport. "This your luggage, correct?"

"Yup, that's it. Just the two bags."

"Your name is Douglas Pearce? From America?"

"Yes, that's me." The man behind the desk was unzipping every pocket on his black, nylon bag, peering inside and then spinning them around with a practiced hand.

"Why are you in Egypt?"

"Tourism, I guess. Is there a problem?"

Zip, peer, zip, spin. Zip, peer, zip, spin.

"No problem. How long will you stay in Egypt?"

Good question, Doug thought. "Ah, about a week or so."

Zip, peer, zip, spin. Zip, peer, zip, spin.

"What do you bring with you to Egypt?"

Zip, peer, zip, spin. Zip.

"Just clothes and papers. Oh, and an ashtray I bought in Morocco."

Peer.

"Nothing else?"

Peer.

"Nope, that's it."

"Nothing?" he asked again, staring at Doug.

"Nothing."

He smiled and nodded towards his partner behind the desk. Doug turned and saw his carry-on bag on the table. The man held open one of the side pockets by the zipper pull. He smiled at Doug, pointed to the pocket and then, with the flourish of a sidewalk magician, slowly pulled out a clear plastic bag, half filled with fine, white powder.

"Nothing?" the man said as he gripped Doug firmly by the wrists.

Chapter 13

It was the gray meat with the flat bread again.

For breakfast it had been the gray meat with rice and last night, for dinner, it was the gray meat with what was probably potatoes. It had been the gray meat with every meal, although the three meals he missed due to vomiting and diarrhea might have offered lobster and steak, he couldn't say for sure.

It wasn't beef—that he had deduced by the second day—and it certainly wasn't chicken. That left, he reasoned, goat, lamb, horse, dog, camel, and rat, none of which he had ever tried but any of which he felt were reasonable candidates for the gray meat. The size of the bones should have ruled out rat, but the greasy texture and musky flavor kept it in the running. Despite several days of eating little other than the bread, rice, and probable potatoes, the gray meat still looked and smelled as unappetizing as it had looked when he was offered his first jailhouse meal, over a week ago.

Between the illness, brought on, no doubt, by the one serving of gray meat he had thought he could stomach, and all the small meals, Doug had dropped the fat that he had built up since leaving high school. Two days ago he had looked lean and fit, today he looked emaciated and weak. The lack of sleep didn't help. There was a constant echoing roar in the jail, all the words in Arabic, all the sounds produced by metal on metal, metal on concrete, metal on flesh, flesh on flesh.

But even if it had been peaceful he could have hoped for little sleep. He had spent all of his time in a windowless concrete space smaller than his hotel room in Casablanca. There was a bunk bed, taken right from every prison movie, and a ceramic tiled hole in the floor that served as a toilet. A small plastic bucket of water was kept full by a dripping pipe that poked through the wall, and this was used in lieu of toilet paper and for any other hygiene needs. A steel door with a grated window and no inside knob broke up the uniformity of the concrete walls. It was roomy for one, cozy for two, intimate for three, and home for Doug and eleven of his newest friends.

He had sat on the bed once his first day, but this had caused such a commotion that he never tried again. The four men that claimed each of the two beds guarded their territory like pit bulls and, by the smell, probably marked it the same way. There was the gut-turning stink of body odor that got worse every day, the poisonous smells produced as the gray meat worked its way through the bowels of his cellmates, and the pervasive smell of sweat-soaked concrete. But the smell that wafted up from the hole, a smell that Doug was certain carried diseases deadlier than the plague, a smell he was sure he could see, made it impossible to ever get comfortable.

True to the Pearce line, his beard grew in spotty and disheveled. He wore the khakis and polo shirt he had put on that morning at Aisha's but they had taken his shoes and belt when they signed him in. He spent the day, like his roommates, sitting on the floor, back propped against the wall. At night, like the three others not squeezed on to the beds, he slept in the same position, his head balanced on his crossed arms.

It was his second full day, just before the vomiting started, when John Wayne spoke to him.

"I reckon you're not from around these parts, are you pilgrim?" It was an excellent John Wayne with not even a hint of Arabic. "Abdoulrahim Abdulrazzaq," he said, extending his hand. "Call me Abe."

"Douglas Pearce. Call me Doug." They shook hands and Abe slid down next to Doug. He was a good-looking man, even Doug could see that. He wore his thick, black hair short, and he needed a shave, but it only made his angular jaw seem more masculine. He had a young face and athletic build, but deep crow's feet made his eyes look as if they belonged to an older man. His clothes—jeans and a tee shirt—were even dirtier than Doug's.

"Wow, you don't look so good," Abe said, this time in his normal voice, an accentless English of a Middle American variety.

"I feel like shit. It might have been something I ate."

"No doubt. You are what you eat, you know. My first time here—Egypt, not this jail—I got sick too. I guess I'm immune to it now."

"That was a pretty good John Wayne you did there," Doug said, pulling his knees in closer to his chest. His stomach was starting to rumble ominously.

"John Wayne?" Abe said, smiling. "Shit, that was my Bogart."

"You pick that up here in the jail?"

"No, here I picked up lice, crabs, scabies, and the nasty habit of burping loudly. The John Wayne I learned to do growing up in Michigan." He thought a moment and then said, "Not a lot a call for John Wayne imitations here."

"I guess I picked up the lice too, that would explain the itching."

"No, that would be the scabies. They deloused the cell the day before you got here. They use some derivative of DDT, kills everything. Probably killing us all right now. What you also have is an intestinal disorder brought on by bacteria, probably from the food. It's not fatal but I bet it feels that way. You'll get sicker before you get better, but in two days you'll be back to your cheery self. I'll talk to the guard, have him get you some Lomotil, and make sure you drink a lot of water. Believe it or not, it's safe."

"Are you a doctor, Abe?" Doug said.

"No," he said slipping into a Groucho Marx, raising his eyebrows and holding an invisible cigar, "but I've played one in the women's dorm."

Soon after, the vomiting started. The diarrhea started the next morning. Doug added his bit to the smells in the jail, but it was hardly noticeable. The cramping in his back and stomach, from the dry heaves and his wringing intestines, doubled him over in pain. Abe had him lie as flat as he could on the floor, the bunk men offering the cleanest blanket they had. Despite the fever and the sweats, Doug could tell the other prisoners were genuinely concerned. When a guard checked in around noon, they were on their feet, shouting at the guard, pointing to Doug on the floor and gesturing heavenward, either seeking divine assistance or divine retribution. Later, one of the men—grossly overweight with a fat sweaty face that glistened like a glazed ham—knelt down beside Doug and began rubbing his back. Doug tried to protest but was too weak to really care. After five minutes he felt his back relax, the pain melting away. The man spent two hours massaging Doug's back, stomach, shoulders, and legs. When he finished the pain was gone and Doug fell asleep. Later, when the drugs had stopped the mad dashes to the porcelain hole, Doug tried to thank the man, who smiled and said *"Maleesh, maleesh. Al Hamdu Allah."*

"He's trying to say forget about it, it was no big deal. Thanks be to God. That kind of stuff," Abe translated.

"Tell him how grateful I am, will you?" Doug asked.

"Ah, he knows. *Maleesh*. Forget about it."

Abe said a few words to the fat man, who smiled again and patted Doug on the knee. "While you were sleeping the guards came and took five of the guys out. Sent 'em home I guess. They put six more in their place and you already missed out on the bed."

"That's okay, I'll pass. Look, who do I talk to to get in touch with my embassy? No one has said a word to me since they brought me in about how long I'll be here or what happens next."

"Get used to it. I've been here two weeks already and I was never even charged with anything. Eventually your name will come up on somebody's list and, if they can remember where they stored you, they'll come and get you."

"Then how come you're still here?" Doug said and added, "I mean, if you don't want to talk about it, that's cool."

"*Sadeeqakee*—my friend," Abe laughed and put his arm around Doug, "I'm here because somebody wanted me here. It may be my asshole brother-in-law who is pissed off about me refusing to help him secure a loan from the bank, it could be the man who owns the building next to my family's shop who wants my dad to sell out cheaply, it could be the father of some young lady I may or may not have helped to corrupt. I haven't figured it out yet. This is Egypt," he said, holding his hands out, palms up, "it could be a thousand things, it could be nothing. But what it will be is slow, inefficient, and costly."

"And you'll just sit there and take it? You won't say anything? You won't get a lawyer?"

"*Maleesh, sadeeq.* It'll all work out. Nothing happens from the inside. My family is no doubt making all the right calls, finding the *baksheesh*—the bribe money—like I said, *maleesh.* And you? They don't get many Americans in here, well, non-Arab Americans anyway. What are you in here for?"

"They found drugs in my suitcase at the airport."

Abe looked at him. He made a low, long whistling sound as he leaned his head back against the wall. "That, Doug, is deep shit."

"It wasn't mine, really," Doug said.

"Sure, and you didn't inhale."

"No really," Doug insisted, "somebody planted it on me."

"Like who?" Abe was smiling again. "Come on Doug, listen to yourself. This jail is full of people who were framed, who are innocent."

"You are, aren't you?"

"*Touché, touché,*" Abe said, holding up a finger as if he was conceding a point. "Okay, Sherlock, if it's not yours, whose is it?"

From the moment the twins at the airport wrestled his arms behind his back and clamped on the cuffs, Doug had struggled with that question. It had to be cocaine, a drug Doug had never even tried, and it could only have come from one place. He had tried to imagine a dozen different scenarios explaining its appearance in his bag—slipped in by an airline steward who knew the police were on to him, stashed by an Islamic fundamentalist eager to see the godless American suffer, spontaneously created by a bizarre combination of shaving cream, aspirin, and the increased cabin pressure. He wanted to believe anything other than what he knew was the truth.

"Some girl I met in Morocco put it in my bag. She has 'business connections' here in Cairo and I assume they would have stopped by my hotel to pick it up." It didn't feel any better saying it out loud.

Again Abe whistled, it sounding more like a bomb dropping from a great height. "Well *sadeeqakee*, you know what that means?"

"Yeah, *maleesh*."

"Doug, *maleesh* means no problem," Abe said. "What you have here is *mushkila kabeer*."

"*Mushkila kabeer?*"

"Right. A big problem."

◇◇◇

The gray meat looked out from under the flat bread.

"If you're not going to eat it," Abe said, making a thick, gray sandwich, "give it to Yasser over there. He loves the stuff."

It had been eight days since Doug arrived in the cell. Many of the faces had changed but the cell stayed as crowded. Abe's cousin had managed a visit to let him know that the family was working to get him out and, *insha' Allah*, he'd be home by Friday. Doug sat with his back against the cold wall, his spot strategically selected to be as far from the porcelain hole as possible, looking forward to another day of watching the ceiling.

Despite the crowded conditions, five times a day Doug's cellmates, including Abe, answered the call to prayer. In shifts of four, they lined up, shoulder to shoulder, and faced one of the walls. They stood, they knelt, they placed their foreheads to the floor, repeating the movements three times.

"The Quibla," Abe explained as he started into his sandwich, "is the direction to Mecca. We face that way since that's where the Ka'ba is located. The bowing and gestures are all quite symbolic, but basically it reminds us what Islam is all about, submission to the will of God. We're Muslims," he said, pointing around the room, "those who submit. But really everything is Muslim, everything submits to the will of God. Muslims just do it willingly."

Doug pulled the flat bread apart into small pieces, trying to stretch out his noon meal. He was uncomfortable with the topic. "I don't think about religion much."

"Me either," Abe said.

"What are you talking about? You're up there praying every few hours. And with all your *salama lakums* and your *Al Hamdu Allahs*, you're thinking about religion all the time."

"I'm not thinking about religion, I'm thinking about God."

"Same difference," Doug said, eager to end the discussion.

"Religions are fucked up, every one of them. But we all still submit to God's will, even you, my little atheist friend."

"I never said I was an atheist, but since you don't see me up there," Doug said, pointing to the last group of men finishing up their prayers, "how can you say I submit?"

"I see you sitting here, next to me, in this jail cell. Like it or not, this is where God wants you."

"I wish God'd get me the hell outta here."

"*Insha' Allah*. If God wills it, it'll happen."

"So I suppose God willed that girl to put the drugs in my bag?" He didn't want to come across too sarcastic but it came out that way.

"Somebody say amen, brothers," Abe said, now in the voice of a TV evangelist. "The *Lord*," he continued, stretching the word out to four syllables, "works in strange and mysterious ways."

"No offense, Abe, but I think it had less to do with the Lord than it did with…."

"Satan!" Abe shouted as he stood, warmed up to his role now, but trying hard not to laugh. "Yes, *Satan* had you by the very balls, sinner. Your very balls! The devil in the shape of a woman, sinner! And she lured you—oh *Lord* did she lure you—into her den where you made the beast with two backs!" Abe gyrated his hips, driving home the image. "And now, sinner," he said, dodging a pillow thrown from the bed and ignoring the Arabic jokes, "now you reap what you have sown. But it is not too late, sinner! No, not too late! Tell Satan to get behind you, sinner. Shout it out: 'Get thee behind me, Satan!' And when the Devil is behind thee, for *God's* sake, sinner," he said, eyes wild and pointing at Doug, "don't drop the soap."

For the first time since he got off the plane in Cairo, Doug was laughing. And so were the other men in the cell, Abe's broad theatrics entertaining despite the language barrier. The laughter stretched out, led to other imitations, these in Arabic, which led to singing and, cramped and crowded, traditional Arabic dancing. Several of the men tried to teach Doug an Arabic line dance Abe called a debka, but with little success. For half an hour Doug forgot all about Edna, all about the jewel, all about the drugs, all about Aisha.

But that night, like every night in the cell, he squatted, staring at the ceiling, trying to make sense of it all. He quit, that he decided in the police van as it pin-balled through the streets of Cairo. Sorry, Edna. Sorry I didn't find your jewel, sorry I didn't clear Charley's name, sorry I spent all your money, sorry…but I quit. He decided to be polite about it and had been mentally drafting his Final Report that he'd mail from Pottsville. "Dear Ms. Bowers," it would read. "I quit." He'd explain why, of course, and, as the professional detective that he was, he'd send along a summary of his findings. A short summary, since he hadn't found much.

"First," it would start, "I believe that the jewel really does, or did, exist. It may have been a very famous diamond with a long history, or it may have been just a hundred years old, I'm not sure, as my sources—a washed-up museum director and a drug-dealing tramp—are divided on this point.

"Second, it was indeed stolen in Morocco. If my source in the Moroccan police force, a sadistic egotist and an admitted embezzler, is to be believed, it was a violent and bloody robbery, masterminded by the one relative I had foolishly thought was interesting, but who was nothing but a punk."

All those years I pestered my father with those questions. That had to be painful. At what point, he wondered, did Russ turn bad? He couldn't have always been like that. He played baseball, for God's sake.

"Third, the jewel was taken from Morocco to Egypt, which you already know because you typed out the notes and paid for the ticket. Fourth, ….." Here is where he was stuck since he had no fourth—and, given his first, second and third were all things Edna had already known—he didn't even have a summary.

How about expenses? Every good detective submitted an expense report. Edna had paid for everything, but Doug still felt there were some unexpected costs, costs he had picked up but felt justified to pass on to his employer. His questions had cost Mr. Ahmed/Fahad his life. How you going pay for that one, Edna? No, that's cruel, he thought, and unfair, too. Besides, it may have been a coincidence. What could the old man possibly have known that got him killed? And why wait until *that* day to kill him? Okay, so he's off the expense list for now.

How about those two pimps he beat up? In a just world they should get something. But it had been Doug's idea to cruise the red light district and it would be stretching it to pin that on Edna. Unless of course they were not pimps and were hired thugs, out to get him off the trail. If that were the case, he thought, they were pretty lame tough guys. Doug had been in enough fights to know his abilities and, while he'd been in a few with worse odds, and done all right too, it was strange how easy it had been. Even if they were just pimps, they should have been able to beat the crap out of him. He thought about the incident for a while, deciding in the end to leave them off the list as well. Maybe he'd cryptically footnote them, "two incompetent assassins, soundly beaten by an out-of-shape former bottle washer: no charge." Then there was Aisha.

On one hand was the fact that she had used him as her delivery man, was responsible for him landing in an Egyptian jail, and, if Abe was right, might be ultimately responsible for his unexplained and unfortunate death, or his formal state-sponsored execution.

On the other was the sex. Doug thought about this for a while, careful to focus on the concept of the sex and not the actual sex itself as he wanted to avoid any hint of arousal while in this tightly packed, all male environment. No reason to give anybody any ideas. It was difficult since just the concept of sex with Aisha was better than most of the real sex in his life. After what he thought was an hour of analysis, but was really less than ten minutes, he decided that, for now, Aisha was off the list.

But there was the cocaine. Or was it heroin? No one had ever mentioned what it was, specifically, that he was carrying, but Doug doubted it made any real difference. 'Oh, it's only *cocaine?* We're *so* sorry to have detained you, Mr. Pearce, *please* enjoy your stay in Cairo.' More likely it would be 'Oh it's only *cocaine?* Then *just* ninety-nine years for you, Mr. Pearce.' What could it have weighed? If a can of beer weighed twelve ounces—was liquid measure the same as dry weight?—then it had to weigh a lot less than a pound, probably less than three ounces. Assuming cocaine costs about four hundred dollars an ounce, then he had brought in only around eight hundred dollars worth of cocaine. Aisha had set him up for less than the cost of one of those designer LBDs she made look so sexy. It didn't seem worth the trouble. Doug thought about this as he tried not to watch one of his cellmates piss down the porcelain hole. Drug dealers dealt in huge quantities, or at least he assumed they did, so why would Aisha need to transport about a quarter of a pound—a pound was less than a kilo, right?—all the way from Morocco to Egypt? The plane ticket cost more than that.

The man stumbled back to his quarter of the upper bunk. In the semi-darkness of the cell, Doug watched as he tried to climb over his sleeping bedmates, curling up between the wall and someone's backside. Doug sat up, stretched, and leaned back against the wall. Was a pound more than a kilo? In an algebraic equation, did one night of great sex cancel out ninety-nine years in jail? How many questions do you have to ask an old man before he gets hit by a car? If two pimps left the train station at the same time, how long would it be before they would get beaten up? Did an ounce of beer weigh the same as an ounce of cocaine? What if it was light beer? A freakin' C+ in eleventh grade math, he thought, and I can't add this up.

Somewhere down the hall, the loudspeaker began blasting the early morning call to prayer. Several of his cellmates woke up and began washing their feet, arms, and hands, the ablutions required before prayers. Doug rested his head back on his raised knees and somehow managed to drift to sleep.

Chapter 14

"What's your last name again?" Abe asked as they stacked the breakfast dishes on the plastic tray by the door. It was gray meat and rice, the breakfast of champions.

"Pearce. Why?"

Abe held up his hand to quiet Doug and turned his ear to the barred window as he listened to the voices in the hall.

"They're coming for you, Doug."

For a moment Doug had no idea what Abe meant, then, as the voices drew nearer and he heard his own name in the middle of a long Arabic sentence, Doug remembered. He had lost count of the number of men who had passed through the cell over the last two weeks. Some came back, eyes blackened, maybe a thin trail of blood snaking out of their ears. Some didn't come back. "Were they released?" Doug had asked. "One way or another," Abe had said.

"Abe," he said, his voice shaky, all the fear that he had swallowed over the days and nights suddenly bubbling up. "Abe…I… I don't know…."

Abe walked over and put his hands on Doug's shoulders, and Humphrey Bogart spoke. "Doug, the lives of two little people don't amount to a hill of beans in this crazy world. Where you gotta go, I can't follow. What you gotta do, I don't want any part of. But if you don't go outta that door, you're going to regret it. Maybe not today, maybe not tomorrow, but soon and for the rest of your life. We'll always have this cell."

"What the fuck are you talking about, you crazy Arab?" Doug said, trying to laugh but too scared now to do more than manage a weak smile.

Abe pulled Doug in and gave him a hug, and, before Doug could react, kissed him on both cheeks.

"You're fucking crazy, Abe."

"Here's looking at you, kid."

"Douglas Pearce? *Hal anta* Douglas Pearce?" the guard said through the bars.

"*Aywaha*," Doug said, using one of the few Arabic words he had picked up, "I'm Douglas Pearce."

"Come," the guard said as he opened the door.

Doug looked back at the other men in the cell. The fat man, Fozan, who gave him the back rub, crazy Yasser who actually ate everything on his plate and looked for more. It was strange, he thought, I'm going to miss these guys. He looked at Abe, who was sliding back down the wall to his chosen spot. "That was an excellent Bogart," Doug said.

"Bogart?" he said, shaking his head. "Shit, that was my best John Wayne."

A hand reached in and grabbed Doug by the shoulder, pulling him from the room. The door slammed shut and Doug wished he were on the other side.

"Come," the guard said, exhausting his English vocabulary, pushing Doug forward down the long hall. Dozens of identical doors lined both wall, each housing another dozen men, each with their own Fozans and Yassers and Abes and maybe a Doug here and there. They passed through doors, climbed some stairs and made enough confusing turns to thoroughly disorient him. The halls became brighter, drop ceilings were added, bulletin boards on painted walls appeared, then polished floors, noisy air conditioning and plastic potted plants. He could hear phones ringing in the offices they passed, the rhythmless tap of computer keys filling in the forms that keep the headless bureaucracy breathing. The guard led him into a desk-filled work area and at the far end he saw Sergei leap up from his chair and walk toward him, accompanied by a heavily mustached officer.

"Oh thank God you're all right," he said as he wrapped his thin arms around Doug's chest. "I have been so worried." The guard said something to him in Arabic and he released Doug, stepping back. "Yes, I'm sorry, please forgive me, it's just I'm so happy to see my son. Are you a father yourself?" he said to the officer. "*Three* sons? *Al Hamdu Allah, Al Hamdu Allah.* But he is my only son so I'm sure you understand, don't you?"

The guard replied in Arabic and he and Sergei shared a laugh, no doubt about wayward sons and a father's love. The escort guard was waved off by the father of three sons and he and Sergei continued to chat in Arabic as they sat at a nearby desk, passing folders of paperwork between them, pulling out forms now and then to sign or pound into submission with a rubber stamp. Doug sat on the bench near the desk trying to piece it all together. He watched as Sergei nonchalantly removed a sealed envelope from his coat pocket and slipped it into the folder he then handed to the guard, the man too polite, too proud, or too professional to notice. They shook hands again and the man checked his watch, not wanting to be late for his next appointment with another nervous father.

"Thanks, Dad," Doug said, as they walked through the office labyrinth.

"Yes, well, that," Sergei said. "I couldn't think of anything else. I hope you're not offended."

"Offended? You could have told them I was your wife, as long as it got me out of there," Doug said. "I should explain how I got there."

"Certainly not here, Douglas," Sergei said as they made their way through the crowded lobby toward the entrance. "And certainly not in the cab—all the drivers outside the police station are paid informants for this lovely organization. There will be plenty of time to talk once you get cleaned up. And speaking of that, what have your mother and I told you about playing in your church clothes?" Sergei laughed and put his arm around Doug's shoulders as they pushed open the glass doors and entered the blinding blast furnace that was downtown Cairo.

Chapter 15

The felucca glided along the Nile, its triangular sail and ancient design contrasting with the triple-decked, diesel powered dinner cruise barge that plowed through the dark waters, its rows of lights multiplied by the ripples of its wake. The felucca's pilot was dressed in the traditional galabiyya and white headscarf, not because it was part of his tourist shtick, but because that was all he ever wore. The dinner barge carried over-charged diners vacationing from London and Australia. The felucca carried six cases of Gordon's Gin and a replacement computer modem from a downriver warehouse to the Sheraton. In his quaint costume and in his unhurried way as he guided his craft towards the shore, he was picturesque without meaning to be. In a few weeks, fuzzy and poorly lit photos of his sailboat would be passed around dinner tables in Derby and Perth, and he would be described as historical and fascinating. But at that moment he was being described as late and fucking worthless by the assistant manager who paced the edge of the riverside restaurant.

Doug had watched the manager through most of his meal and now, as he relaxed with an apple-flavored tobacco water pipe, he watched as the manager, in his haste to unload the felucca, dropped the modem off the dock and into the ancient river. The man in the boat said nothing but the diners who watched silently filled in what they knew he was thinking.

It had been a good meal and the dockside entertainment only made it better. Forty-eight hours ago he was mopping up stray grains of rice with the piece of bread he had kept from lunch. Now a small swarm of restaurant employees bused away the remainder of the steak and potato dinners he and Sergei had enjoyed. The Osiris beer had a strange, chemical taste, but Sergei insisted that if they didn't dine in the style of the Egyptian they would at least drink that way.

"Have you ever had a hubbly-bubbly before, Douglas?"

"Depends," he said. "What is it?"

"This," Sergei said, holding up the long wooden handle of the water pipe. "They call it hubbly-bubbly here. Over in the Gulf it's called *sheesha*. In Istanbul you order *nagillia*."

"I had it once in Morocco," Doug said, remembering the night with Aisha, not sure if he should smile or shake his stupid head.

"What do they call it there?"

"I think the lady said it was *kif.*"

"Oh dear," Sergei said. "Well, I don't pass judgment, but if it's somehow tied into later events I don't want to know."

Doug had told Sergei about his arrest at the airport, his time in the jail, and his decision to call Edna and quit. He told him about his adventure in Casablanca's red light zone, his run-in with the pimps/assassins, his day at the beach, and his time in the old souk. He told him everything—except for Aisha. It wasn't that he was ashamed of his time with her—far from it since he knew he'd get his drinks bought for weeks with that story back in Pottsville. He just wasn't sure what to say about her. Was she an earnest grad student really on the trail of a historical relic and family obsession, or was she, as Doug had seen her more than once as he sat in the sweltering jail cell, the sultry ring-mistress of an international cocaine cartel? Was she the *kif*-smoking, whiskey-chugging sex goddess of his dreams, or was she playing a role she knew would lure the foolish Yankee into acting as her drug-toting mule? He had spent most of the last two weeks hating her for one of the things she did to him and fantasizing about the rest. If I don't say anything about her, he reasoned, maybe the bad parts will go away.

Sergei explained everything to Doug as well. He had cleared customs long before Doug but became concerned when Doug never showed up near the taxi stand. He went back inside just in time to see Doug, handcuffed and shackled, being hurried through a security door. "At first, of course, no one would tell me anything," Sergei had said, "not that it was top secret but because no one in Egypt does *anything* without *baksheesh*, a 'tip,' which is at best a bribe and more typically extortion money."

Sergei didn't say that he had paid *baksheesh* to find Doug, and more *baksheesh*, a lot of *baksheesh*, to get him released, but Doug was sure that he had. Sergei refused to discuss the matter. "What was I supposed to do Douglas?" he asked, "Leave you there? Please." But he did apologize for taking so long to find him, and the reason made Doug shudder every time he thought about it. "They lost you. Really. Couldn't find you in any of the records. Who knows how long you would have been there."

Sergei had also convinced him not to run out on Edna, not in so many words but that was how Doug had heard it. "You can't possibly blame this woman, thousands of miles away, for your regrettable problems in Egypt. In good faith she has financed your trip and, in good faith, you should stick with it Douglas, until either you find what you are looking for or she calls it off. You are only as good as your word, you know."

"Sergei, weren't you the guy back in Casablanca who told me to play it careful? Told me pretty much to go back to Pennsylvania? Told me that there were a lot of dangers playing this game? Why the change of heart?"

"Not a change of heart, Douglas. Everything I said before still holds true. It is a dangerous game you are playing, stirring up dust that settled years ago and likely to find some nasty things buried in the process. But your problems with the gentlemen from customs had nothing to do with this affair and so you have no real reason to resign now. See it through, Douglas," he said, blowing out a cloud of blue *sheesha* smoke; "if not, you may wake one day to find that not finishing the job was the cause of all the regrets that followed."

While Doug had found Sergei's advice a bit extreme, when he called Edna that night he didn't mention quitting.

"Oh my God, Douglas," Edna said, "where have you been? I've been so worried. Egypt Air said you arrived but you never showed at the hotel and you didn't call. Where were you?"

He lied, of course, creating an old high school friend whom he met on the plane—the odds being so astronomical that it sounded plausible—and they had gone on a bit of a binge.... He let it trail off so it sounded like the old story about the irresponsible former-brewery employee and his rich, jet-set friend from Pottsville, that swinging place, closing bars and breaking hearts. He apologized, a bit too much he thought later, and assured her that he wouldn't let her down, that he'd be back on the case right away and that he'd already set up some appointments. "I gave you my word," he found himself saying, "and you're only as good as your word, you know."

Sergei took care of everything. While he had recovered Doug's bag, all that remained were the guidebooks and the papers, everything else having "disappeared" while it sat in a secured locker at the police station. He had bought Doug new clothes, a bit conservative for his tastes and a little loose given his prison diet, but name brand and selected with care. He had managed to locate Doug's passport, no doubt with the help of more *baksheesh*, and even had him looked over by a Swiss doctor he knew. The room, the meals, the wardrobe, it all had to cost a considerable sum of money and Doug had recalled Sergei's comments about a tight budget.

"I contacted the museum," Sergei explained, "and told them I had located a few small items from the Mamluk era—a mosque lamp, some quality pieces of pottery—things that won't be on any list of non-exportable antiquities, and that if they sent me a draft I could make some arrangements. I know the museum business. 'Arrangement' is the term for 'if you are lucky' and since it wasn't a huge sum and since they know the items are either stolen or about to be stolen…."

"Wait a second, the museum would know they were stolen? Isn't that illegal? And unethical?"

Sergei smiled as he exhaled another blue cloud. "If the museums of the world each gave back what was technically stolen goods, I doubt that together they could mount a decent exhibition. That's an exaggeration, of course, but there is more truth to it than you'd realize. Forged letters of provenance, dubious background checks, a most liberal reading of treaties and contracts, not to mention outright theft and plunder. In my years with the museum I have seen it all, and, truthfully, participated in it as well. It is the nature of the beast, I believe. It consumes as much as it can find, gorging itself in the times of plenty, like during the war, and hunting, constantly hunting, in the lean times."

"But I'm always hearing about how some museum shelled out a million bucks for a painting or some thingamajig."

"Oh they do, they do. Museums worldwide spend billions and billions each year to lawfully acquire objects for their collections. But the beast is not stupid. Why should it spend more than it must to satisfy its hunger? Just like you, the beast tries to get as much as possible by spending the least. It is patient, it is greedy, and it is always hungry."

"What about the real owners?" Doug asked. "Don't they ever get wise and try to get the stuff back?"

"Have you ever heard of the Elgin Marbles? No? Well, on a hill in Greece is a building, perhaps one of the most famous in the world. It's called the Parthenon."

"Yeah, I think I may have heard of it," Doug said, annoyed that Sergei would think he was that stupid.

"When it was built in the fifth century BC," Sergei continued, oblivious to Doug's tone, "its pediments were adorned with statues, each larger than life, depicting mythological events, and along its frieze ran a series of sculptures depicting life in Athens during the Classical era, all of it either done by, or at least supervised by, the great Phidias. And there they remained, surviving disasters both natural and man-made. They were relatively intact during the Ottoman occupation of the city and it was then, this would be around 1800, that a British official, one Lord Elgin, negotiated with some petty officials in the occupation forces and 'bought' the statues.

"Using methods that were crude even for that era, he had the statutes hacked from the building. Some fell as they were being removed, shattering on the steps below. Others were too hacked up to bother with and they were left behind. But the bulk of the sculpture, a world treasure if there was ever one, ended up in Lord Elgin's estate and eventually in the British Museum.

"Now this is a good example of your rightful owners trying to get the stolen works returned. Everyone knows this story and no one disputes the Greek claim that the Elgin Marbles are really the Parthenon's marbles, but, despite constant pressure from the Greek government, the marbles stay in England."

"And I assume Lord Elgin ended up fat and happy," Doug said.

"Poetic justice intervened, I'm happy to say. His young and beautiful wife left him when his nose literally rotted off, the outward effects of an advanced stage of syphilis."

Doug whistled between his teeth. "And I'm sure you'll tell me that this is just an example, that you could tell me dozens of other stories...."

"Hundreds, actually. Not always with the syphilis."

"...and that people and whole countries are robbed of fortunes and everybody knows and nobody can do jack about it and that's just the way of the world, right?"

"The museum world, yes. Not to be confused with the real world I'm afraid."

"Geeze, Sergei," Doug said, "and here I thought Captain Yehia was rough company. Don't you know any nice, sweet, normal people?"

Sergei laughed as he signed for the meal, slipping in an Egyptian fifty-pound note as a tip. "There's you, and there's this fine gentleman here," he said, handing the leather case to the waiter, "and that about sums it up. And to be honest," he added in his stage whisper, "I'm not so sure about the waiter. He *said* the salad was fresh, but…."

Chapter 16

Stuck inside one of the guidebooks was the book of matches with Aisha's minute scrawl providing directions to Uncle Nasser's shop in the Khan al-Khalili. The Ashkananis had had one stall or another in the Khan since the sultan Salim the Grim brought Ottoman rule to Cairo in the early 1500s. In the current shop, located near the Bab al-Badistan—the gate of the domes—Ashkananis were selling locally made gold necklaces, pearls from the Arabian Gulf, and precious stones and jewels when Napoleon rode by. Most of the stock was imported from India now, but it was still high-quality merchandise. Nasser, son of Nasser, son of Ali, son of Mohamad, son of Nasser, the latest Ashkanani to own the shop, sat on a folding chair behind a wooden and glass display case, sipping tea.

Few of the shop owners, and certainly none of his sons or his grandsons, knew as much about the type of things sold in this part of the souk as Nasser, but his opinion was only cautiously sought. A slight tilting of his head or a barely audible click of his tongue was enough to knock thirty percent off any previously appraised value. But, and this was rare, if his left eyebrow twitched upward the piece could double in price.

His expertise was jewelry, his passion was mosques. Not the whole mosque, just the minarets, the spindly towers that rose alongside of each mosque and from which the call to prayer was made. He loved the diversity of the minarets, the subtle changes in architectural details that signalled a radical shift in local politics, royal favor, or theology. There were hundreds of minarets in Cairo, and Nasser had seen them all. He saw beauty in each of them, from the smooth simplicity of the winding minaret at the Mosque of Ibn-Tulun, the oldest still standing in the city, to the exquisite carved details on the minaret of Jamin al-Bahlawan, to the stark pencil shapes favored by the Ottomans. Like old friends they greeted him as he drove through the city each morning, and he watched as they slowly decayed, the constant fog of pollution accomplishing in twenty years what the wind and the sun had not done in five hundred. And when one finally collapsed, or was pulled down, Nasser mourned its passing. Nearing ninety, he knew they would outlast him, but probably not by much.

But this morning he had seen an old friend he had not seen for years. The latest urban renewal project—how many thousands of those had this city seen?—had pulled down a condemned boarding house a ten-minute walk away. A modest little minaret in the Fatimid style now peeked out from behind the rubble, the sun lighting four of its eight sides for the first time in sixty years. When he had seen it he laughed out loud and slapped his hands together. They had a lot to catch up on, Nasser and this minaret.

He was still smiling when Doug found the shop just before noon.

"Aisha Al-Kady! That little devil," Nasser said. "What kind of trouble is she making in Morocco now?" To Doug's surprise, it took him little time to find the shop—only an hour and a half, which, given the warren of shops and alleys, Doug thought was rather impressive. More surprising, Nasser Ashkanani seemed pleased to meet him and eager to talk. Should he be surprised, he thought, that her own uncle described her as a trouble-seeking devil?

"The last time I was in Morocco, that would be five years ago, Aisha was off to some museum somewhere. Crete? Tehran? Should have been home, looking after the family business. She was just here, Aisha was, not two months ago. I don't think she mentioned you, I'm afraid."

"Oh, we just met a few weeks ago. I was in Casablanca to ask her grandfather some questions about some old friends he had. One of them was my uncle. Maybe you knew him. Russell Pearce?"

Nasser Ashkanani didn't say anything, but leaned over in his chair and began rummaging under the counter. After a minute he reemerged with an inch-thick stack of photographs. He patted each of his coat pockets until he found his glasses, which were sitting on the counter in front of him, and hooked the wire frames around his large ears. He looked at each photo and then tossed it on the glass top of the case displaying finely wrought gold bracelets. Some were in color but most were black and white, with thin white borders and scalloped edges like the old Kodak prints Doug's father got at the drug store. Some showed Nasser, his arm around a tourist, holding the expensive trinket that he had just sold, others were of Arab men sitting around the shop, in front of the shop, at the coffee shop just down the narrow alley from the shop. Nasser Ashkanani had spent half his life not more than twenty feet from where he sat now. There were many shots of mosques and minarets, and over these Nasser seemed to linger a bit longer. He looked at one photo and set it down for Doug to look at. It showed an older Arab woman in oversized, dark sunglasses and fashionable black clothes. "Umm Kulsoum," he said, and when he saw no reaction in Doug, he added "the most beloved singer ever. The Nightingale of the Nile. She came here often." He set down the stack of photos and disappeared under the counter again. Doug could hear the sound of cassette tapes clacking together and then the hiss that comes before the music. A live recording; there was much appreciative crowd noise before the voice started. It sounded like every other Arabic singer he heard, but Nasser smiled as the lyrics started. "Umm Kulsoum," he said, pointing up to the music that flowed overhead.

He continued to flip through the stack till he came to a black and white photo, which he held up to get a better view. Doug could see the holes left by thumbtacks, the Arabic script on the back and the date 1948, written in pencil. "Recognize your uncle?" he said as he set the photo down for Doug to see.

The photo was taken outside the shop—you could see the arch of the Bab al-Badistan over the heads of the four people in the group. Although he was much older now, Doug recognized Nasser. He was taller then, a full head of jet-black hair and a finely trimmed mustache. He still had the mustache, not so neatly trimmed, but the hair was now white and there was a lot less of it. Somehow, in the heat of Cairo, he looked cool in a tan suit and tightly knotted tie. He stood with his arm around Russell Pearce, whom Doug recognized despite the open-mouthed smile and fact that he had blinked as the picture was snapped. The black and white photo still captured the dark tan in tints of gray, and the rolled-up sleeves of his white shirt showed the muscular forearms of a ball player or bully. Sweat stains showed through the band on his Panama hat.

At the far end of the group was another man, an Arab, wearing a white linen suit and tie, but who also wore a nervous smile, probably because his arm was gingerly placed around the shoulders of a young and stunning Edna Bowers. This was a closer shot than the photos in her Toronto apartment, but she improved in close-ups. Her hair, which fell about her shoulders like a black waterfall in the Paris photos, was cut short here and parted on the left. The photo cropped her off just below her narrow waist, her pleated, belt-less khakis drooping to show her navel peeking out from under her tee shirt. She was sweating just enough for her two dark-brown nipples to appear on the film. They looked nothing alike, Edna and Aisha, but they both had that sultry aura, that same heart-stopping face. No wonder the Arab guy looked nervous, Doug thought.

"If you are here about your uncle, and Aisha sent you, then you must be after *Al Ainab*. And if you are, you are in the wrong place and you're a damn fool." At least he smiled when he said it, thought Doug.

"Damn fool. Yup, that'd be me. And yes, it is about the jewel but it's also about my uncle. I didn't know him, he was killed before I was born, and I'm trying to find out what I can about him."

"I didn't know he had a family, but then what I didn't know about him was far more than what I did. His friend here," he said, tapping the photo on the counter, "there was a strange relationship. But yes, I did know him a bit. Tea?" Nasser waved to a passing waiter from the coffee shop who seemed to be delivering single steaming glass cups of tea to all the shops up and down the alley. Doug studied the photo as Nasser exchanged the required *aslamalekums* with the waiter. What was Edna's connection in all of this? Did she know more than she was letting on, or far, far less?

"I'm certain my niece bored you to tears with her history of the jewel. She has spent so much of her life in one university or another and so little of it doing something useful. Her English is excellent, as is mine, yes, but I learned English, and of course French, and a bit of German to better serve my customers. It is so much easier getting a man to part with his money when you can speak his language. Her and that jewel."

"She did seem quite well informed about it," Doug said.

"Yes and to what point? That is what her grandfather could never understand. She wants to make a name for herself in the academic world. Publish her book. She hunts the world for anything on that stupid grape and pesters me constantly with the same questions, over and over. She needs to settle down, meet a nice man. But no, that damn book comes first. Her *career*. I ask you, what man would want a woman like Aisha?"

Me, for one, Doug thought but nodded sympathetically.

"Now Hammad's interest in *Al Ainab* is far more practical. To this day he checks his sources all over the world, keeps a list of prospective buyers and jewel cutters. That's how I know for certain our families are related," Nasser said, holding up his finger to emphasize the point. "In our blood we are shopkeepers."

Doug thought back to his meeting with the mumbling Hammad Al-Kady. "I'm sure his stroke slowed him down a lot. I really wish I had met him before."

"Stroke?" Nasser said, looking up, his glasses slipping part way off. "Hammad has had a stroke. *Wallah*, no one has told me, no one called. When was this, while you were there?"

"I assumed it was years ago," Doug said, remembering back. "Aisha had said that it happened about four years ago."

"Four years ago? No, no, you are mistaken. Hammad was here in Cairo not more than a month ago and I have spoken with his son, Aisha's father, just last week."

"But I saw him, right by the pool. He was, well, he was confused. He didn't know who I was and just kept falling asleep."

Nasser laughed out loud and readjusted his glasses. "'I drink so much wine, its aroma will rise from the dust when I am under it.' Omar Khayyam, the great Arab poet, wrote that in the eleventh century. Hammad should have that carved over his doorway. No, I'm happy to say that you just encountered my old friend Hammad when he was in his cups."

"Aisha said that it was a stroke, that he'd been like that for years."

"Oh he's been like that for years," Nasser said, "but it has nothing to do with a stroke. Believe me, if Hammad knew you were looking for *Al Ainab*, he would not let you out of his sight. He lost that diamond once before and I'm sure he would do whatever he could to keep from losing it again. And as for Aisha," he said, shaking his head, "if you know her at all you know that she is quite the little devil, capable of anything."

"I'm beginning to find that out," Doug said.

The tea arrived, scalding hot and over sweet. Doug couldn't pick up the small glass to blow on the tea. Nasser held it in his palm and in one gulp drained half the glass.

"Now about this jewel, tell me what you know."

Doug told him about the request from Edna, the theft in Casablanca, and what Captain Yehia said about the blood. He told him about the vague clues he received and how a man named Sasha played a role as well. It took less time to explain than he thought it would. His tea was still too hot to sip when he finished.

"Yes it did come to me here. It sat right in that strong box over there," Nasser said, pointing to a dark corner of the shop. "It wasn't as large as I had been led to believe, just about the size of the end of my thumb, but its color and clarity were exceptional. Not perfect, of course, but standards change when you have a red diamond. I did not ask questions about how they acquired it and naturally they did not volunteer any information either. I'm not sure how they got it out of Morocco…or how they got themselves out for that matter."

"The notes I've been reading say that you were setting up a sale for them, something about a possible sale in Istanbul or Ceylon."

"Hmmm, did they?" Nasser said as he shuffled the photos into a stack. He finished his tea and reached behind the counter for a pack of cigarettes and a lighter. "Of course I didn't have any sales lined up. How could I with such short notice? I had connections in Istanbul when it was still worth having connections there and perhaps I thought someone would be interested. Ceylon makes no sense. Pearls, yes, but not a diamond of this size. I must have been telling a tale to keep them from doing something stupid."

"From what I read they seemed to have no trouble doing stupid things."

Nasser laughed, which led to a coughing fit that led to more tea and the second side of the Umm Kulsoum tape, which sounded just like the first. A few tourists popped in the shop now and then, but Nasser Ashkanani knew his customers like he knew his jewelry and waited until the window shoppers left before they continued.

"This was in 1948," Nasser said, flipping the photo back over. "It was a difficult time. The war, Farouk, the Brotherhood." He stopped when he realized that none of this registered with the young American. "I don't know what you think of your uncle but he was a good man. He was honest and loyal. I suppose you could say he was brave, too, but it was a criminal bravery so perhaps it does not count for much. As far as the woman in the picture," he said, again tapping the photo with his finger, "I don't remember much about her but I didn't like her."

"Really? That surprises me. She seems so nice." Doug picked up the picture to take another look.

"Too bold. You couldn't tell her anything, she knew it all. God knows I'm not a conservative man, but there are some things that are just not done. Not done here in Cairo, anyway, even back then. The way she carried on with those, those *lovers*. If her family only knew. Believe it or not," Nasser said, leaning forward to emphasize his point, "I think it was all her ideas from the start, the theft, the double crossing of the Russian...."

"Sasha?"

"That may have been his name, but it is a common familiar name in Russia. I only saw him one or two times. She wanted to leave him in Morocco but he followed them here. She told him that they were smuggling the diamond out of Egypt and going somewhere else, I can't remember where she said, but of course it never went there. He did, however, the Russian. Then she and your uncle had a falling out—over someone she was romantically involved with." He made a grunting sound to punctuate his displeasure and sipped the remainder of his tea.

"Those two. Your uncle wanted me to talk to her, help smooth her ruffled feathers, but I just couldn't. She was not the kind of woman I like to talk with. Well, they worked it out on their own, after a fashion. I helped your uncle secure a position on a steamer heading to Japan. Naturally she couldn't sail with him, not on that ship. Arab owners. Not like the Europeans."

A man entered the shop and he and Nasser talked in loud, rapid, gesture-filled Arabic. Doug thought it would end in a fight when suddenly both men started laughing and shaking hands. "My friend Salam here wants me to help him convince this British tourist to spend far too much on a piece of dubious quality."

Doug took one last look at the photo as he stood up. Nasser noticed and said something to the man that Doug couldn't understand. They talked some more and again it led to laughter and handshaking.

"Stop by before you leave Cairo. After tomorrow. I'll have a copy made of that for you."

"That would be great. I don't have any pictures of my uncle. You've been a big help, Mr. Ashkanani. Maybe you could suggest some people I could talk to in Singapore."

"Yes, when you come for the picture, we'll talk. But you'll want to stop by anyway, picture or no picture," Nasser said, laughing with his friend. "Salam tells me Aisha is in town. I'm sure you're anxious to see her again."

Chapter 17

"Well what do you think?"

"Honestly?"

"Honestly."

"It's a fucking let-down."

"Of course! That's why we're here."

Here was in the burial chamber at the center of the Great Pyramid of Cheops, and Doug was fucking let down because, other than a couple of bed-sized slabs of unadorned, dull gray stone and a bare light bulb suspended from an extension cord, duct taped to the ceiling, the room was empty. It had taken twenty minutes to get to this point, the last ten of it stuck in a three-foot-wide, four-foot-tall, sharply sloped passage that served as both the up and down route to the heart of the pyramid. Alone he could have scampered up the incline in twenty seconds, but the passage was crammed, nose to ass, with a busload of British tourists from a retirement home, with Doug and Sergei stuck in the middle. It wasn't the heat, which was mind-numbing, that made it difficult, nor was it the contortionist-like positions everyone assumed, in total darkness, to allow for both up and down traffic. No, it was the smell of urine—an ancient, dust-encrusted reek, pissed down this slope over four hundred centuries. After enduring that, finding Tutankhamen sipping tea in a La-Z-Boy would have been a disappointment.

Most people came in, said, "This is it?" and turned around, ready to endure the downward version of the trip up. Sergei took a seat on one of the slabs and motioned Doug to sit next to him.

"This is one of my favorite spots in Cairo," he said. "Just watching the look of disappointment come over everyone's face, it's so ironic."

"You've got a sick sense of humor, Sergei." Doug took out the already soaked bandana he was using as a sweat rag and wiped the stream from the back of his neck.

"You misunderstand me, Douglas. I don't find it funny, I find it so beautifully ironic. Everyone comes here expecting a treasure and leaves disappointed, the whole time missing the wonder of this space."

"Yeah, I wonder about it too."

"There are tons and tons of stone above us and here we are, safe inside one of the oldest man-made spaces on the planet. It's an engineering marvel, a timeless monument to human ingenuity. A sacred site. Yet everyone comes with their mythological expectations for the pyramid and leaves disappointed when the reality does not match up with their version of what the reality should look like. This place offers so much and people still leave empty handed."

"I guess," Doug said. "But I'm still disappointed."

Sergei kept watching the tourists who, one by one, popped into the chamber, mumbled something in whatever language they spoke, snapped a photo that would turn out to be an unidentifiable gray mass, and forced themselves back down the deadly slope. "You're too young to understand, Douglas."

"Oh, that old line. Believe it or not, Sergei, I've had a few disappointments in my life too." He hadn't, but it sounded good.

"You're missing my point, my friend. I'm not saying that it's about disappointment. We all share that. No, it's about reaching a goal, getting what you think you wanted only to find out that what you wanted never really existed. And then that sudden realization, the realization that they are all missing," he swept his hand in front of him, taking in the never-ending stream of sweaty, stooped-over tour group adventurers, "that what you get is much more valuable than what you sought. You need to reach your goal many times in life to begin to understand."

"The journey being better than the destination, is that it?"

"Yes, but you make it sound so trite. Life is a journey. The goals are so small and fleeting and inherently disappointing. Arriving here these people have the opportunity to consider all that they did to get here, the planning, the saving of loose change in large glass jars, the well wishes of loved ones. They could have a life-altering epiphany yet they settle for an unoriginal *bon mot*. The journey *is* the goal."

"Okay, Socrates, can we get out of here now so I can take a breath that actually contains oxygen?"

On the way down Doug didn't think about the journey being the goal. He thought about the books he saw on the shelf in the Egyptologist's office. Sergei had started him out early with a pre-dawn trip to the desert area near the pyramids. The sunrise was, as Sergei promised, awesome, and the camel ride Sergei arranged was definitely cool. The old man could argue in Arabic as well as any of the dozens of camel drivers that descended on every arriving tour bus or cab like ants on a slow-moving worm. Doug was impressed with his ability to get just what he wanted for just the price he told Doug he would pay.

They had climbed a few blocks up on the main pyramid but the official entrance was closed, Sergei explaining that they would have to come back around noon to get inside. And what about the pyramids, Doug thought. "They are really, really big," he could see himself saying to the guys in Pottsville. Other than that? They would never understand, and I'll never be able to explain. Getting wedged in this shaft, that they'd understand, but since it was his nose on someone else's ass, he'd keep that to himself.

They had breakfast in the National Museum, in the office of an old friend of Sergei's. The museum wasn't open yet but Sergei had no trouble getting them past the legions of under-employed guards and museum workers who congregated by the staff entrance, waiting to start their day so they could get on with their coffee break. Dr. Hawanna and Sergei chatted in Arabic as they drank their tea and ate their cheese, bread, and olives, from time to time consenting to speak in English so Doug wouldn't feel left out for too long.

"You have a most wise friend here," the museum man said. "Dr. Nikolaisen is much respected. I myself refer to his works often."

"Hopelessly out of date," Sergei said.

"Timeless," the man countered. "Look. I've worn out the bindings." He motioned to a shelf across the room, too far away to confirm his claims.

"If you ever have a bout of insomnia, Douglas, I do strongly recommend them to you." Sergei translated his little joke for the man and the two laughed, rattling on in Arabic for another ten minutes.

Bored, Doug found himself wandering about the spacious but cluttered office. Stacks of paper-filled folders that looked as old as the artifacts were scattered on top of desks and crammed in the Victorian styled display cases. Everywhere there was the settled dust that said that it had been years since any real research had been done in this office. He worked his way around the room, coming to the bookshelf the man had pointed to. Wedged among the dog-eared books, Doug saw a small section of books with nearly identical spines, all from the same publishing line. They were all in German, but Doug could make out *Dr. Sergei Nikolaisen* among the foreign words. He pried out a copy and it was as worn as Dr. Hawanna claimed. Doug flipped through the pages, glancing at the impossibly long German words, the typeface making the thirty-year-old book look medieval. There were shiny pages with black and white photographs of small artifacts placed next to a ruler to provide scale. The photos in one book were of what looked like beetles carved out of stone with Egyptian hieroglyphics engraved on their underside. Another book was all on beads, beads in piles, beads strung together, beads up close. Doug was thumbing through a thin volume filled with pictures of small stones and what looked like ancient jewelry. He stopped thumbing when he saw something he recognized. Lying on a white background, a ruler alongside marking off the millimeters, was *Al Ainab*. The Grape.

The words in the white border were undecipherable and nothing looked like it said *Al Ainab*. But Doug did make out the phrase *der Rot Diamant*, which had to be what it looked like. And the tints in the black and white photograph meant that it couldn't be a regular diamond. If it was *Al Ainab* then Sergei knew about it, enough to put it in a book.

"Careful, Douglas," Sergei said from across the room.

"Huh?" was the best Doug could manage.

"Just put the book down slowly and back away," Sergei said, setting his teacup down.

"Huh?"

"My books can bore the average man to death in just three minutes," he said breaking into a smile, "and even short passages can cause irreparable damage."

"Oh? This?" Doug said, holding the book up before he crammed it back into place. "I wish I could read German, I'd love to know what it says."

"You can thank your wonderfully insular educational system for keeping you from ever being harmed by inane vanity tracts by self-absorbed European academics, the most deadly of the species, you know."

Dr. Hawanna objected but Sergei would hear nothing of it. "Come," Sergei finally said, "let's show this young man around the museum before the masses arrive. Museums would be so much better if we could just keep the people out."

They toured around the museum for two hours, stopping at almost every display until Doug was ready to scream. The King Tut artifacts were the highlight, the endless display cases filled with fragments of papyrus or pottery the most painful. An hour after they left the museum they were back at the Great Pyramid, an hour and a half after that they were discussing goals and journeys, and now, with his head wedged between the ass of a

Korean tourist in track pants and the cold and slimy wall of the corridor, Doug thought about the photograph.

He had only seen it for a moment and had looked at Aisha's photograph for not much longer. Was it the same diamond? Could he even tell one diamond from another? Maybe it was just a stone of some kind or another red diamond. But what were the odds it would be a different diamond? About the same as it being the very diamond I'm looking for, he thought.

Later that afternoon, as he floated in the shallow end of the hotel's pool, he thought about the pyramids, the ridiculously tiny locks on the King Tut display cases, the row after row of mummies in the museum's storage area, off limits to tourists.

And he thought about the diamond.

And that led him to think about Aisha and for an hour that's all he thought about.

◇◇◇

Towards the end of the second day of sightseeing, it was clear to Doug why Sergei had wanted to show him around.

Sergei led them through the fifteenth-century spice market, with its ten-foot-tall stacks of garlic, up to the intricately carved timber balcony in the V-shaped building in the middle of al-Mu'izz Street, across the roof of a four-hundred-year-old tenement to climb the tightly twisting staircase of an equally old minaret, clinging to the walls as the steps narrowed and the handrails disappeared. Sergei's stories—of princesses killed off by plagues, slaves who rose to be sultans, the eighty-day rule of the only sultana—were peppered with advice on bargaining, buying aphrodisiacs, and crossing the street. He seemed to draw energy from each site they visited, from every question Doug asked.

Inside the Sultan Hasan Mosque, in the shade created by the four huge *iwans* surrounding the central fountain, Doug and Sergei sipped the cool bottled water they bought on the street.

"Each of these arches, these *iwans*, represents the four branches of Islamic law, and the doorways at the rear of each *iwan* lead to the *madressa*, or school. Students would sit here then, much as we are now, and study their respective disciplines or relax in what I believe is the most restful place in all of Cairo."

"You said that about the first mosque we saw. And about that caravan place...."

"Caravansi."

"Caravansi. And about that house with the wooden windows."

"Ah, no, this is the best place of them all."

"Until we get to the next place."

"Exactly."

Doug looked around the courtyard. "Okay, professor, let's see if I remember. There's the thing that indicates the direction to Mecca...."

"The *minrahb*," Sergei added.

"I knew that. And that thing there, with the steps, that's the minibar."

"*Minbar*. Big difference."

"Right. That's where the Iman does his little chat thing on Fridays. That platform is where the sultan would do his praying to keep him safe from assassins."

"And so he could be seen by the people. That was very important."

Doug noticed a smaller archway next to the *minrahb*. "Where's that lead? Another school?"

"There's an interesting story behind that," Sergei said, sitting upright, ready to continue his lectures.

"You say that about everything, Sergei."

"Through that doorway is the mausoleum of Sultan Hasan. And while his mosque is regarded as one of the crowning achievements in Islamic architecture, Sultan Hasan himself was of little importance. He came to power as a small boy and was therefore himself ruled by his ministers. When he did reign on his own he was ineffective and was eventually killed, his body hidden, never to be found again."

"And the tomb?"

"In the late fourteen hundreds, more than a century after Hasan was murdered, they placed the body of some minor amir in the tomb. Today no one bothers to read the rather informative plaque and everyone assumes Sultan Hasan is in there."

Doug laughed. "Sergei, you are amazing. You can even make that story sound interesting."

They sat in silence for a time.

"You miss the academic world, don't you?"

Sergei sighed and didn't answer, and for a minute Doug thought that he had upset him. He sighed again and turned to better see Doug.

"When I was a small boy I had a collection of buttons. Military buttons off old uniforms. I used to arrange them in my room, sketch them, list them from oldest to most recent, group them by regiment or by nationality, and line them up for battle. They were my link to the past. They had actually been in the battles I had read about, battles that took place a hundred years before. I'd think of the soldiers who wore them and how they fought and, naively, how they died. I'd always found that exciting. Then a real war came along and swept me along with it. I fought against the Nazis on the Eastern Front. I lost my interest in things military.

"But I was still fascinated by artifacts from the past. After the war I found myself in Munich where I earned my Ph.D., jumped into the museum circuit, and, for almost forty years, was blissfully happy. I was paid to research, to travel, to study and teach. I published my little books and I established what I thought was a rather secure reputation, ready to live out my final years doing pretty much what I had done for almost all of them. It was dull, routine and monotonous. And I loved it."

Sergei paused and shifted again, this time so he could look above the high walls that enclosed the courtyard and up to the perfect blue sky. "Publish or perish, they said. Well, not in those words, but that's what they said. But I've already written a whole series of books. Yes, that is true, but that was ages ago. But can't

I just advise, serve as a consultant? No you cannot. What is left for me to do? What indeed, Dr. Nikolaisen."

They sat in silence again till Doug couldn't take it any longer. "Well that sucks."

Sergei looked at Doug and let out a loud laugh that echoed in the *iwan*. "Perfect, Douglas, perfect," he said. "Yes, it sucks but you know, in a way I see their point. I was getting to be a burden on the museum and I really didn't do much truly fine academic work after the early Seventies. And I was, I'll admit, a bit arrogant, looking down my nose at the young people who were publishing well received monographs and organizing exhibitions that drew big crowds. Pandering to the masses, I cried, forgetting it was the masses that kept the museum going."

"You know what I would like?" Sergei continued. "I'd like one last big find, one last moment to show them that old Dr. Nikolaisen still has something to say. Maybe publish one more book. My opus. My swan song."

"How many books have you written?" Doug asked, nudging towards the question he wanted to ask and away from the somber mood his first question brought.

"Alone, fifteen. With colleagues, another dozen or two. And I honestly can't say how many articles I've written. Hundreds, I suppose."

"Mostly on Egypt?"

"Oh no, on many subjects."

"Hey, ever do anything on diamonds? Maybe I can look in your books and find out where mine is."

"The Jagersfontien Diamond? No, I'm afraid not. Other than its adventure in Casablanca, there isn't much to write about." He placed the empty water bottle in the small bag he carried. "Ready to go?"

They walked through the courtyard and into the winding corridors of the old building. "When I was flipping through the books in Dr. Hawanna's office, I thought I saw a picture of the diamond I'm looking for." There, he thought. It's out.

"My books?" he said, sounding surprised. "Not in my books. What was the title?"

"It was in German, I don't know."

"Was it on the Royal Collection at the Soffia Museum? There was some mention of a blue diamond in that work."

"Like I said, I don't read German."

"Was the title *Eighteenth Century Acquisitions of the Uthman Katkhuda?* There's several diamonds in that one, but all too small to be yours."

"Yeah, maybe. I don't know, Sergei."

"If it *was* in that book then it would have to be a later edition since the first two editions had no color plates."

"It wasn't in color. It was a black and white photograph."

"Tisk, tisk, Douglas," he said as the zigzagging corridor gave way to the three-story vestibule and the equally tall wooden doors, the bright sun blinding after their short walk through the building. Sergei fished his sunglasses out from his bag. "Identifying a rare object, a jewel no less, from one black and white photograph? That's a bold claim for an expert to make. Do you know more about jewels than you're letting on?"

No, Doug said to himself, but I thought you might.

"Miss Monroe was right, diamonds may indeed be a girl's best friend. But to museum curators, they are over-priced security risks. We leave them to the jewelers. Up for one more site? It's that one there, on the top of that hill. The Ottoman mosque of Muhammad Ali—the ruler, not the boxer. Like all things Ottoman, it's too ornate, too showy. After this beautiful mosque, this masterpiece of simplicity, I do hope you'll be disappointed."

"Come on then," Doug said, putting his arm around Sergei's shoulder. "I promise not to let you down."

Chapter 18

Doug had been sitting in the café for two hours already when he decided he would continue sitting there for about another two. Sitting. Just sitting. Not wandering around some historical site, not getting yet another lecture from Sergei, not having every other person trying to sell him something from a carpet to a chess set to a washing machine.

Sitting was good. The waiter, who spoke no English, kept the pots of coffee full and added a plate of pastry as dry and crumbly as papyrus. He left Doug alone to write out his dozen postcards, each saying just about the same thing. Left him alone to half-start and re-start a list under the heading *The Mystery of the Grape*. Left him alone to observe the tough guy sitting by the door, the one with the overly hairy mustache, overly hairy eyebrows, and overly hairy ears. Left him alone to glance down the alley and through the medieval gateway, watching for the unmistakable shape of Aisha Al-Kady heading towards the jewelry shop of Nasser Ashkanani. The waiter left him so alone that when a man entered from the rear of the café, pulled up a chair behind Doug, and placed a knife against the small of Doug's back, Doug didn't even bother to look up for help.

They sat silently long enough for Doug to feel the cold bead of sweat roll down his neck and under the collar of his short-sleeved shirt. He sensed the man lean forward, felt his breath on his ear. "So tell me, punk," Clint Eastwood said, "do you feel lucky?"

Doug's sigh was so long that Clint had time to pull his chair around to Doug's table and set the butter knife down onto the tray of papyrus pastries.

"So, you smuggle any drugs for Moroccan tarts lately?" Abe said as he tried to get the waiter's attention.

"Couldn't you say hello like normal people?" Doug said.

"Could. But what fun would that be? I walked by the front window and waved like a fuckin' tourist, but you didn't see me. Consider it a lesson on being aware of your surroundings. You're like an American Express commercial waiting to happen. I'd do a Karl Malden right now, but I'm not sure what he sounds like."

"So I take it you got out of the jail alright."

"Told you I would. It was that rarest of all things that got me locked up—an honest mistake. They wanted to grab another Abdoulrahim Al Abdulrazzaq, there being many of us in Cairo saddled with that name. A mere good ol' American C note got me sprung, with the apologies of the man who put me in. The same man who, in fact, was able to get me out at that bargain price. The coincidence is sublime."

"I don't know how much it cost Sergei to get me out. Will you look at this, my hand is still shaking." Doug held up his hand and watched as it twitched uncontrollably. "You're an ass."

"Oh I bet you say that to all the boys you shared a jail cell with. Yes, finally," Abe said as the waiter approached the table. Abe ordered a coffee and a second plate of pastries. "So, Kimosabe, what are you doing here? Most tourists go to Fishawi's."

"I think that woman you called the Moroccan Tart will be coming by here."

"Ooohh, an ambush. What are you going to do, sneak up behind her and give her a whack from your blackjack? Chloroform maybe? Or are you going to trail her to her mountain hideout to get the drop on her?"

"No, I just want to talk with her."

"Talk? Okay, slick, let's see if I have this right. You're going to walk up to this woman and say 'Excuse me, I am the gentleman on whom you chose to plant a pound of cocaine and I would like to discuss with you my displeasure at your most uncivil actions.' Get real."

"Well, your ideas were no better. How can you eat those things?"

"These are great, man," Abe said, emphasizing his point by raising the half-eaten cookie. "And those were not my plans. Those are things I figured you might try. I, of course, have a better idea. Here's what we do. I got a friend who owns a shop not far from here...."

"Everyone seems to say that."

"Of course. Every *real* Egyptian knows someone with a shop. Anyway, I'll show you where it is. He's got some rooms on the floors above the shop. Then we'll come back here, you point out the chick, skip on back to the shop and, the suave and debonair man that I am, I'll convince the young lady that she has to come to the shop with me."

"That's your plan? The blackjack was better. Aisha is no tourist, there's no way she'll fall for that line."

Abe shook his head. "Oh ye of little faith." He said something to the waiter as he stood up. "I'll show you the back route. Then we'll sit here and you can tell me all about your years of success with women. That'll kill ten minutes."

The shop turned out to be just two blocks over, which of course meant five hundred yards of twisting alleyways and side streets to get there. Abe was quick with introductions and Doug looked around the cloth shop while Abe explained in Arabic his plans to the shop owner. Doug looked at the thousands of bolts of black cloth—and only black cloth—used to create the ninja-like abayahs that the most traditional women wore. Sergei had pointed out that they were worn by Muslim and Christian alike, but in either case Doug thought it was ridiculous. A hundred plus degrees and they cover themselves in black, on top of their regular clothes. The men, of course, Doug noted, wore white.

The spare rooms were three flights up a narrow, back staircase, the only light filtering down from a pigeon-shit encrusted skylight five stories above. The room was littered with fragments of remnants of black cloth, too small to sell, yet, damn it, too valuable to just throw away. There were boxes crammed tight with odd-shaped pieces, and plastic bags overfilled with factory seconds and other shop discards, but mostly the rooms were filled with loose piles of off-black strips, moth-eaten end-runs and miles and miles of frayed-free strings that entangled anything that stayed too long in the room. The desert-dry wood shelves and the football-sized mounds of black lint added to the firetrap feel of the place. It was a good thing that the air conditioning below kept the room at a chilly ninety degrees.

"Perfect," Abe said as he looked around. "You two can have such a lovely chat. It's as good as soundproof up here."

"I'm not going to shoot her, Abe, just talk," Doug said. Black strings inched their way towards his legs.

"I hope she feels the same way about you, Dougie."

◇◇◇

Back at the coffee shop, Abe got the waiter to find Doug a cold can of 7-Up and a small bag of Chips Ahoy cookies, while he ordered another pot of coffee—"*Qahawa*, Doug, say it right."—and more dry pastries. They arranged the table so they could lean their chairs back against the wall and still see down the narrow street that sloped toward the coffee shop before branching off towards the Bab al-Badistan and the shop of Nasser Ashkanani. Doug explained that it might be a long wait and that Aisha might not even go by. "What else have I got to do?" Abe asked, "I'm not scheduled to get re-arrested until next Monday."

After a half hour they had exhausted the standard small talk topics and got down to serious girl watching. The coffee shop was near the center of the tourist area and there was a constant stream of tourists, mostly organized groups of retirees, off-loading from the buses at the far end of the street. But, interspersed among the blue-hairs and the practical walking shoes, there were enough college-aged backpackers in baggy tank tops and shorts to keep them alert.

"What about that one, the one with the bandana? She your type?" Doug asked.

Abe tilted his head, a connoisseur appraising the specimen carefully. "I'm not a big fan of long hair, but on her, yes, it looks good. So, yes, I'll take her."

"But will she take you?"

"It's funny," Abe said as he watched the touts strike up conversations with the girls in the hope that they would end in a big sale and a nice commission, "if I met a girl like that back in the States, she'd have nothing to do with me. But here she'd sleep with me simply to be able to say 'Once, when I was in Egypt, I met this really sexy guy....'"

"Oh Jesus, I think somebody's got themselves an ego problem," Doug said.

"No, you don't get it. She's not sleeping with *me*, she's sleeping with her exotic, foreign, swarthy fantasy. I'm Aladdin, I'm Omar Sharif. I don't matter. I could be as ugly as you and still get laid. It's part of their tour package, right up there with a moonrise over the pyramids. I think the *Lonely Planet* even has a section called Sleeping With a Local."

"So, Mr. Fantasy, why doesn't it work in the States?"

"Here I'm a Letter to Cosmo. There I'm another dark-skinned nobody. Except when they find out I'm a dark-skinned Arab Muslim nobody. Then I become a terrorist." Abe looked across the table at Doug. "It ain't easy being different in America."

"Oh get off it," Doug said. "I hear this crap all the time from the black guys at the brewery. They're always screaming racism whenever things don't go their way. Sure, some people got a problem with race, but mostly that's all gone. It's not like that anymore."

"Spoken like a good white male," Abe said, popping the last half of a dry pastry into his mouth. "If I don't see it, it don't exist. The problem is, you've never been a minority. You'd think your time in prison...."

"I wasn't in prison."

"You'd think your time in prison," Abe repeated, his voice rising to cut off Doug's interruption, "would have changed you. How'd it feel to be ignored and powerless? God gives you this great chance to learn...."

"Oh shit, back to God again."

"Everything comes back to God, my foolish little friend," Abe said, and drained the rest of Doug's now warm 7-Up into his coffee cup. "And, speaking of God—Oh my God, look at the rack on that chick."

Doug followed Abe's stare out the window and down the street. It was easy to spot Aisha, she was the one every guy was looking at. She wore a white tee shirt knotted at the side, loose-cut men's jeans that slung low, exposing her flat stomach, thick gold navel ring and her bikini line. Other women wore something similar, no one wore it like Aisha. Doug smiled, both because it was Aisha and because he got to say, "That is the woman I slept with in Morocco."

"*That's* the Moroccan Tart? My God, Doug, I have grossly underestimated you."

Doug couldn't get the smile off his face, even when he remembered that she probably hid the drugs in his bag as he recuperated in her huge bed. "I still need to talk things over with her. Can you manage to convince her to get to the shop? Without stepping on your tongue?"

"I guess it all comes down to me. Cover me boys, I'm going in," Abe said in a flat, mid-American voice. "That was my Audie Murphy, by the way."

"I'll have to take your word on it," Doug said as he stood up, "I've got no idea what Audie Murphy sounded like."

"Me either. Meet you at the shop." Abe brushed the crumbs off his shirt and headed out the door.

Doug went out the back exit, through the maze of streets and was surprised to find he made it back to the shop, and the black cloth filled storeroom, without a problem. He sat on one of the firmer boxes and listened to his heart pounding in his chest. It dawned on him then that Abe was right, he had no idea what he would say. He thought through a few opening lines and settled on "Hello, Aisha. We need to talk." He chose a half-sitting-on-the-box-half-leaning-against-the-wall-arms-crossed-tough-guy pose to go with his hard talk. He hoped that she'd take one look at him, break down, confess everything, and beg his forgiveness. He hoped that it would turn out this way since he didn't have another plan.

As he was testing whether or not crossing his ankles made him look relaxed or just put him off balance, he heard Aisha's unmistakable laugh coming up the stairs. Abe stepped up to the landing first, then into the room. He extended his arm out as if guiding Aisha into the place. She came up looking at the swaths of cloth on the ground and had surveyed half the room before she saw Doug.

"Oh my God," she yelled and came at him with her arms outstretched. Before he could uncross his ankles, she had her arms wrapped around Doug's neck, knocking them both backwards into a pile of black cloth that reached halfway to the ceiling. And it seemed she was trying to kill him by sticking her tongue so far down his throat he couldn't breathe.

"I believe you know my friend, Douglas Pearce," Doug heard Abe say as Aisha rolled him around in the pile. When she stopped to catch her breath, Doug managed to pry himself partially free and sit up as best as he could. "Aisha," he said, "we need to...."

"Oh my God, Doug, what a great surprise, I thought you were avoiding me, you shit-head, my uncle told me you were still in town, but you never checked in at the Shepheard and I've been here doing nothing, waiting for you to call, and then I figure, fuck him, I mean, no offense, but I was hurt, you stupid ass," a quick kiss and a breath, "and so I decided to come on down to his shop, my uncle that is, and then this guy, oh my God, he is *so* funny, says he has something for my uncle and like an idiot I believe him and he brings me—*me*—to an abaya shop, and I'm thinking, what's going on here? and then I see *you*, you are *so* romantic," she said and, refreshed, renewed her assault.

"And Doug, I believe you know Aisha."

"Oh I'm sorry," Aisha said as she spun off the top of Doug to sit on the pile. "I'm just rather fond of Doug and I'm *really* surprised."

"Oh I understand," Abe said. "I get the same way around him myself."

Doug was trying to pull black strings out of his mouth. The dust cloud they raised in the room gave the few shafts of light a defined shape. He tried to figure out how to get his plan back on track. "Aisha, uh, I wanted to get you up here because I wanted...."

"Oh I can *guess* what *you* wanted," she said, punching him on the arm, her inflection indicating something lewd, something erotic, and something she was all in favor of.

"My work here is done," Abe said in a superhero voice. "I'll leave you two kids alone to get reacquainted. I'll catch up with the boys downstairs. Play nice, now." He went out onto the landing and pulled a black curtain from the shadows across the doorway.

Doug tried just once to stop her, but gave up when she unzipped his pants. The unusual location seemed to inspire Aisha as her tongue mauled other parts of his body. Doug bit down hard on a fistful of dusty cloth, not fully trusting the soundproofing. The heat, the dust, holding his breath—ten minutes of this, he was sure, and he'd pass out. Fortunately, his survival instincts kicked in and hurried him along.

There was a lot more dust in the air, and the shafts of light looked like columns of white marble. They lay on the pile, breathing so hard Doug was certain that they could be heard down the street. Black threads like spiderwebs clung to every surface, and small pieces of black fabric, held in place by sweat, dotted his face. He could feel the damp cotton on the back of his neck, but couldn't feel anything below his chest. His breathing was settling down to a rhythm of puffs and sighs.

"Comfy?" Aisha asked, looking at the centuries-old wooden beam of the ceiling.

"I feel like I've just been mugged," Doug said.

"Oh, thanks a lot," she said, trying to get a hair or a string off her tongue. "I've never had a guy equate sex with a mugging."

"I meant it as a compliment."

"Hmmm," she said, and then they said nothing for another five minutes. Doug had the time to figure out what to say, the time to come up with a way to turn the situation around, the time to get back to his master plan and Aisha's confession....

"So where have you been hiding?" Aisha asked, startling Doug who, completely spent, had started to drift off to sleep.

"I'm staying over at the Sheraton. Been there a few days. Before that I was in prison."

Aisha turned her head but still couldn't see Doug from where she was lying. "Really? Or you just saying that?"

"Are you impressed? I'm sure it'll look good on my résumé."

"What were you doing in prison?" she asked. Doug was alert now, listening for hints of clues in her voice.

"The airport police found a bag of cocaine in my carry-on bag."

"How could you be so fucking stupid?"

"I didn't put the drugs there, someone planted them on me," he said.

"Did the police buy that story? I wouldn't."

"No, they did not buy it. I sat in jail for two weeks because of it." Doug told her what happened. He tried to read her face, or what he could see of it, but he couldn't tell if she was acting, if she already knew what happened, or if she even cared. And if she was faking it, Doug decided, she was good. She laughed at his attempts at jokes and told him it was a really exciting story, unlike anything she'd heard before. Now that was a lie, he knew, but it was a good lie. He didn't want to think that she might have faked *everything*.

"So your dad bailed you out, did he? How sweet. Now this Sergei, he's not some sort of sugar daddy looking for a cute little boy-toy, is he?" She reached down and patted his thigh as she said it.

"No, it's not like that. He's just a nice guy. If you met him you'd know what I mean." He tried to sit up but the pile of cloth kept him reclined. Twenty years, worth of dust was settling back around him.

"I'd like to meet the guy that put the coke in your bag," Aisha said, which made Doug smile. "Wouldn't you have seen somebody messing with your bag?"

"I was asleep most of the flight."

"On Egyptian Air? You're kidding."

"If you recall," he said, turning to see her face, "I didn't get much sleep the night before."

"Hey, I was up. I packed your bags, remember?"

He didn't bite his tongue, but that was because there was still enough lint in his mouth to chew on instead. "Maybe Sergei put it in when he came to visit us peasants in steerage."

"Oh that makes sense," Aisha said as she stood up, brushing off her wrinkled shirt. "He plants five hundred bucks' worth of coke on you so he can then later spend hundreds more just to get you out. You'd make a shrewd drug dealer, Doug."

There were the awkward looks when they came down the stairs, but Aisha seemed immune to shame. She asked something in Arabic and was directed to a small, but filthy bathroom at the rear of the building. Abe waited until she had shut the door before he spoke.

"Boy, you sure showed her."

"Cut it out, okay?" Doug tried not to look embarrassed but the room suddenly felt much warmer. "She didn't say anything."

"Oh, we heard some things pretty clearly down here," Abe said, and then said something in Arabic to the men in the shop, who found whatever it was quite funny. The more they talked in Arabic, the more they laughed and the more Doug was sure it was all at his expense.

"Gentlemen, save something for the locker room," Aisha said, sweeping back into the room. Abe said something to her in Arabic and her response, whatever it was, brought howls of laughter from the old men. Abe was as red as Doug now, and he could only force a slight smile as Aisha strode past him, waving over her shoulder to the old men, and taking Doug by the arm and out into the always crowded souk.

Chapter 19

Aisha knew her way around the dead ends and dark alleys, which was good since Doug had already forgotten the route back to the coffee shop. With Aisha leading the way, he could focus on the shops and the tourists and the locals who tolerated the tourists as they attempted to get the weekly shopping done. The bazaar was different from the one in Morocco—older, more intimidating in a dark, gothic way. It was mid-afternoon, the sun should have been almost overhead, but the narrow streets and the layer after layer of striped awnings and smog-soaked laundry gave the streets a menacing feel.

Everything was for sale. Pots big enough to boil a missionary? You want two or four handles? Laptops with bootleg Windows in Arabic? Hey, free modem if you buy today. Got a goat head? So fresh the goat don't know it yet. Need a cheap gold bracelet? Need a thousand of them? And everything that could be hauled out of the shop and stuck on a peg or tied to a wire was hung around the wall-sized doorways like parts of an over-decorated Baroque gilt frame, which could also be had, complete with a black velvet painting of the moon over the pyramids. Red and white Coca-Cola signs that advertised Pepsi, Leevye Jeans, Ralf Lauren toilet seat covers, video cassettes of movies that were due to premiere next month. And everything at a *special* price.

Aisha ignored the touts, ignored the special offers, and ignored the hard stares from the old women and another type of stare from the young men. "Anyway," she continued, Doug having missed much of what she had already said, "after he didn't show at the party and he didn't call, I said the hell with it and decided to head to Cairo a few days early. So that's what I've been doing. Same old bunch of nothing. There's my uncle's shop. You didn't tell him anything about us, did you?"

"Why? Is he supposed to think you're all innocent?"

"No," she said, with a look that said both "he's not ignorant" and "what do you think I am?" "I just don't want him to start lecturing me about settling down and how all I ever bring home are losers and what a disappointment I am to the family, that's all."

It was Doug's turn to look offended but Aisha ignored that, too, and adjusted her hair in an "antique" plastic framed mirror hung outside a shop, pulling a few black strings from her shiny black hair. "That's strange," she said as she tried to shake a string off her finger, "the gate's down."

"Maybe he closed up early, taking some time off."

"Time off?" she said, her tone making it clear that he had just said something blasphemous. They reached the front of the shop and, despite the two industrial-sized double-key padlocks and quarter-inch steel hasps, Aisha pulled on the doorknob. They tried to peer inside but the roll-down gate and the closed blinds made it impossible to see a thing.

"This is not good," Aisha said as she surveyed the neighborhood. She walked across the narrow alley to a shop that specialized in brightly colored enamelled souvenir plates, the kind that Eastern Europeans bought by the gross. Doug watched from the street as she spoke to the owner in rapid fire, full volume Arabic, the only type of Arabic that seemed to be spoken here. After a few minutes of pointing and yelling and plate slamming Aisha stepped back to the alley, hands on her hips, searching for her next victim.

"He didn't see a thing. Bastard." She stood biting her lip and breathing through her nose. This was a side of Aisha he had not expected. Oh, she was still stunning, he had just not expected it.

"Nasser Ashkanani closes his shop up early and you didn't fucking *notice?*" She yelled something in Arabic back at the shop, which seemed to calm her down. "Better odds of the Sphinx walking off."

"Can we call him?" Doug asked. "I mean, just to see if everything's okay...."

"Everything's not okay. His shop is fucking closed, understand? Something is wrong."

"Alright, so call him and...."

"Somebody had to see something," she said, ignoring him. She did that a lot, he noticed. "Come on, let's try the other shops."

Aisha pushed her way into a couple of shops and bullied the staff until she was sure they had seen nothing. Doug was tempted to suggest that she might find the salespeople a bit more helpful if she wasn't so insulting, but changed his mind when she swung at a one-legged shop owner with a souvenir bamboo back-scratcher. Doug backed out of that shop like a startled tourist who had come upon some of that Middle Eastern violence he'd read so much about, and took up position across the alleyway, leaning against a bare spot on the wall. From here he could observe her inquiring technique. She'd start out with her most polite demanding tone, the same kind used by secret police wielding rubber hoses in half-lit interrogation rooms. At the first hint of an "I didn't see a thing" answer, she'd adopt a more focused demeanor, sounding much like a professional wrestler calling for a folding chair to use in the ring. Then, just before she'd throw something, her voice would drop to a low growl and she'd let her narrowed eyes do the talking.

Doug was certain that the people in the area had no idea why Nasser Ashkanani would close his shop early. As distracting as he found Aisha's approach, most of the people in the Khan walked on as if this kind of ear-splitting, stock-tossing tirade was an everyday occurrence, which, of course, it probably was. Doug watched as the other shop owners continued to wave in backpackers, watched as the tea guy continued to weave in and out of every doorway, and watched the locals standing around, watching him. Like the guy standing in front of the Ashkanani shop, the tough guy with the hairy mustache, hairy eyebrows, and hairy ears.

Doug stared at the man for a full minute. He watched as the man looked down the alleyway, across from where Doug stood, to where Aisha was currently at level two of her questioning of a postcard and bootleg video vendor. When Doug first saw him in the coffee shop, he thought he was a large man, maybe as tall as himself, with a bulky build, like an out-of-shape former Marine. Seeing him now, in the daylight, Doug realized that his first impression had been wrong; the man was not built like that at all. He was huge, freakishly unbelievably huge. Huge like biker-strip-club-bouncer huge. And the black shirt, black pants, and black boots provided no slimming effect. His arms, which Doug was comparing favorably with his own legs, were crossed in front of his steroid enhanced chest. There was no room for a neck.

When the man turned to look at him, Doug felt his own eyes lock onto the white parts visible just under the heap of black hair that on a normal-sized person would have been eyebrows. He stared at Doug—the white parts did, anyway—long enough for Doug to feel his heart beat double. Then he turned his hairy gaze back down the street, just under the Bab al-Badistan. He raised his hand to get the attention of someone in the crowd, then, moving his hand a few inches, pointed at Doug.

"Aisha, we gotta go," he shouted into the phone booth sized shop.

"Look, pharaoh, my uncle's had a shop here before your family wandered in out of the desert...."

"Aisha, we gotta go."

"Just a second, Doug," she said without turning around, "so don't you go telling me that you don't have no...."

"Aisha!" Doug could see the hairy man working his way down the street.

"I said just a second," she said, glancing backwards while she reached for a copy of *Titanic* to throw. "If my uncle hears that...."

"Now!" Doug said, grabbing her wrist and pulling her out of the shop and dragging her behind as he started to run down the street.

"What the fuck are you doing?" she said, pulling her wrist free. Doug turned to explain, stepping back just in time to avoid a pretty decent left hook. "Don't *ever* do that to me," she said, and got ready to swing again, this time a right. Just over her shoulder, Doug could make out the yard-wide shoulders of the black suit cutting around a tall blue backpack with a Canadian flag patch.

"They're after us. Let's go. Now." The words came out sharp and hard, and Aisha was as surprised as Doug. Her expression changed and she only half turned around to look before extending her hand out to Doug, who grabbed it as he started to run.

They ran down the alley, cutting onto a smaller side walkway which twisted back and forth a half dozen times before emerging back onto the alley, just four shops down from the now running hairy black mass. "Oh shit!" Aisha said when she saw the man coming, "he's huge."

"Come on," Doug said, darting across the alley and down another side street. Overhanging awnings slung way too low and burlap bags filled with empty burlap bags turned the cross street into a maze. It didn't help that all the old women had picked *that moment* to step out of their doorways with large, empty baskets on their heads. "Excuse me, excuse me," Doug said, trying to get by the short little grandmother types, busy adjusting their headscarves. "Get the fuck out of the way," yelled Aisha, knocking baskets and short little grandmother types to the ground. This led to a lot more people stepping out of their homes, but fortunately for Doug, a good forty feet behind them and right in front of the rapidly gaining black suit. When Doug slowed down to let a donkey cart squeeze past, Aisha cut in front and started pulling him along. She made a quick turn down one alleyway and then down another and another until Doug was certain that even she was lost. She made a few more quick turns and then pulled him in through a large wooden doorway.

A tarnished brass placard identified the building as the Mosque of Hossam Bin Ahmed Al-Shaloub, dating from 1698, but it was hidden behind the open door and written in Arabic.

"Aisha, this is a mosque," Doug said, noticing the *minrahb* and *minbar*—Sergei would be so proud. "Aren't we supposed to take off our shoes?"

"Whatever," Aisha said, cutting across the threadbare carpets to a narrow doorway in a shadowy *iwan*. An old man in a light blue galabiyya shuffled across the mosque, a turban balanced on his head like a week's worth of laundry. His pointing and waving let Doug know that yes, they should have taken off their shoes. Before he could catch up with them—long before, really—Doug and Aisha were climbing a tiny spiral staircase made of the same stone as the entire mosque. The twist of the stairs was so tight it seemed as if they weren't climbing at all but merely going around in circles. Narrow slits in the walls provided the only light. The steps were close together and never more than four inches wide and every five steps produced a stumble with Doug's face slamming against Aisha's ass.

Over the rhythmic shuffle of their steps, and his own breath, which was loud and panting, Doug heard the sound of someone else climbing the steps below them. At first he thought it was an echo but the pattern of the steps was different and then he heard the voices, deep voices that didn't sound out of breath. It was impossible to tell how far behind they were, the stone steps offering not the slightest view down, and there was no way to tell they had reached the top until they spilled out a half-sized doorway and onto the small platform from which, for centuries, the call to prayer was made. If they had stopped to read the tarnished brass placard by the entrance, they would have known that the minaret of the Mosque of Hossam Bin Ahmed Al-Shaloub, dating from 1698, was twenty-one meters tall. As they both grabbed for the low handrail, heads and shoulders sailing under the bar and off the platform, it looked a hell of a lot farther.

"Go, go, go," Aisha was yelling as they climbed back onto the platform and edged their way to the far side of the minaret. The sounds of the men on the stairs were much clearer now and much closer.

The minaret was built into the side wall of the mosque and, while the door side of the platform dropped straight to the street, the back side of the minaret dropped to the roof of the mosque, no more than ten feet below. They ducked under the handrail, hung on to the base and swung down.

"You okay?" Doug asked.

"Shit," Aisha said as the black suit stepped onto the platform. "This way." She grabbed his arm and led him across the roof, not a flat, level roof that would allow an easy getaway, but a roof that, due to seventeenth-century Islamic building methods, was set with knee-high walls, sudden horizontal shifts, and half-hidden ventilation shafts. The satellite TV dishes and the randomly strung cables were of more recent origin. A rare flat, wireless area allowed Doug a look behind. There were two men, the hairy giant and a shorter, lighter man in a green tracksuit, and they were only half a roof away now. When he looked forward again, he saw the open space.

"We're outta roof?" he yelled. "We're outta fucking roof?" A sound like a small firecracker went off behind them and they both looked back in time to see the man in the black suit level the pistol again. Instinct should have made him duck, like it did Aisha, but Doug stood there and stared as he heard *something* zip over his head, the sound of the shot a fraction of a second behind the muzzle flash and puff of smoke. He looked over at Aisha, and they both looked across the next roof. It was lower than this roof, there was no wall by the edge to clear, and it connected to every other roof in the neighborhood. But it was definitely not jumpable.

"Ready?" Aisha asked, stepping backwards from the edge and scraping the toe of her shoe on the roof, trying to build up some traction. Doug was about to say never when two more some-things zipped much closer to his head and two more firecrackers went off behind him. He was running before he knew it and, for what he thought was an amazingly long time, he hung in the air, one arm flapping like a wing-shot duck, the other holding onto Aisha's hand. They hit the roof of the next building with almost four feet to spare. Small stones and dust sprayed up like a fountain a few yards away and more firecrackers went off on the roof of the mosque. Doug pulled Aisha to her feet and they ran, clearing the low walls with uncoordinated grace.

Aisha looked back to the mosque. "I think they're gonna jump it," she said.

"Don't stop now, look for a way down, a stairway or something," Doug said, but Aisha grabbed Doug's shoulder and froze.

"Oh my God," she said as she drew in a deep breath.

Doug turned, expecting the hairy man an arm's length away, but there was no one. He looked back and saw the man in the green tracksuit leaning forward, standing at the edge of the mosque roof. He was looking down to the street.

"Oh God, Doug, I saw him fall." Aisha's voice sounded tiny and far away. "He wasn't even close. I watched him fall."

Doug hadn't seen or heard a thing, but he wasn't about to go to the edge and look. He swallowed—his throat was quite dry and burning—and reached for Aisha's hand. "Let's go." She stood fixed to the spot for a moment, then slowly allowed Doug to get her walking again. She turned back twice and both times said "Oh my God."

"Aisha, what could we do?" Doug asked. "It was a long jump and nobody told him to try it."

"Besides," he said after they climbed over a series of pipes and wires and were heading for what looked like a fire escape a few rooftops away, "he was trying to kill us. I mean, sure I feel bad for him, but he was shooting at us."

She glanced over at Doug as if he had suddenly appeared. "Fuck *him*," Aisha said. "I'm thinking about *me*. I mean, that could have been *me* falling there."

"Us," Doug reminded her. "It could have been us."

"I could be dead right now. Flat on the side of a street like some...some *dog*. Me. Dead. Just like *that*." She snapped her fingers for effect but it looked more like she was calling an inattentive waiter. "Who do you think he was, and why was he chasing us? Or does this stuff happen all the time around here?" The ladder was a fire escape and only two families had expanded out from bedroom windows to turn their section of the rusted iron stairs into an open-air closet. And no one, not even the old man whose reclining chair they had to climb over to get around, seemed at all inconvenienced by their passing.

"How would I know who they were?" Aisha asked as she ducked under a row of birdcages and stepped around a kettle of tea on a hotplate. "You're the one that pointed them out to me. I thought you knew who they were."

Doug tried to figure out a way to grab a hold of the last handrail without touching the line of bras drying in the non-existent breeze. In the end he just hoped the stairway wouldn't collapse and risked not holding on. "I just saw them in the crowd. I thought they might have something to do with your uncle's shop. I guess you'll have to jump," he said noticing that the last five steps had been removed and were being used nearby to prop up air conditioning units in the ground floor windows.

"I'll kill them if they did anything to Uncle Nasser," Aisha said. "Well, the guy in the tracksuit, anyway."

Back on the ground, Aisha got her bearings and a three-minute walk took them to an open square filled with more shops and street vendors. That was the number one industry in Cairo, Doug decided, selling things—selling the same thing the guy next to you sold, the same packet of socks, the same alarm clocks, the same knock-off Barbie dolls, the same basket of rotting vegetables. You bought it, then you sold it. The same handful of goods could keep a neighborhood employed for months.

"I want to call my uncle," Aisha announced, "I don't have my phone with me. Wait here while I find a phone." Before Doug could ask if she thought it was smart that they split up like this, she dove into the crowd. He could tell where she was for a few seconds by watching for the men whose heads were turned one way while they walked another. Doug found a lamp pole to lean against and tried not to look conspicuous. This proved difficult since everyone who passed by, even the man leading the camel—the only one in downtown Cairo—stopped to stare. At least the touts left him alone, tourists being so rare in this area that they didn't know what to do with him. Other than stare, that is. Doug stared back, not directly, of course, but in a casual, friendly way, smiling as he scanned the crowd for other homicidal maniacs who might be stalking him.

And why him? It's not like he had the diamond—he didn't even have a clue. And who would know where he was or anything about the Ashkanani connection? Maybe it was Aisha they were after, God knows she must have enemies all over the world. But why today, and why was the hairy guy following him? Something Sergei said rolled in from the back of his mind. "I'm not suggesting that the original killers are out there…." But maybe they were. And maybe they had assumed he knew something.

And now some guy was dead, Doug thought, and how do you think *that* makes me feel? So he thought about it for a moment and realized he didn't feel anything at all. No guilt, no remorse, no regrets. Then he thought about that, since not feeling anything didn't feel right, but after ten minutes he realized his thoughts had drifted to trying to figure out how the woman with the four-foot-tall basket on her head managed to maneuver through the shopping area without once reaching up to steady the load. He took a deep breath and tried again to focus on the diamond and all the trouble it had caused.

Back in Morocco he had written up a list of things he knew and now, weeks later, he had little more to add to that list. The diamond left Casablanca and came to Cairo, and left Cairo for Singapore and no one seemed to know what happened to it there. This was the easy stuff and if it was so easy for him to find out, why didn't Edna already know? Oh boy, Edna. He called when he got out of jail but he was vague about what he was doing. It didn't seem to matter what he told her though, she was happy with anything he did, even when it was obvious to anybody he wasn't doing anything. He thought about feeling guilty and then remembered the gray meat in the jail and decided to follow Aisha's advice—take the money and keep her happy.

And where was Aisha? It couldn't be that hard to find a phone around here, especially for someone as pushy as her. Doug bought a cold bottle of Coke from a passing vendor, overpaying again since he had still not figured out the exchange rate or buying power of the Egyptian pound notes. Other than a few professional level gawkers who still found him fascinating to watch, the locals ignored Doug, which gave him more time to watch them. It was mostly men in the crowd and all of them, perhaps by some harshly enforced law, sported the same thick, black mustache that hung down over their top lip. A few wore the traditional galabiyya, but most wore long-sleeved shirts buttoned to the top, despite oven-like heat. Doug was roasting in his khakis and polo shirt, both, he noticed, still carrying stray black strings from the abaya shop.

And everybody smoked, all the males anyway. Packs of kids young enough to get into movies for free puffed away on unfiltered Camels while the adult men seemed to keep two cigarettes going, one to smoke and one to point with. But given the amount of exhaust fumes that flooded the street, thick fumes you could feel slide up your skin and roll down your throat, what difference would it make if you smoked a carton or two a day? Greasy smoke from greasy trucks that idled so high you'd expect an explosion added to the noise and heat of the whole area. And add to that the dust, the city-wide layer of litter, and the pervasive smell of sewage that had gone bad in the sun and you had Cairo. How do people live here, he thought.

That's when he realized that the background music to this whole scene, more pervasive than the diesel trucks, more common than the hawkers' nonstop shouts of *aywah!*, louder than the call to prayer that had just started up, was the laughter. Everybody seemed to be having a great time, slapping hands with a sideways low five, stopping only to cough up a lung or light up another cigarette. The kids hacked out a smoky laugh, the old men wore big, one-tooth grins and there were high-pitched giggles coming from under the black sheets that hid teenaged girls as they wove through the crowd. Maybe the fumes had got to them, he thought, since they were sure starting to get to him. Or maybe, despite the totally shitty reality that was their lives, they were happy. Fathers bought their children bags of out-of-date candy, friends greeted friends with hugs and kisses as if they had been separated for years instead of minutes. There were happy couples holding hands as they strolled through the market. Granted, they were both guys, but that seemed to be normal around here. They're not gay, Abe had said, they just look that way.

An idea started to form in Doug's mind, a fundamental idea that held together a worldview, a core philosophy. He found it hard to pull his thoughts together and it took his focused thinking for a full five minutes until he could attach words to these feelings. Maybe the environment didn't matter. Maybe happiness was something you found inside you, not in your surroundings. Maybe his whole way of looking at the world—Pottsville, the brewery, Egyptian jail, this intersection—maybe everything was neither good nor bad, maybe it was all what you made of it. Maybe the keys to happiness and despair, to your own personal heaven or hell, were yours all along. Life could be good, you could be happy, if you wanted it to be so.

Doug thought about this for a while and decided that no, it was the fumes. Nobody could be happy here.

He looked at the digital watch he bought the day before from a street vendor. It still flashed 99:99 like it did ten minutes after he bought it. He waited another forty minutes until his watch said 99:99 before he decided to take a cab back to the hotel. Aisha was a big girl, she could find her way back home. Whether he could or not remained to be seen.

Chapter 20

"That funny taste? That's formaldehyde."

Doug held his beer up to the light, as if he could check chemical content by sight, and wondered if it really was formaldehyde. He'd never tasted formaldehyde but was willing to believe that's what the strange taste was. It would explain the smell.

"The people that make Osiris beer? They also own a chemical company and their main product is formaldehyde." Jeff Willett, twenty-four, from Norman, Oklahoma, was staying at the Sheraton with his new wife, Stacey, also twenty-four, also from Norman, Oklahoma. "That's what the guy at the papyrus shop said."

Jeff had sat down at the hotel bar, the Nile Sunset, the one with the excellent view of the river, less than twenty minutes ago, and in that time Doug learned just about everything he wanted to know about Jeff and Stacey Willett from Norman, Oklahoma. Like the fact that this was their first trip out of the States, that they were on their honeymoon which they had been planning since their first date at the sophomore Halloween dance where he went as King Tut and she as Cleopatra, that Stacey's Uncle Frank gave them two hundred dollars to spend "just on drinks," and that in two days they were going to take a Nile river cruise all the way from Aswan back to Cairo. Jeff provided intense details about his job—he "sold, maintained and repaired commercial swimming pool pumps and filters"—as if Doug was about to fill in for him while he took his Nile cruise. Jeff Willett found it exciting work and naturally assumed so did everyone else. And he lectured about his first impressions of Cairo, since, having been here for three days, he was now an expert.

"Know what you should go see? You should see the light and sound show at Giza. Man, you really start to understand just how old the place is. Plus they got a lot of good souvenir shops over that way, good stuff. Stacey picked up this real nice model of the pyramids in a glass ball, not one of those snow ball things that you shake, just a glass ball," he said and paused for dramatic effect. "Ten bucks."

Doug took a long pull on his Osiris beer. It was his fourth since Jeff Willett sat down and Doug was hoping that if it indeed were formaldehyde, it would soon kick in. He wasn't sure what formaldehyde would do to you if you drank it, but, as Jeff Willett described how everyone at the wedding reception got such a laugh when he and his two brothers—Steve and Little Jimmy—got up and danced the Macarena, Doug hoped it would at least make him deaf.

"…but Stacey's aunt is really two years *younger* than Stacey, so we all went to Hooter's to celebrate and who should be there? Right! Mr. Keiffer, our old math teacher…."

The bar, with its unique and breathtaking view of the ancient river, was decorated in the American Style Family Orientated Theme Restaurant motif, all dark woods and phony antiques hanging from the ceiling. A Texaco gas pump stood by the men's room door and sepia-toned team photos covered the walls. Lacquered to the bar top were high-quality photocopies of "old tyme" beer ads and 1930s era baseball programs. The bartender wore a starched white apron and a little red fez, the signature headgear for the hotel. Other than the fez, it could be Anybar, USA. For some reason, Doug found that depressing.

"…The way we figure it, why pay someone else's mortgage when we can use that money on a place of our own…."

There wasn't anything really wrong with Jeff Willett. Hadn't he bought all the beer and an order of nachos?

"…it's a little par three with a wicked slope to the green and this pocket bunker that has to be five feet deep…."

I know this guy, Doug thought.

"…I pointed out the sign clearly said 'three day rental on all first run movies,' and it was only two days anyway…."

Not him, not Jeff Willett from Norman, Oklahoma, but Jeff Willett, typical guy.

"…she's got a rack out to here and legs that just don't quit…."

I know what he likes, what he does in his spare time and what he'll do when he retires.

"…sixteen Buds, four shots of tequila, four of JD, *and* a rum and Coke…."

I went to school with Jeff Willetts, worked with them, hung out at the Rusty Nail with them.

"…so we put the housing back on and it's *still* leaking so I'm thinking gasket…."

Jeff Willetts made up just about everybody he knew in Pottsville. They wore jeans, drove pickup trucks or Trans Ams, cheered on the Steelers in October and the Pirates in June. They liked to hunt but were just as happy when they came home without a thing. They married women they had screwed in high school and lived and died fifty miles from where they were born.

"…he goes 'who you calling stupid?' and I go 'I just call 'em like I see 'em' which really pisses him off, right? So he goes…."

He knew Jeff Willett.

"…but as a designated hitter? He's *unreal*. If he was with, say, the Yankees…."

He was Jeff Willett.

"Whoa, Doug, you look like you could use another. Yeah, a couple more beers down here and how about a bowl of peanuts? Put your money away, this is on Uncle Frank."

This can't be me, Doug thought as he drained half the Osiris beer in one swig. I can't be this….

"…just give me a cold beer and a game on cable and color me happy…."

…this…

"...but the highlight is the three-day layover in Minneapolis 'cuz they got that Mall of America...."

...boring.

"...Led Zeppelin II. Enough said."

Don't panic, Doug thought. Think. Do Jeff Willetts jet off to Morocco? Do they end up in jail in Cairo? Are they hired as detectives to find stolen jewels and are they tracked down by professional killers? Are they shot at and do they make daring leaps across mile-wide alleyways? Do Jeff Willetts have exotic sex with hot Arab women?

"Hey Stacey! Finally. Pull up a stool and meet my friend Doug."

No, they do not.

"I got *such* a great deal on a carpet. I talked him down to just fifty dollars!" She looked at both Jeff and Doug to see if they were as amazed. "Fifty!"

So maybe he wasn't a Jeff Willett. Not now, anyway.

"...I'm not sure, but I think the mosques are a lot like a church, just the wrong god is all...."

On the tenth beer, the formaldehyde kicked in.

Chapter 21

"We met over breakfast, it's only fitting that it is over breakfast that we say farewell."

A formaldehyde hangover isn't much different from an alcohol hangover, except for the undulating band of visual distortion. It snakes through the air, disrupting solid objects, like a confined heat shimmer or bad tracking on a VCR. Doug was watching one of these lines roll across his plate while Sergei explained his itinerary.

"The train ride to Alexandria is much safer and more comfortable than the Egyptian Air flight, and it's usually an hour or two faster. The ship to Cyprus leaves quite early tomorrow morning but I have a cabin so it should be pleasant enough. Then a day trip to Paphos. By this time Saturday I'll be sipping wine on the terrace, working on my tan."

Doug had noticed the flashing message light on his hotel room phone when he got out of bed to throw up, but couldn't figure out how to get the message out of the damn thing until six, when the dry heaves made it impossible for him to continue trying to sleep. He showered for an hour and met Sergei in the Nile Dawn breakfast buffet lounge, which was actually the Nile Sunset with tablecloths covering the beer ads.

"I think you should tell your Canadian friend that you are just *certain* that the Jagersfontien Diamond made a side trip to Cyprus and join us for a week or so." The "us" part was the big surprise Sergei had mentioned in his phone message. He had run into an old friend while visiting the Islamic Arts Museum and the two had decided to run off to Paphos "like giddy teens."

"The weather will be a tad warm but that will only mean less in the way of clothes, I imagine." Sergei raised and lowered his eyebrows suggestively, which only made Doug feel nauseous again.

"We spent a torrid July together in Barcelona some time ago and swore that we'd relive it one day. You should come along, you'd have a great time."

As much as Doug admitted that he enjoyed Sergei's company, the thought of spending a week with him and his "companion" on an island—Cyprus was an island, wasn't it?—didn't sound like fun. "So what's there to do at Paphos?" he asked, trying to change the subject a bit.

"Absolutely nothing. And that's what we'll do. Well, not *absolutely* nothing." The eyebrows bounced up and down again. "We shared some…moments, you could say, in Spain. We hope to share them all again. And some new ones, I suspect."

"So…you leave this morning?" Change the subject, please, Doug prayed.

"My train was scheduled to leave twenty minutes ago, so I'll leave for the station in an hour and only have forty minutes to wait. My friend leaves for Cyprus Friday, her husband has business in Beirut and won't be leaving till tomorrow."

"Her *husband?*" Doug didn't drop his fork or anything so dramatic, but he was nonetheless stunned. The wavy formaldehyde band jumped off his plate and clung to the Texaco gas pump.

Sergei smiled a tight-lipped smile and lowered his eyes in mock shame. "I'm afraid you now know my dark side, Douglas. I hope this doesn't lower your opinion of me."

"Sergei," he said laughing, "what am I going to do without you?"

"Well Douglas, you seem to be keeping yourself quite busy. And, by the looks of you this morning, not using your time to catch up on your sleep. I trust that you've made a few friends here in Cairo?"

"And a few enemies," Doug added, imitating Sergei's eyebrow gesture.

"And what about you? Still looking for that diamond? Hot on the trail, as they say?"

Good question, Doug thought. Now what? He'd killed a man—well, sort of—and possibly caused something bad to happen to Aisha's uncle. He could track down Aisha and take it from there, or look for Abe and see what he suggested. Or he could call Edna and find out how she wanted him to spend her money. He didn't have any real idea what to do.

"Me?" he said, pushing his half-eaten eggs into a pile with his fork. "Eh, I'll think of something."

"I'm going to miss you, Douglas. You've become quite the *bon vivant*," Sergei said, holding up his tea in salute.

"If that means hung over, I agree," he said and raised his orange juice in reply.

◇◇◇

Cairo is more than just the pyramids, more than the mosques, more than the old souks. But since the new parts are not nearly as interesting, or as well built, as the ancient ruins, most visitors to the city never see it. There are thousands of shops that never see a tourist, that don't sell tiny pyramids, and whose owners don't stand in the doorway, enticing you to come in with claims of insanely discounted prices on unspeakably valuable items. For three hours Doug wandered around in one of these areas, hoping for inspiration, waiting for the wavy band to disappear, and trying to decide if he needed a rubber stamp.

The hotel had thoughtfully provided a copy of *Cairo!* magazine in every room, and, mixed in among the lengthy restaurant "reviews" written by the restaurant owners and the three color maps pointing out the locations of these highly praised establishments, there were real articles, reprinted each month, about life in Cairo. Squeezed in between mouthwatering descriptions of specially selected and masterfully prepared braised lamb chops, and accounts of how heads of state, when they are in the city, always dine at Maroosh, was a piece on the tradition of the souk.

According to A. Carieen, Arabic rulers required like shops to be located together in the same part of town to encourage competitive pricing and make shopping easier. "No need to traipse from shop to shop, across town and back again, to find what was needed. Oh, the ease of shopping then!" Whether by tradition or a still enforced law, whole streets were dedicated to one product. As Doug walked the half-mile of the rubber stamp and small engraved signs with no borders souk—quite separate from the rubber stamp and small engraved signs *with* borders souk—he wondered how any of these places could stay in business. There were no hordes of price conscious shoppers traipsing from shop to shop, keeping the area financially healthy. There were, however, hordes of underemployed rubber stamp and small engraved sign makers wandering about. Doug tried to picture the entire Reading mall selling only one thing—say, truck-bed liners or sneakers—but it just didn't make sense. Sort of like the rubber stamp and small engraved signs with no borders souk.

Mixed in with the specialty shops, perhaps by that same ancient decree, were small restaurants and at one of these, in the middle of the electrical motor and arc welding supply souk, he stopped for a Coke. The electrical motor and arc welding supply community sees itself as a cosmopolitan crowd, unlike those commoners over in the lead-based paint souk, so Doug didn't attract too much attention.

On the paper placemat he wrote the heading *What To Do Now* and, for two Cokes and a Snickers bar, he made boxes around all the letters in *What To Do Now*, turned the boxes into three-dimensional cubes, shaded in all the Os, rewrote the heading in fancy cursive, shaded in all the Os in that heading, and copied the Arabic letters used to write Coca-Cola. With the mat nearly filled, he checked his pants pockets for something else to write on, this list being too messy now to use for any real work. On a folded, round paper coaster used by the coffee shop near the Bab al-Badistan was the phone number Abe had given him yesterday morning.

"Where the hell are you?" Abe said. Even over the phone Doug could tell Abe's teeth were tightly clenched.

"I'm sorry, have I reached the home of Charlton Heston?" Doug asked.

"Cut the crap, where the hell are you?"

"I'm not sure. Want me to pick you up some welding rods?"

"What the hell are you talking about? We've been trying to reach you all day. The hotel said you were at breakfast but nobody's seen you since."

"Calm down, I went for a walk. Who's we?"

"Me and Aisha. She called here about ten this morning. She went to the hotel to look for you but you were gone. And don't tell me to calm down, asshole."

"What's going on?" Doug asked but was thinking about Aisha going to his hotel room.

"You've got to get the hell outta Cairo, that's what's going on. There's some mean motherfuckers looking for you and they're going to kill you if they catch you."

"What?" Doug could feel his testicles retreating up into his stomach. Instinctively, he looked up and down the street. "What did Aisha say?"

"She said that there's some mean motherfuckers looking for you and they're going to kill you if they catch you, that's what she said. Where the hell are you?"

"I said I don't know. I'll catch a cab back to the hotel…."

"No man, don't go there," Abe said. "She checked out for you and dropped your stuff off here."

"How'd she get my passport from the front desk?"

"It's Aisha. How do you think she got it? Look," he said, and paused long enough for Doug to think the line was cut, "get a cab and meet me at T.G.I. Friday's, the one on the boat."

"They got a *Friday's* on a boat?"

"Oh Jesus," Abe said, his teeth clenching again, "just get there." Now the line did go dead, but Doug had clearly heard Abe slam the phone down.

Chapter 22

When he got back to Pottsville, if he got back, Doug was considering looking for work in the fake antique business.

The walls of the Friday's on the boat—yes, there really was a Friday's on a boat—like the walls of the other two Friday's he'd been in, and like the walls of the Nile Sunset/Dawn, and a dozen or so restaurants and bars in the greater Pottsville area, were covered in retro Americana antiques. There were signs advertising Beech-Nut Chewing Tobacco, Hershey's Chocolate Syrup, Esso Gasoline, and one that said "Learn to like Moxie!" but gave no clue what Moxie was or why one had to learn to like it. There were musical instruments, a couple of sleds, scores of old team photos in unusual-shaped frames, a traffic light, some toy fire trucks and train tracks, and a suitcase or two. There were enough balls—National League Spalding, American League Reach, and sandlot no-names—bats and gloves to outfit a team, the kind that would wear the thick cotton uniform that was hanging above the men's room door. And everything, from the wooden Adirondack canoe to the Old West sheriff's badges, was rusted or tarnished or bent in a way that was aesthetically pleasing and sort of homey. The red Texaco gas pump, identical to the one at the Nile Sunset/Dawn, identical to the one at the Friday's in Reading, blocked his view of the Elvis tribute section, displayed over the bright lights of the non-functioning jukebox. But that was all right, he knew exactly what he'd find there. He wondered what it must be like working at the factory that pumped out enough phony antiques to supply the world's bars and restaurants. Probably three shifts. Probably union. "I work in the stain and tarnish section," he could picture himself saying, "part of the weathering division."

Doug had just finished his second Osiris when Abe pulled up a chair.

"Anybody follow you here?" Abe asked as he motioned to a passing waiter to bring the check.

"I didn't think to look," Doug said. "Did anybody follow you?"

"Nobody's trying to kill *me*, Dougie. And if I work this right, no one will." He threw some multicolored pound notes on the table. "Let's get going, we've got a five-hour drive to get to Sharm el-Shiek if you're gonna catch that flight."

"Who's Sharm el-Shiek?" Doug asked as they headed down the covered gangway and to the tiny street-side parking lot.

"It's a resort town on the Red Sea. You're catching a Gulf Air flight outta here. It's the first flight we could get you on that didn't fly out of Cairo."

"Why? You think someone's actually watching the airport for me?"

Abe stopped to unlock his car door and looked over the roof at Doug. "Yeah, Doug, I do."

For over an hour they drove in silence, not counting Abe's running commentary on the fucking stupidity of every driver on the goddamn road. In heavy traffic the cars bumped into each other, pushing with a fender, nudging with the whole left side of the car, but since this didn't even elicit so much as a "bastard" from Abe, it probably meant that this was considered courteous driving in Cairo. Doug stared out the window at the identical-looking buildings that raced by, and at the other drivers every time they pulled up to a stoplight. The other drivers, however, ignored Doug, glued to the traffic light, waiting for their chance to sprint ahead a half a car length. And at every traffic light, motorcycles snaked their way up to the front of the line, so when the light did change it looked like the starting flag at a motocross rally.

Finally Doug said, "Where's Aisha?"

"No idea," Abe said and then yelled something in Arabic, something that probably ended in *learn to drive, you dumb fuck.*

"Well how'd you get the ticket?"

"I got an uncle who owns a travel agency—no smart-assed comments, Dougie—he took care of the flight. Your name won't be officially listed until you land, too late to catch you here."

"So where am I going?"

"I told you, Sharm el-Shiek. After that, we'll have to see the ticket."

◇◇◇

Doug passed the time watching the darkening horizon. When the sun set in Egypt, it set fast, and all that was left of the blinding sun was a thin band of orange glow in the sky behind them. An hour later, even that was gone. He had started off trying to figure out what to tell Edna, but his mind drifted to a thousand different areas, few of them having anything to do with jewels, killers, or Egypt.

"We're being followed," Abe said, breaking the silence.

"Huh?"

"The car behind us, it's following us," Abe said as he checked his rearview mirror.

Doug turned around to look out the back window. There was nothing to be seen other than a sliver of the moon, a thousand stars and a pair of yellow headlights.

"How do you know they are following us? They could be going to Sharm el-Shiek, too."

"Because I thought we were being followed about an hour ago so I took a back route I know. They took it. So I took a few other back roads. They took all of them. No, they're following us," he said, looking out to the side mirror, "and they're getting closer."

"Now what?" Doug asked.

"I've got one more road to try, a real back route but it'll get us around to the main road eventually. If they take that one too, I'm gonna try to lose them."

Doug looked around the area, trying to make out something in the blackness. "I don't see anything out there. There's nothing to hide behind and no traffic either. How you gonna lose them?"

"Well, first with moves like…THIS." Abe slammed on the brakes, sledding the car along the thin layer of sand like it was ice, pulled the wheel hard to his left, whipping the back of the car around, dropped it into first and shot off the paved road and onto a gravel track that ran into the desert. The car bottomed out hard and the sound of rocks hitting the axels made Doug cringe. Behind them, two headlights bounced down the short embankment and onto the gravel road.

"I knew it, I fuckin' knew it," Abe shouted as he leaned forward in his seat, trying to make out a road. The floorboard shook with the impact of desert rocks kicked up by the tires and the headlights behind them seemed dimmer through the dust. Dimmer but larger.

"I think they're getting closer. Go faster," Doug shouted over the noise of the road.

"Oh brilliant," Abe said, taking his eyes off the road long enough to roll them at Doug. "I didn't think of *that*." He pushed the pedal harder against the floor, trying to force more out of the redlined engine.

The interior of the car grew brighter as the two headlights drew closer. Doug braced himself with one arm on the roof and the other on the dashboard. He twisted his neck to watch the headlights disappear behind the trunk of their car and he prepared for the impact. It was a slight nudge but enough to force Abe to wrestle the car back under control.

The headlights pulled back to ready for another hit.

"Get ready," Doug shouted.

"*You* get ready," Abe yelled, "they're trying to flip us."

The headlights came at them again, this time faster, and the hit sent Doug hard into the windshield. He looked over at Abe, who somehow kept the car straight, and saw the blood from his busted lip. Doug held on, trying to turn to see out the back window. There was less light—one of the headlights busted on the last hit—but it stayed with them, just peeking over the top of the trunk. The tires sent up a steady stream of stones and unseen holes in the road threatened to rip off a wheel.

"If I remember right," Abe said as he stared ahead, "there's going to be an intersection up here. If they try to hit us there I'm going to try something."

The lone headlight kept pace but didn't try to ram again.

"Get the gun," Abe said, "and be ready."

"What gun?" Doug yelled and thought oh shit, oh shit, oh shit.

"There, there," Abe said, pointing to the glove box.

Doug pulled out a handgun, an automatic, he had no idea what kind, and felt for the safety. He turned to look out the rear window and shifted in his seat.

"What are you doing?" Abe yelled. "Don't shoot out my back window. Are you crazy?"

"Hey," Doug said, "they're the ones trying to kill us. And you told me to get the gun."

"I don't care. Don't shoot through my windows."

Doug twisted back around and started to open the passenger window. I'm not really going to do this, am I, he thought, but before he could decide, a slight nudge from behind forced him to hold on again.

Abe took his right hand off the wheel long enough to smack Doug on the leg. "Forget that. Here's the spot. Hold on."

Doug tossed the gun on the floor and braced himself.

As if on cue, the headlight backed off a few yards and lunged forward. Abe yanked the wheel one way, then back, pumping the brakes each time they were hit. Above the noise of crumpling metal and flying rocks, Doug knew he heard gunshots and tried to reach for the automatic on the floor but was thrown back in his seat by a hard hit from behind. There was one more hard hit, and the interior of the car filled with light again as the single headlight shot up over the trunk and arched away into the desert. Doug couldn't make out the car but watched as the light bounced off the road and disappeared behind a sand dune, briefly backlit by a bright yellow flash. The sound of the explosion was just audible above the gravel and the engine's roar.

"Holy shit," Abe yelled, "did you see that?"

"What'd you *do?* How'd you do that?"

"I was just trying to force them off the road," Abe said, and started to laugh but stopped himself. "Holy shit," he added and slowed the car down, but not by much. The gravel still made it hard to hear.

"I couldn't make out what happened. I couldn't really see anything," Doug said, and then said, "Should we go back?"

"Hell no, what are you crazy? They'd kill us."

"If they aren't already dead," Doug said.

Abe was licking his lip, trying to determine how bad the cut was. The air conditioning was gone and they were sweating.

"No. They ain't dead," Abe said.

"What? Did you see the explosion?"

"They were just busted up. They're fine."

Doug wiped his eyes, the sweat was starting to run down his face. "Abe, how can you say they are fine? I mean, with a crash like that…."

Abe turned in his seat and pointed a finger at Doug. "*Look,*" Abe said and then paused. He turned back around to stare down the road. Doug didn't say anything. Ten minutes later they merged onto the main road and he said, "How much farther?"

"They're not dead, okay?"

"Okay, okay," Doug said. "How much farther?"

"About two hours. See I told you I knew a shortcut."

"Famous last words," Doug said and then wished he hadn't. "Roll down your window, it's like an oven in here."

The desert night air was cold and Doug had to roll the window back up part way. Abe left his window open.

"Is it worth it?" Abe said. They had been driving in silence for over an hour.

"Is what worth it?"

"This little adventure of yours, this mystery diamond, this whole uncle thing? Is it worth it?"

"Seriously?" Doug said. "I don't know. I don't even know what the hell is going on." He leaned back in his seat and stretched his arms over his head. "I mean, when it first started I was like, yeah, this is going to be great. I remember thinking, when I was in Casablanca, that I was some, I don't know, what's the word?" and he looked around the car as if he had the right word but had dropped it somewhere. "Adventurer? Detective? Indiana Jones? I've never done anything with my life and here I was doing something. But now…."

"So why are you still doing it? Quit. Go home. Screw the diamond." Traffic started to pick up and there were more road signs now as they approached Sharm el-Shiek.

"Well," Doug said, "it's not just the diamond, it's Edna, that woman I told you about, and all that crap about my uncle…."

"Fuck 'em. If you don't want to be doing this shit, go home."

Doug ran both hands up his face and through his hair, grabbing a handful and tugging. "That's what I'm supposed to do."

"I thought this Edna woman…."

"Not her," Doug said, "me. That's the story of my life. I could go home, get a job—I know enough people in Pottsville where I could get a job—that's not a problem. A week, two weeks…it would be like I never left."

"So there you go. Problem solved."

Doug laughed and it startled Abe. "That *is* the problem. I'm the problem. My dull, stupid life's the problem." He laughed again and slapped his thighs hard.

"You're getting weird on me Doug. I asked one simple question…."

"Okay, a quick simple answer: No, it's not worth it."

"But?"

"But I am."

Abe turned to speak but changed his mind, looked back out to the growing traffic and shook his head. They drove on in silence until Abe began a running commentary on the traffic and the questionable parentage of the other drivers, all delivered in cartoon character voices. Hearing Daffy Duck shout obscenities was believable, but Doug couldn't buy it when it came from Mickey Mouse.

Nobody, in any voice, mentioned the desert.

◇◇◇

Abe swung the car into an empty spot, the airport parking lot already filling up for the start of the night flights. Half the vehicles were hotel shuttle buses, the other half taxis waiting to pick up the backpack crowd. Abe managed to get the trunk open and neither mentioned the busted taillight, missing chrome trim, or the slightly skewed bumper. Doug grabbed his bag from the trunk—who knew what Aisha packed this time—and stepped away as Abe wedged the trunk shut.

The airport was much smaller than the one in Cairo and the crowds of passengers and well-wishers were subdued and even polite, as if, unable to compete with the capital city's airport in size, they gave up on the frenzied behavior as well. They walked through the metal detector at the door, the red light flashing and the buzzer sounding, as it did for everyone who passed through. The guard, picking up his tea from the security desk across the room, didn't even glance up. Abe's uncle was waiting for them by the departure board. Doug was introduced and then left out of the Arabic conversation that concluded with the passing of envelopes and kissing of cheeks.

"Here's the deal, Doug," Abe said as they left the Gulf Air counter. "You're flying out in twenty minutes to Bahrain, from there you'll transfer to a Singapore Airlines flight that will get you into Singapore about four tomorrow afternoon, their time."

"Singapore? What the hell are you doing? I thought you were sending me back to the States?"

"Yeah well, now you're going to Singapore. Here's your ticket, it's all set."

"I can't pay you for this," Doug said, just realizing that he only had a couple hundred dollars' worth of Egyptian money on him anyway. "Can you cash a traveler's check?"

"It's all taken care of," Abe said, and before Doug could ask he added, "Aisha." He handed Doug a second envelope. "And she sent this for you."

"I can't leave just yet," the note started, "I gotta straighten some things out on this end. I'm going to try to meet you in Singapore in about a week. I always stay at Raffles, so you can reach me there. Watch yourself, okay?" After the loopy signature that filled half the page she added, "So far I've had a great time," along with a smile face. She didn't strike him as the smile face type, but then he didn't think she was having such a great time, either.

"Come on, boss," Abe said in a heavy jowled, southern accent, "youze gotta get outta here."

"Huh?"

"The Nazis done got a price on your head and they'll be here any minute."

"What are you talking about? And why are you talking like that?"

"Dooley Wilson? *Casablanca?* The train station scene?" Abe paused, hoping Doug would make the connection. "Oh forget it. My best material is wasted on you. They're calling your flight. Don't lose your passport. And when you get to Bahrain there'll be a guy there who will pick up the cocaine I put in your checked bag."

"*What?*" Doug tried to yell but nothing came out.

"Joking, Doug, only joking. You'd better get going."

"Abe, you're still an ass," he said as he reached for Abe's outstretched hand. And when Abe kissed him on his cheeks, Doug tensed up but didn't pull away.

"Maybe I'll see you in Pottsville sometime," Abe said as Doug walked to the customs check.

Doug smiled and shook his head. "And the next time I'm in a jail somewhere, I'll look around for you," he said and passed through the security door.

Chapter 23

Singapore Airlines flight 340 from Bahrain banked sharply to the right as it began its long approach. The morning sun, still low on the horizon, beamed through the windows, sending twenty squares of light racing above the seats on the far side of the cabin. Doug kept his eyes clamped shut and tried to picture himself sitting in a nice, quiet room, a room that wasn't spiraling down from thirty-five thousand feet.

He wasn't hung over, not yet anyway. He was still somewhat drunk which was impressive considering the last thing he had to drink was a gin and tonic an hour out of Bahrain. But he had four full days of alcohol to process before he could begin sobering up.

If he had only stayed on the plane, he told himself for the hundredth time, everything would have been just fine. But no, a four-hour delay in Bahrain—and he still had no real idea where Bahrain was—gave him the opportunity to stretch his legs in the airport, catch a complimentary meal and maybe a beer or two. That was, what, five days ago? He should have just stayed on the plane.

But that wasn't an option. The Gulf Air flight from Sharm el-Shiek terminated at Bahrain and he was supposed to transfer to a Singapore Air flight which was delayed due to a sandstorm in Riyadh which, given the sandstorm part, Doug assumed was somewhere in the desert. The late-night four-hour layover stretched into a six-hour early-morning delay before the nice

Indian woman at the counter announced in Arabic, Chinese, Hindi, and finally English that on behalf of Gulf Air and Singapore Air she was truly sorry for the delay, that their bags would be transferred to the new flight, and would they all mind getting on the shuttle bus that would take them into town so they could rest before their flight resumed around nine p.m.

The processing through customs was so quick Doug didn't even have time to panic and the ride to the hotel was over before he realized he was in another country. He was heading to his second-floor room when a hand shot in between the closing elevator doors, tripping the safety and springing them back open.

"An emergency," a big man said in a British accent so thick that Doug had to strain to decipher. "Need your help." Days later, as the Singapore Airlines flight attendant informed the passengers that they should return their tray tables to the upright and locked position, Doug replayed the elevator scene in his mind. If I had only taken the stairs, he thought.

"Sure," Doug said. "What's up?"

"Big problems. Cheeky bastard. Need one more to make it a go." The man held the door open as it tried to close again and gave it an extra shove as if to teach it a lesson. "Come on, then," he said and led Doug down the corridor.

The man was big, but not in a tall, all around big way, more like a small car, one of those boxy European imports, thick and low to the ground. He was a few inches shorter than Doug but his deep chest and thigh-like forearms and the way his neck tapered down from his ears out to his shoulders made him look bigger. A fistful of fat cigars stuck out of the pocket of his Hawaiian shirt. They reached a frosted glass door at the end of the hall. "Right, in ya go."

The windowless room was dark, made darker by the mahogany-stained wood that covered everything that wasn't already covered in shiny brass. Fake antiques, of course, hung on the walls, mostly from the European Sports/English Pub collection. The neon Guinness sign reflected off the neat rows of wine glasses, suspended upside down above the bar, and gave the group of men clustered by the taps a cherubic glow. They glanced over at Doug and most smiled. "About time, ya fuckin' twat."

"Piss off, Rebecca. Here," the big man said—and they were all big men, cut from the same squat, bulldog cloth—as he propelled Doug towards the bar. "Here's the tenth. Start pouring."

"I thought there was an emergency," Doug said as the big man sat him down at the bar.

"Is. Low-caste Paki twit. Won't serve. Needed ten at the bar."

"Gentlemen, I am sorry but the rules are most clear," the bartender said in his practiced subservient-but-still-firm voice. "I know it is not a popular rule but...."

"Piss off. Keep pouring," the big man said and reached across the bar for a bottle of Wild Turkey, which he handed to Doug. "We'll need this."

"Look, guys, I appreciate this, but I just got in and I haven't had anything to eat so I'm going to have to say no...."

Nine sets of eyes locked onto Doug and the only sound was a nervous whistle coming from the bartender, who stared at the suspended wine glasses.

"Nice job, Rachael. You grab the only wanker in the lobby."

"Steady, Sally," the big man said as he put his heavy hand on Doug's shoulder. "Doesn't know what he's saying. *Meant* to say he needs some food. Anne, a menu."

Anne, the Neanderthal with the full beard and shaved head, leaned past the whistling bartender and grabbed a menu from the back counter. "Order us up some crisps while you're at it, Rachael."

"Here mate," the big man said as he handed Doug the menu, "order what you will. Under five dinars." Doug started to say no but the grumblings of both the big men and his stomach made him change his mind. "Right, Ladies. It's half seven. Left hand drinking only. Gladys has the golf ball...." Gladys raised his thick arm and waved the golf ball between his fingers. "...Watch your drinks. Ante up. Cheers." He turned to Doug and said, "Chug, mate. Don't be last. Buy the next round if you are." He looked back down the bar. "Sorry. Too late. It's beers around, mate."

Twenty minutes, two beers and an Arabic version of a Spanish omelet later, Doug was in the mood to talk. "Is your name really Rachael?" he asked the big guy.

"For the weekend. Reminds me. You need a name. Fancy Crystal?"

"Can't," said a red-haired troll who was trying to fish a golf ball out of his beer, "there's a Crystal on the Dubai team."

"Can be two Crystals," Rachael said. "Got five Bettys, Betty. Not the same team. No law."

"Still," said Betty, "he's rather protective of the name. Remember what happened to the guy from Qatar?"

"Oh yeah. Right. Okay. Not Crystal."

"He looks like a Terri to me," said a voice from the far end of the bar.

"No. He's a Cindy," said another, followed by a wine glass-shaking burp.

The big guy poked Doug in the chest with a hot dog sized finger. "Call you what? Terri or Cindy?"

"How about Doug?" Doug asked.

"Doug?"

"Not likely, mate."

"Told you. Fucking wanker."

"Easy, easy," Rachel said, "not from the Gulf."

"He's a Yank is what he is," Betty the troll said, popping the golf ball out of his mouth.

"Like this," Rachael said. "Every year. Tourney here in Bahrain. Teams. Expats. The Gulf. Good times. Traditions. Aloha shirts. Ladies' names. This tourney," he said, pointing to his chest, "Rachel."

"Sounds like fun," Doug said, trying hard not to sound sarcastic.

"Fun, yeah, of course, but it makes it hard to meet women," said Anne, as if it was just this damn tradition that slowed him up.

"And you? You're a Heather," pronounced the big guy.

"Heather? I don't think...."

"Heather, Heather, Heather..." the ladies chanted until Doug raised his beer in acknowledgment, only to find a golf ball sitting at the bottom of the glass.

"Sorry mate," Rachael said, "eyes open. Keep it covered. Gotta drain it. That a boy. Shame though. The time. Five after the hour. Right hand drinking. Chug another. Or a shot. Take the shot. Won't bloat up fast."

"Drinking games at eight in the morning. You guys don't get out much, do you?"

"Work in Kuwait," explained Rachael. "Dry."

"In more ways than one," shouted Betty the troll. He had to shout to be heard over the singing, part of another drinking game.

"Right. Dry. Don't get out at all. Come here to party. Wives, girlfriends at home. Start drinking. Rugby tourney just bonus."

"Rugby?" Doug said. "Hey, I've watched it on ESPN. I never really understood the game but I always wanted to give it a try." The singing stopped and everyone at the bar—even the bartender—was staring at Doug, smiling.

"You know rugby?" asked Anne.

"Always wanted to play?" asked Rebecca.

"Give it a try, right?" asked Sally.

"Are you *sure?*" asked Betty.

"Shut up, ya twat," Rachael said, slapping the troll on the top of his bald head. "So. Wanted to give it a try?" Rachael said, plopping his arm on top of Doug's shoulders. "That's funny. Isn't it, ladies?"

"Oh yeah, funny," said Anne.

"What a coincidence," said Gladys.

"A sign from the gods, if you ask me," said Sally.

"Like this, Heather," the big guy said. "Big tournament. Paperwork. Passports. Customs. Trouble. Travel ban. Mate stuck in Kuwait. Us here. One player short. So...."

Chapter 24

Singapore, according to the in-flight magazine, was a "miracle of modernity, poised for global economic leadership in the new millennium." Doug leaned his forehead against the window, feeling the vibrations as the flaps shifted for the landing. The vibrations echoed off the back of his skull and prompted a throbbing deep behind his eyes that he knew would stay with him the rest of the day, perhaps through the new millennium as well.

From the air, everything looked green. Doug didn't know if it was the lack of vegetation in Egypt that made the greenery here stand out or if this miracle of modernity was built in the heart of a jungle. He didn't know much about Singapore other than what the in-flight magazine tried, in vain, to explain to him. He didn't know if it was above or below the equator since the lines on the Singapore Airlines map kept jumping around when he tried to look at it. He didn't know what he was going to do when the plane landed or why he was even here. There was so much he didn't know.

But he was learning. He learned that what should have been called a touchdown in rugby was called a try. This had bothered him much of the game, this and hearing members of the other team saying "hit the Yank." He learned through observation that a man with a broken arm just needs to be taped up and handed a half a glass of whiskey and he's ready to play some more. He learned that a rugby-playing regional manager for British Airways can pull enough strings to get a Singapore Airlines ticket changed—irreversibly changed, as Doug also learned—stranding a traveler in Bahrain so that he can play rugby too. "Who got you that ticket?" Sally asked. "There were more chiggers on it than a Bombay bint."

"What?" Doug said. It was early afternoon of the day he should have been on a nine a.m. flight, but there he was, in the hotel coffee shop, trying to keep down dry toast.

"That ticket. There were all sorts of 'hang-ons'...electric bugs and special instructions—automated crap—so somebody could keep tabs on you. You a terrorist or something?"

"Yeah. Osama bin-drinking. Who put the...."

"Chiggers."

"Yeah, whatever. Who put them on the ticket?" The toast was staying down all right, but the hair of the dog—Anne's idea—was beginning to growl.

"No way of telling, mate. All deleted now. You're free as a bird. But," Sally said, slapping the ticket on the bar, "no more favors."

"Favors?" Doug said. He would have yelled but it would have hurt too much. "I never wanted it changed."

"Not you, mate. Rachael. Every trip he pulls this stunt. I've only got so many connections."

And Doug had learned that, despite his total lack of progress, Edna was thrilled.

"This is going *so* well," she said when Doug explained his time in Egypt, leaving out just about everything significant that had happened there. "And now you're off to Singapore—how *exciting* for you!" They had tried to make arrangements for her to send the last installment of memoirs and anecdotes and some expense money but decided that it was smarter to wait until he arrived in Singapore. "The more you learn about your uncle..." she said. The more I cheer on his killer, he thought.

The stewardess was passing out white and red landing cards and Doug fished his passport out of his carry-on bag. Printed on both sides of the card, in impossible to miss, seventy-eight point red boldface type, was a simple declarative sentence:

The punishment for drug smuggling is death.

Doug felt his stomach roll over. As he sat in the prison cell in Cairo, Doug had sworn that he would always double-check his bag and here he was, flying into a place where, with great civic pride, the number of executions for drug smuggling was printed in the in-flight magazine, with luggage packed by the same person who had a history of putting drugs in his bag. The more he thought about it, the more his stomach rolled.

The approach, the smooth landing, the fifteen-minute taxi to the gate and the ten-minute wait for his checked bag all passed without Doug really noticing. When the customs man asked if he had anything to declare, Doug mouthed a weak no, and didn't start breathing again until he was wading through the crowd of well wishers who filled the lobby, waiting for someone else. After eight hours of sitting on the plane he found he needed to sit some more and by the time his blood pressure and stomach had returned to normal, he had exchanged what was left of the traveler's checks, picked a budget hotel from a discarded tourism magazine, and arranged for a cab to the city.

The forty-minute ride as a front seat passenger in a car with the steering wheel on the right was not as traumatic as he thought it would be, although several times his foot shot out, looking for the missing brake pedal. If it had been Cairo, where driving is a contact sport, neither his heart nor his stomach would have lasted the full ride. But this was Singapore and the ride had a soothing effect.

At a hundred and eighty dollars per night—U.S. dollars—the budget hotel was out of his budget. "Ask your cab driver," the beautiful and efficient desk clerk had told him, "he will know of other places that are more within your price range." And she didn't even sound condescending when she said it.

"I've got a place, real cheap. You like, yes," the cab driver said, all smiles. "I have an uncle who owns a hotel. Real nice for you."

The Geylang area of Singapore was twenty minutes back towards the airport and well off the tourist track. It wasn't as bad as the bad areas of Cairo—the worst parts of Singapore were better than the best areas of Cairo—but it lacked that miracle of modernity feel to it that downtown Singapore promised. Turn-of-the-century buildings, with thick concrete pillars and ornate, pre-cast moldings, all soot-stained and chipped, were wedged between modern concrete buildings in a nondescript international style, equally soot-stained and chipped. The signs, suspended above every doorway or screwed to any available wall space, were mostly in what Doug guessed was Chinese, and the few that were in English announced Coke, Kentucky Fried Chicken, and 7-Eleven. After ten minutes of driving around what Doug would have sworn was the same street, the cab pulled up in front of a building that looked like the front of every other building, the cab driver springing out to fling open the passenger door and grabbing the luggage in one artistic sweep. He led Doug up a short, narrow flight of steps to a landing in front of a solid door. The cab driver shouted something into the speaker by the door and they were buzzed in.

It wasn't a lobby as much as it was a hallway between office cubicles. Through openings in the frosted glass walls, Doug saw desks piled with papers, massive two-ring binders and Post-it-notes clinging like little yellow butterflies that swayed under the low-hanging ceiling fans. He could hear the clicking of computer keyboards and the antique metal clacking of a real typewriter, but the cubicles near the door were empty.

"I think you got the wrong place," Doug said. "I'm looking for a hotel."

"This is hotel. Just wait you here." The driver set down the bag and ran from cubicle to cubicle, poking his head in and saying something that Doug could not make out. Down the glass row, a middle-aged Asian woman poked her head out of her doorway, smiled and waved to Doug. While he was deciding whether or not he should just leave and find another cab, the driver came around the corner with a tall, well-dressed man who seemed to be in charge. The driver was trying to keep up with the man's long strides while trying to tell his story in both his version of English and through elaborate mime-like gestures. Deciphering one of these, the man nodded and, twenty feet away, extended his hand to Doug, guiding it in with the last three giant steps.

"Welcome to the ZRZ Publishing Group," the man said, pronouncing it "zed-r-zed." "My name is Dexter Lee. How can I help you?"

"There seems to be some mistake. The driver said he was taking me to a hotel. I'm sorry to bother you. Perhaps you could explain to the driver...."

"This is a hotel," Lee said, "and a publishing company. It may not look like much, but my family is starting to turn it from an office building to a fine hotel. We haven't had many guests yet so we're excited that you chose to stay with us. Everyone is buzzing each other on the intercom system," he said sweeping his arm back, suggesting hordes of Lees, all peering over the tops of cubicles scattered throughout the building. "Until we get it all finished we won't get many walk-ins, so your business really means a lot. And we'll give you the best rates in town. Can I show you one of the rooms?"

Doug sighed. He was a sucker for that kind of talk and he knew it. He had wanted a hotel in the heart of the city, a real hotel with a pool and room service, but the sad-story sales pitch was hard to resist, especially when he had no real idea where he was anyway. "Yeah sure, why not," he said and pulled out his wallet to pay for the cab.

The publisher/innkeeper said, "The tip, you can understand, is on me."

"Great. Thanks." That sealed it, he had to stay now.

At the end of the cubicles, the corridor branched left and right. To the left were dozens of filing cabinets and bookshelves, to the right, plastic potted plants and a dozen identical framed prints of the English countryside. A freight elevator took them up and the sales pitch continued during the slow elevator ride.

"It was my grandfather who started Zed-R-Zed Publishing shortly after the war. His picture is down by the door, did you see it? It's the classic rags to riches tale. He started with wedding invitations and business fliers and moved on to short-run books and technical manuals. He worked a thousand hours a week and passed the business off to his son and his son passed it off to his eldest son."

"That would be you?" Doug asked.

"That would be my brother. When my dad died my brother got out of the business and passed it to me. I was studying business law in San Francisco, now I'm here. A lot has changed since my grandfather's time. At one point we were one of the largest publishing houses on the island, now we're not even the biggest one on the street. The competition is fierce and when you have a family business you have to think of the family first and business second—well, you don't have to but we did. My father decided to specialize in publishing encyclopedias."

"Like *Encyclopedia Britannica?* That kind of thing?"

"Sort of. We focused more on the low end of the scale, *Robert's Encyclopedia, Encyclopedia Gallactica,* that sort of thing. Maybe you've heard of them? They were sold mostly at supermarkets as part of a promotion."

"Yeah, I remember that," Doug said, smiling. He did, too. Over at the Smart-Shopper about twenty years ago. Every week there would be a new volume on sale. What was the name of the encyclopedia they had? He could see the fancy gold binding and red stripe but the name was lost. His family, like everyone's family, started strong, getting the free A, the ninety-nine cent B-C, and the dollar ninety-eight D-Em. But En through Z was where the supermarkets made their profit and the price went up noticeably with each alphabetic jump. Doug had turned in school projects on airplanes, bears, Cincinnati, diseases and the Empire State Building. The big holes in his education began with England.

The elevator inched to a stop and Dexter Lee waited for the main doors to open before sliding back the black iron grate.

Clones of the plastic plant and the English countryside print lined the wall. Maybe a side business, Doug thought.

"Business was good in the Sixties and Seventies—it's just down the hall here—but with home computers and on-line encyclopedias, no one buys print encyclopedias anymore. We were too specialized to change, the market was already filled with high-quality publishers, so we decided to sell off the remaining stock and convert the building to a hotel. It's kind of sad, but that's business, right?"

Dexter Lee stopped at a room with a black stenciled A on the door, turned the key in the lock and held open the door for Doug. It was a large room with polished hardwood floors and slowly rotating ceiling fans, fifteen feet overhead. White Venetian blinds covered the floor to ceiling windows, obscuring the view of a brick wall. There was a deep, walk-in closet and an industrial-looking bathroom across from the windows and a king-sized bed in between. A television sat on a rolling cart beside the bed. And along all the open walls stretched ten-shelf bookcases crammed full of encyclopedias. Shelves lined the walls of the closet and the narrow spaces between the windows.

"Great room," Doug said, tossing his bag on the bed, "I can even catch up with my reading."

"Sort of," Lee said, handing Doug the key. "Until we get rid of our stock, we keep the books separated by letter. Nobody buys full sets, just replacement volumes. This is the A room. You can catch up on your reading, as long as you want to read about something that starts with A. It's funny," Lee said, looking around the room, "we always sold more As."

Chapter 25

Plans for a quick cold shower, a cup of coffee to wake up, and a full day exploring the city turned into a long hot shower and a five-hour nap. A quick cold shower, a cup of coffee to wake up, and Doug was ready for a full evening of exploring the city.

The woman at the cubicle that served as the reception desk and the overseas phone order center assured Doug that four p.m. in Singapore was the perfect time to call Toronto, adding—just as Edna was saying hello—that would be four in the morning there.

"Damn, Edna, I'm so sorry. I didn't think it would be so early," Doug stammered.

"Hold on a second, Douglas," Edna said. "Hey guys, hold it down please. I've got a call." Doug heard her hand cover the mouthpiece, muffled laughter and then she was back. "Sorry about that. How *are* you?" Four a.m. and she's got a party going. Doug felt old.

"I'm doing good, Edna. Look, I'm in Singapore."

"Of course you are, dear. Isn't that where you were heading? You're not in jail are you?" Doug heard her laugh before she was able to cover the mouthpiece again. Was she drunk? "Sorry. Back again. Shall I send you a file in a cake?" The word "cake" slid into an uncovered howl of laughter.

"Uh, Edna? Should I call you later?"

"Oh, *definitely* don't call later. He shouldn't call later, should he?" More laughter, more muffled voices. "I'm glad you called, you little rascal. I want to send you some money. How much should I send him?" she said off the phone. "You are *soooo* generous. Yes you are so. *Stop* that. Oh Doug, are you still there?"

"I haven't gone anywhere Edna. Look, I'm staying at this hotel...."

"Good. Don't sleep on the subway, baby...." More laughter with singing this time. "Look, Doug, are you still there?"

"Yes, Edna, I'm still here."

"Look, Doug. Look. I've got this caller ID thingy. *Stop* that. Not you Doug. Look. I'll call you back, okay? Doug? Are you still there?"

Oh boy, Doug thought. "Yeah. Sounds good," he said, just as the line went dead.

"See?" the cubicle lady said. "You call now. Best time."

◇◇◇

The SMRT station was less than a quarter mile away and easy to find. Down the short escalator Doug encountered some of that miracle of modernity promised in the vaguely remembered in-flight magazine. The subway looked like something out of a movie that was set just a bit in the future. It was the best—and first—subway Doug had ever seen. Everything was in English, the *lingua franca* as the magazine said—whatever the hell that meant. He took it to the Orchard Road exit, just like the cubicle lady instructed, and exited into a seven-story, two-block-long shopping mall. It took Doug thirty minutes to get oriented and almost as long to notice he was standing around with his mouth half open, looking like a backwoods, "golly-they-don't-have-*this*-back-at-home" yahoo.

But they *didn't* have this back at home, and he noticed he wasn't the only slack-jawed shopper in the place, either. Two hundred feet overhead the bright lights hanging from the glass ceiling obscured the late afternoon sky but illuminated a space big enough to taxi a couple of 747s. Chrome and smoked glass elevators raced up and down and escalators, suspended like spiderwebs, crisscrossed in open space. They had malls, and huge K-Marts, in central Pennsylvania, but this, this was different.

It had everything every mall had—the food court, the Gap, the Hallmark card store—but it was the scale of these standard fixtures that shocked Doug and he tried to put it in perspective. There was a CD store the size of the Frackville K-Mart, a shoe store the size of the Centralia K-Mart, an arcade the size of the Pottsville K-Mart and a K-Mart-like department store twice the size of the K-Mart at the Schuylkill County Mall. Doug realized two things: that there were many different chain stores out there, and that he shopped at K-Mart a lot.

The illuminated, 3-D map, with a blinking You Are Here red dot, indicated his insignificant position and hinted at the real size of the place. The map showed how this massive structure was but one of six mega-sized malls, all connected by canyon-like corridors, moving walkways, skyways and trams, with the subway providing three stops. It wasn't like the souks of Casablanca or Cairo, but it wasn't like home, either. Home wasn't this good.

Doug didn't like shopping. Most of his clothes were Christmas presents or things old girlfriends had picked up for him. But he loved going to the mall for the action he always found there. He liked seeing all the people rushing and he liked that no matter how lousy it was outside, inside it was always sunny and pleasant. He seldom had a good reason for going to the mall, he didn't get much out of it and wasted a whole lot of time doing nothing there, but for years that's where everybody else was so he went, too. It was a lot like high school.

Since he had turned twenty-one, Doug didn't need to hang out at the mall all that much. Now he could do the same thing at a bar. But here in Singapore, he remembered the number one reason he had spent years hanging out at the mall: women. Well, it was girls back then, but it was women now. Having been raised on a steady diet of the blonde, blue-eyed variety, he tried not to stare as each beautiful woman walked by, her long, black hair—and they all seemed to have long, black hair—looking blue when the light hit it just right. Along with the uniform black hair went the uniform LBD—the Little Black Dress that he didn't even know existed before he met Aisha. He tried to picture Aisha in each dress that went by but decided it was more enjoyable picturing her out of each dress that went by.

The food court was cavernous, but it seemed to offer only two hundred different types of Chinese foods, all listed by numbers. "What's Number 47 like?" he had asked.

"Ever have Number 18? Taste like Number 18."

"What's Number 18 like?"

"Taste same as Number 47."

After the best Number 47 he ever had, and two hours of blissful wandering, Doug found the subway to take him back to the Geylang area where his hotel/warehouse was located. On the subway he noticed an advertisement for The Historic Raffles Hotel and remembered Aisha's note that Abe had given him in Sharm el-Shiek. The poster showed an antique photograph of the hotel with the edges blurred so that it was less a building and more a dream. *The Truth Must Be Told!* the banner on the poster shouted and below what appeared to be an enlarged column from an old newspaper, "Providence led me to a place called RAFFLES HOTEL, where the food is excellent as the rooms are good. Let the traveler note: Eat at Raffles and Sleep at Raffles." It was signed *Rudyard Kipling* in a firm, manly hand. Raffles Place was the next stop on the subway and the small type at the bottom of the poster whispered that a "10% discount" could be had at the Long Bar if this ad was mentioned.

Raffles Hotel was everything Casablanca was supposed to be. The architecture was the same ornate, late Victorian/Neo-Classical excess, but where in Casablanca everything had a worn, crumbling look, Raffles appeared as if it had just opened that weekend. The building filled a full city block with snow-white walls and darkly stained wood trim that glistened with fresh oil. The floodlights, perfectly placed in the surrounding gardens, shot up through the plants making the building look much taller than its three stories. But it wasn't size that made the hotel a landmark, it was the strange sensation, and Doug felt it as he stood in front of the main entrance, that you were looking back in time.

There was a small army of doormen and porters, each division wearing distinct and elaborate uniforms, what used to be called livery, and there were men whose only job seemed to be to stand around in military poses, wearing jackets even whiter than the hotel, held taut with brass buttons and black leather belts. Tourists and locals hurried to have their pictures taken standing next to the Depression-era Rolls Royce that had just pulled up, discharging an elegantly dressed couple and their trunkload of luggage. Small swarms of lightning bugs—purchased each month from a distributor in Malaysia—flashed among the football-sized flowers and, floating out of dozens of hidden and acoustically perfect speakers, soft jazz glazed over any of the inappropriate street sounds but somehow enhanced the clinking of champagne flutes and the high-pitched laughter of women who knew which fork to use with the fish course. Now and then a camera flash tried to compete with the light that sparkled off every polished surface, but all the prints would later show would be an overdeveloped glare associated with angelic visitations. Even the full moon and star-filled, cloudless sky disappeared in Raffles' presence.

Inside the lobby—the lobby that was open to the general public, not the one that real guests were privileged to use—the theme of colonial superiority continued, with the perfect combination of roll top writing desks, splayed-out plants with leaves the size of an elephant's ear, brass spittoons which never saw as much as a candy wrapper, brown leather chairs that could seat a family of four, and more uniformed lackeys—these wearing turbans—holding open doors or balancing silver trays full of martini glasses on fingertips as they navigated the veranda.

Everything seemed designed to elicit a feeling of nostalgia for the days of British Raj and even though Doug didn't know what that meant, he felt it too.

◇◇◇

Andrew Chan tapped the stack of blank forms against the marble countertop, perfectly aligning the already perfectly aligned papers for the tenth time that evening. He positioned the stack tight along the return key box, just left of the Long-Term Luggage Storage labels and the Tiffin Room Table Reservation book. He made a mental note to restock all the blank forms. This was Andrew's fourth full day as an Outer-Lobby Desk Assistant and he wanted to be noticed. He glanced down the sharp crease of his uniform trousers to see if his shoes had retained their shine since he last buffed them, ten minutes ago, then checked to ensure that his tie just touched the top of his belt buckle, even though it was hidden under his navy blue Raffles sport coat. "Always remember," Mr. Fung Kee Fung had said when he personally notified Andrew of his promotion, "Raffles is the greatest hotel in the world. One piece of lint, one hair out of place, detracts from this standard. If you don't think the guests will notice, you don't belong at this hotel." Andrew knew his uniform was impeccable so he worked on the friendly smile that had more to do with his promotion than his work as a back office clerk.

Andrew beamed his smile into the cavernous outer lobby. There was the usual assortment of tourists and locals, all trying not to look like tourists or locals, trying to look as if they were guests here at the hotel and not mere gawkers, imagining they were part of the international jet-set crowd that calls Raffles home when they swing by this part of the world. Another thing Mr. Fung Kee Fung had told him to "always remember" was that there were two types of people in the world, guests and everyone else. "We don't treat them with any sort of disrespect, Andrew," he had said, "but they are not really *our* type of people. Be courteous, be efficient, be a Raffles employee, but be sure that when you deal with a guest of the hotel—*if* you deal with a guest of the hotel, and you really shouldn't until you have finished your training—that you are at *your very best*." Even Mr. Fung Kee Fung couldn't define it any better than that, but every employee knew just what he meant.

Andrew watched the tourists as they roamed about conspicuously in the lobby. They photographed the floral arrangements. They photographed the dual staircases that led to the *real* lobby. They photographed the carpets. They photographed each other and they photographed the smiling Andrew Chan. He could keep the same infectious smile on his face for hours and it always looked fresh and sincere. So when the American tourist in the wrinkled khakis and the black and yellow striped rugby shirt approached the desk, Andrew knew he would feel welcome.

"Good evening, sir. Welcome to Raffles. How may I be of assistance?"

"Yeah, I'm looking for a friend of mine. She said she'd be staying at the hotel. Her name's Aisha Al-Kady." Doug found that he couldn't help but smile back at the man behind the desk.

"I'm sorry, sir," Andrew said, his smile switching slightly to indicate that he was, truly, very sorry. "I am not allowed to give out the names of our guests."

"No, I know her name, I just want to see if she's here or not."

"Again, I'm sorry, sir, but I am not allowed to give any information about our guests. I'm sure you understand," Andrew said, as if Doug was the kind of worldly gentleman who was accustomed to this level of guest anonymity.

"Well can I leave her a note?" Doug asked.

"Unless you can provide me with a room number, sir, I'm afraid I will not be able to have it delivered. However, you can contact the guest information center," he said, pointing to a house phone at a small, round table that was being photographed by an Australian tourist. "I'm sure they can be of assistance."

Andrew watched the American walk across the lobby to the round table before he reached under the marble counter top for the phone. "Good evening Mr. Fung Kee Fung," he said, switching to a more subservient smile. "This is Andrew Chan at the Outer-Lobby Desk…. Fine, thank you sir…. No sir, there's no problem." His hand instinctively reached up to check the knot of his tie. "I wanted to inform you that the gentleman in the photograph is here…. Yes he did, sir…. No, sir, I don't think so…. He's on the house phone now, sir…. Very good, sir."

Andrew hung up the phone and immediately adjusted the phone's base so that it was parallel to the back of the counter.

He watched as the American tourist left a message with the information center operator then, after checking the discreet brass signs, walked out along the south veranda, heading, like all tourists, to the Long Bar. For precisely ten seconds Andrew thought about the American, the photograph, the guest, and Mr. Fung Kee Fung's instructions, and then removed the entire incident from his mind. "Always remember," Mr. Fung Kee Fung had said, "a *good* employee—a *Raffles* employee—is attentive to the needs of our guests but never curious. Curiosity is not in your job description."

Andrew was smiling his real smile, which looked no different from his work smile. There were many things to remember about this job, he thought as he watched a group of Korean tourists take turns photographing each other as they stood by the main entrance. But most important, Andrew said to himself, always remember to look good in front of the boss.

Chapter 26

"Something wrong with your drink, sir?" The bartender had noticed Doug probing the bottom of the glass with his straw, shoving chips of ice out of the way. It was a Singapore Sling, the signature drink of Raffles Hotel and, according to the bar menu and the brass plaque by the door, invented here at the Long Bar.

Doug wrinkled his nose and smacked his lips. "It tastes like there's something missing," he said even though these were the first two Singapore Slings he had ever had.

"It's the alcohol," the bartender said, smiling. "There's virtually none of it. It's a tourist drink, really. You'll get a sugar high before you start feeling any effects of the gin. Let me take care of that."

The bartender whisked away the glass and, nearly as fast, set down a round coaster, a napkin and a neon blue drink. A gold and black nametag said he was Yeo Cheow Tong.

"It's called a Hurricane. I think you'll like it."

Doug took a sip and agreed that it was a lot better than the Singapore Sling.

"Did they invent this one here as well." Doug asked.

"It's not even on the menu. I learned to make it from my girlfriend. She grew up outside of New Orleans and tended bar for a bit when she was at LSU. It's a good drink but not what people are looking for here. Here they want a Singha beer, sometimes a Murree's. If they're American they want a Bud. Gin and tonics are popular. But everybody starts off with a Sling.

"Ngiam Tong Boon," the bartender said suddenly.

"Uh, good, thanks," Doug said.

"What's good?" Cheow asked.

"The drink?"

"Oh, thanks. Anyway," he continued, "Ngiam Tong Boon."

"Boom?"

"Boon. Ngiam Tong Boon."

"Okay," Doug said, "I'll try one."

"Try what?" Cheow asked.

"Ngiam Tong Boon."

"You know Ngiam Tong Boon?"

"No, but if it's as good as this here Hurricane, I'll try one."

"Ngiam Tong Boon," the bartender said one more time, the patience of a saint in his voice. "He's the one who invented the Singapore Sling. Everyone always asks."

"Oh," Doug said. He wasn't going to ask but now he knew.

"And, no, it wasn't even in this room," Cheow said, anticipating questions Doug would never pose. "The original Long Bar was over in the first part of the building, but it's all gone. This," he waved to take in the belt-driven ceiling fans, the rattan chairs, the open stairway to the second floor, the dark woods and the polished brass fixtures, "this was all recreated when they redid the whole place back in the Eighties. Even she's a repro," Cheow said, pointing out the painting of a reclining nude redhead behind the bar. "Peanuts?"

"Sure, why not," Doug said, sipping the much stronger drink.

"Ngiam Tong Boon," Cheow said as he set down a basket of nuts.

"We're going to do this again?"

"Ngiam Tong Boon. The guy who invented the Sling. He's dead now, but they still keep his original recipe book in a safe over at the hotel's museum. Everybody usually asks."

"The hotel has a museum?" Doug asked, trying to remember if Pottsville had a museum.

"Sure, you should see it. It's really nice. It's got lots of old photos and things from the hotel. Lots of famous people stayed here—Charlie Chaplin, Douglas Fairbanks, Michael Jackson...."

"Not at the same time, I bet."

"And the hotel itself has an interesting history. Once a tiger wandered into the lobby and they shot it under the pool table. Really," Cheow said, noticing Doug's expression. "They've got a newspaper clipping all about it over at the museum. Sure, you can read all about when the Japanese were here in the war and the story about the diamonds, and the time, back in the Fifties...."

"Diamonds?" Doug asked, the Hurricane in a holding pattern, two inches off the bar.

"Sure. Hang on a second. What can I get you?" Cheow said as a couple of smartly dressed retirees sat down at the bar. Doug watched as Cheow prepared two Singapore Slings. Uncle Russ was killed in Singapore. He might have even been killed at this hotel, Doug didn't know. But he was killed and it was probably over a diamond. Doug noticed that he was leaning so far forward it looked as if he was about to spring over the bar and make himself a Ngiam Tong Boon, so he leaned back until he felt the bar stool start to topple. He settled for a slouch-like lean that he felt looked natural. It didn't.

"Sure, the diamonds," Cheow picked up the story as he returned. Doug slouched in even farther. "This goes back about, oh, what, forty, fifty years or so. There was this Italian manager of the hotel, I think his name was Guido...."

"Guido? Come on, you have to be kidding."

Yeo Cheow Tong didn't know enough Italians to understand, so he continued with his story. "Well during the war, the Japanese sent Guido to some POW camp...."

"The Japanese? Wasn't Italy on the same side as Japan?"

"I guess," Cheow said. "Anyway, they sent him to Australia."

"Wasn't Australia fighting against Japan?" Doug was trying hard to recall that mini-series that covered all of this.

"You're right, they did fight Japan, so it must have been someone else who sent Guido."

"Okay, so somebody sends Guido to Australia...."

"Sure, and before he goes he asks a British guy named Smith...."

"Smith? An Italian guy named Guido and a British guy named Smith?"

"Yeah, why not?" asked Cheow. "So he asks Smith to hold on to these jewels that have been in his family for years because he doesn't want the Japanese soldiers to get them."

"Wait a second," Doug said, holding up his hand. He drew in a breath to speak, held it a second or two, and finally settled on "never mind, go ahead."

"So Smith has to hide the jewels because the Japanese are looking everywhere for them, so he makes a false bottom in a milk can, the big kind that they used to deliver milk in, you know what I mean? He makes this false bottom and puts the jewels in and to cover up for the weight he keeps the milk can half filled with water all the time so the Japanese soldiers won't be suspicious."

"Wouldn't they think it was strange that this Smith guy kept a big milk can half filled with water?"

"Sure. You know, I think Smith thought of that because he hollowed out the heels of his wooden clogs and hid jewels in there, too."

"Wooden clogs? Wouldn't they have to be pretty big if you were going to hide jewels inside of them?"

"Yeah, I guess," Cheow said as he started to fix Doug a second Hurricane, "but you can make clogs, eight, ten centimeters tall. This big," he said, holding up a large shot glass.

"I've never been a Japanese soldier," Doug said as he drained the last of the first Hurricane and transferred his straw to the second big, blue drink, "but I think I might have found it suspicious if there was a British guy named Smith prancing around in high-heel wooden clogs, hauling a big milk can half filled with water everywhere."

"After the war Guido comes back to Singapore and Smith gives him the jewels and the experts say that there was no damage at all."

"So the moral of the story," Doug said, holding up his *really* strong drink, "is that if I'm hunting for jewels I should look in milk cans and wooden shoes."

"Sure, why not," Yeo Cheow Tong said as he blended up a big batch of Singapore Slings for the next round of tourists.

Chapter 27

A dedicated team of research scientists could spend the better part of a hefty government grant determining the specific combination of alcohol, jet-lag, nap time, sugary tourist drinks, salted peanuts and won-ton soup (purchased from a street vendor near the ZRZ Publishing House and Guest Hotel) that would induce an otherwise exhausted traveler to pop wide awake at four-thirty in the morning. By chance, Doug had hit on that specific combination and he was using that bonus time to catch up on adobe.

"This versatile building material was developed independently in arid and semi-arid climates across the globe. A mixture, in various combinations, of clay, sand and silt, adobe can be formed into bricks or applied in thin layers. The use of adobe pre-dates human history and was most likely first adopted in areas where wood, suitable for building, was in short supply. It may have also been favored for its qualities as an insulator against both heat and cold."

As fascinating as this was—and he really did find it fascinating—Doug was simply killing time until the security system would let him leave his room.

"I really feel bad about this," Dexter Lee had said last night when the COBRA Security Company's Rapid Response Team representatives had finally taken the shackles, blindfold, gag, black hood, and their polished black boots off of Doug. "I forgot all about the security system. Naturally, there will be no charge for tonight."

Doug had found the hotel without a problem and had remembered the four-digit access code number he had to punch in before he used his key. Sure, he had made a left turn at the end of that first hallway, but he had only walked ten feet before he realized his mistake and turned back towards the freight elevator, tripping for the second time the silent electric eye alarm which set in motion the crack task force and the automated phone call to Lee.

And there probably wouldn't have been any trouble—certainly wouldn't have been any screaming or mad chases or smashing English countryside prints or slamming of bodies into plastic potted plants and filing cabinets—if Doug had known that, in most of the world outside of the U.S., the second floor of a building is usually called the first floor. The first floor, which he assumed would be called "the first floor," often has no number associated with it at all. And if he had known that to get to his room on the first floor—his second floor, their first—he needed to push one not two, then Dexter Lee would not have had to apologize and Doug would not feel obligated then to stay another night. But when the Rapid Response Team found an unknown individual wandering around on the second (third) floor, trying doorknobs and peeking into rooms, and when that individual, upon seeing the black jump-suited, riot helmet-wearing, flash-light-mounted, gun-toting paramilitary professionals creeping around the corner, screamed and ran off, it set into motion a series of linked events, culminating with Lee's apology and Doug's assurance that he was not upset and that it was all his fault and that of course he wouldn't be checking out of such a friendly hotel.

"Adobe walls and structures need to be built on top of a solid, waterproof foundation, such as fieldstone or concrete. If not, *capillary action* (see Vol. 2) will draw groundwater and the lower section of the structure will disintegrate. Properly maintained, adobe can last centuries."

Fascinating.

Doug was showered, shaved and fully dressed and packed and reading up on letter A topics, when the four loud beeps of the building's security system told him that the alarms had been deactivated and that it was safe to leave his room and put into effect Plan B. Taking the stairs, he exited into the cubicle/lobby section and was greeted by the phone lady, who gave Doug a hug, saying, "You nice man. You not leave us." So much for Plan B.

The Friday morning traffic looked just like the Thursday morning traffic and the weather, hot and humid, was the same all day long. There were days like this in Pottsville, maybe one or two a summer. Doug tried to imagine the same sunny, hot weather three hundred sixty-five days a year, no brisk autumn mornings, no pristine blankets of new-fallen snow, no chilly spring afternoons, just hot weather, blue skies and a predictable and short afternoon rain. It sounded pretty good.

He re-checked the guidebook map—his only purchase during his mall adventure—picking the quickest way to the main police building. The guidebook had noted that crime was almost nonexistent in Singapore, thanks in small part to cultural traditions and in a much larger part to the draconian laws and the swift and sure justice system. "Our advice is simple," the guidebook said, "don't get arrested." Doug had already seen the tee shirts with "Singapore: A FINE, FINE city" silk-screened on the front, and running down the back, in two small-print columns, lists of various criminal activities and the fines they would earn. Some were strange: five hundred dollars for spitting on the sidewalk, not flushing a public toilet, or cutting in line at a taxi cab stand. There were some things on the list that Doug knew from experience would get you in trouble in central Pennsylvania: don't litter, don't vandalize, don't wander around the streets late at night like a drunken fool, alternately singing "I am Ironman" and crying that Stacey Moore dumped you for that stupid jock, Tommy Roth.

The shirt didn't say that exactly but the idea was there.

Then there were things that, if they weren't already illegal, sure ought to be, like urinating in an elevator or breeding rats. Doug thought that a five-hundred-dollar fine was a bit low for these offenses.

Of course there was the famous No Chewing Gum rule on the list, but Doug had seen dozens of people chewing gum and didn't recall a single cop wrestling these felons to the ground. He hadn't seen any gum for sale in the store, though he really hadn't been looking. But he had noticed that all the sidewalks were free of those black splotches created when spit-out chewing gum morphed into that nameless material that was harder and longer lasting than the concrete it fused to. Yes, Singapore was a spit/dog shit/gum free place where you were never greeted by someone else's bowel movement, where you could ride an elevator without fear of being pissed on, where law breakers—easily caught thanks to the omnipresent security cameras and legions of police and military types in riot gear—were given the choice between paying the fine or getting whacked on the ass by a bamboo pole. When he thought about it that way, Singapore did seem a bit restrictive. But then he remembered Cairo, where, if you were lucky, you'd only find someone pissing in an elevator, and then Singapore didn't seem so bad.

The police headquarters was easy to find and the receptionists efficient and friendly, but it still took over an hour to finally locate someone who could help. Sort of.

"Can I get you a cuppa coffee? A doughnut? Geeze, what am I saying, you guys don't eat that crap. I can probably find you a whiskey, but it might take a few minutes."

"It's ten in the morning," Doug said as he watched his arm get pumped like a car jack.

"Oh yeah, it is. Right. Well you never know with you guys." The "you guys" twenty-year-old intern Chong Kim Siap kept referring to were private detectives. *American* private detectives. And Kim knew all about private detectives.

"Still, if you change your mind, just give me a nod," Kim said as he led Doug to his cubicle that doubled as the photocopier supply room at the end of a dead end corridor. Doug had started off talking with the duty officer, a lieutenant, who handed Doug off to the desk sergeant, who referred him to a rookie patrolman, who passed him down the line until a temp secretary waved over Kim. And there was no way Kim was going to let go of this private detective. This *American* private detective.

"Sorry about the clutter, Doug. Can I call you Doug? Cool. Yeah, just push this stuff out of the way—a bunch of cases I'm helping out on. You know the drill, paperwork for everything." Doug watched as Kim stacked up and swept off notices about coffee filters, parking spaces, and T.V. raffles mixed in with copies of *Guns and Ammo, Soldier of Fortune* and *Maxim*. "Not for you guys though, I bet."

"Oh, there's a bit," Doug said, massaging blood back into his forearm. "Actually it's paperwork that brings me to see you."

Kim beamed at that direct reference to himself. "Whatever I can do. Professional courtesy and all." You see, Kim had explained to his kid brother just last week, private detectives often help the police solve cases. They gather evidence on their own, work out all the complex connections without having to worry about "procedure" and "the rules," confront the criminal in his lair, and arrange it so the police get there just in time to hear the confession, which the detective may have had to beat out of the guy. Sometimes the criminal was a woman and the P.I.—"that's the lingo for a private detective"—had to get the information out of her in a *different* way. But Kim only smiled knowingly when his brother asked "What different way?" "It's a thing that goes with the territory," Kim had said. "Cops and the P.I.s. You wouldn't understand."

"So what kind of case is it? Murder? Robbery?" Kim tried not to look too excited. He remembered how his teachers used to seem nervous when he started to get excited. He leaned back in his chair a bit to show how relaxed he was.

"Both," Doug said, and Kim shot forward, knocking over a box of paperclips.

"Whew," he tried to whistle, "that's some case."

"Yeah, I guess it is. But it happened way back in 1948. I'm trying to see if I can find anything out but it's been tough."

"Gone cold on ya, huh?" Kim smiled and shook his head as if to say, Buddy, ain't we all been there. "Why don't you fill me in—I know, 'client privilege'—but just give me what you think I need, I can fill in the blanks." He flipped over a memo (RE: Department policy on decorative ties) and prepared to take notes.

Doug told Kim what he knew about his uncle's murder, which was next to nothing, but left out any mention of *Al Ainab*. He remembered Aisha's comment about international art theft not having a statute of limitations and figured that it was best left unmentioned. He made it sound as if the theft of some "compromising photographs" were somehow connected to the murder. Kim's smiled widened at this but he didn't press for details.

"Let me see if I've got this straight," Kim said when Doug had finished. "You need copies of any police files related to the murder of one Russell Pearce, American, in the summer of 1948. Wow. It's a safe bet that there won't be too many cases fitting that description. I'll dig around here and see what I can come up with."

"That'd be great. I owe you one."

"Wow. Really? Say, what are doing now? Want to go grab a beer and some lunch?"

"They don't mind you just leaving like that?" Doug asked, hoping they would.

"Me? Heck no. They understand that investigative work means all sorts of strange hours and contacts and that stuff. Come on, there's a place not far from here, The Stowaway, I think you'd like. Not at all like the tourist places near the quay. Kindda rough, but I'm sure you're used to that. Hey, Elena," Kim half-shouted as he guided Doug out of the dead end corridor, "I'm taking an early lunch with this private detective from *America*. Take my calls, will ya?"

The temp didn't even look up as they walked past.

Chapter 28

Doug resisted the urge to reach over and close Kim's mouth and instead reached for his bottle of Singha beer.

Chong Kim Siap balanced at the edge of his seat, leaning so far forward that Doug had had to move his beer off to the side to prevent Kim from knocking it over with his chin. His open-mouthed stare morphed into a full-faced grin, but his face couldn't contain his excitement. He shot out of his chair, sat back down, raced both hands through his thick, black hair, slapped the table and chugged the rest of his beer, all in a five-second burst of pent-up adrenalin.

"God-*damn!*" Kim said, and just to make sure everyone in the nearly empty bar heard him, he said it again. "God-*damn!*"

The Stowaway bar was nearly empty since it wasn't even noon and the drink prices could only attract a better class of drunk. That and the possibility that Kim had scared the others off. The kid made Doug a bit nervous.

But he was a good listener. Doug had told him about "the case," substituting photos—"The old blackmail scam," Kim nodded—for the diamond. He left out some of his suspicions about Aisha, the fact that Russell Pearce was probably the bad guy, and any reference to his own inexperience and self-doubt, but in general he stayed close to the truth. Kim seemed to like it.

"God-*damn!*" he said as he slapped the now-wobbly table. "*That's* the kind of life I want."

"My life? I don't think so. It's not as exciting as you think."

"Not exciting? In the last month you flew halfway around the world, been in four countries, slept with an heiress, been stalked, jumped, and shot at, got thrown in the hoosegow, been in a car chase—*with* a big crash—scored the winning try in a rugby tournament *and* slept with the cheerleaders...."

Okay, maybe not that truthful.

"Sure sounds exciting to me," Kim said. He shot out of his seat again but this time came back with two more beers.

"Compared to *my* life," Kim continued, handing Doug a Singha, "it's exciting. Don't get me wrong, I've got it pretty good at the force. Some of the cases I'm involved with, well, they'd even shock a guy like you. But it's the, I don't know...the *routine* of it all that's driving me batty. Same shit, different day. I got a bumper sticker in my desk drawer, that's what it says, Same Shit, Different Day. I need a job like yours."

"That's funny," Doug said. "When I get done here in Singapore and head back to the States, I'll be looking for a job like yours."

"Yeah, right. You couldn't do a job like mine." Kim's smile dropped and he fumbled on. "No, that's not what I meant. I mean you *could* do it, but you just *couldn't* do it. What I mean is that guys like you, you just can't do a dull job, it's not in you. You're used to the adventure, living by your own rules, every day something different and no paper-pushing desk-jockey telling you to get her coffee or un-jam the photocopier."

Doug looked at his half empty beer bottle. "You'd be surprised at the jobs I've done."

"*Exactly!* That's what I want. I want surprises. There's no adventure in my life."

They sat for a few minutes. Doug played with the paper label of his Singha. It slid off the bottle intact. Too much water in the glue, he thought. He smiled and looked up at Kim.

"Kim, there's a room in the middle of one of the pyramids and there's nothing in it but a light bulb. People go there and get all disappointed since it wasn't adventurous enough for them, but they forget about how hard it was to get there."

"Huh?"

"It's a journey, Kim, not a place."

"So there is no room in the pyramid?"

"No, there is a room, but that's not what's important, what's important is…."

"That there's a light bulb?"

"No, ah, well yes, there *is* a light bulb but the important thing is that people are disappointed."

"Disappointed? Why is that important?"

"Because they need to be disappointed to understand why it's important that there's nothing in the room."

"But you said there was a light bulb."

"That's not why they are disappointed."

"They don't want a light bulb there?"

"No they *do* want a light there, I mean it'd be really dark if they didn't, but they want more there and they are disappointed that there isn't more there."

"How big is the room?"

"That's not important."

"It is if you want to figure out how much more you can put in."

"They don't want to put anything else in, Kim, they…."

"But you just said that they wanted more and if they don't know how big it is, then they'll be *really* disappointed. I mean if I hauled a sofa up there and it didn't fit…."

"How much was the beer?" Doug said, sighing. He dug a wad of light pink bills from his pocket.

"Whoa, hold on, pal. This is my town and my bar. Your money's no good here. It's on me." Kim beamed as if he had been waiting years to say something like that. "Geeze, look at the time. I gotta get back. Big meeting this afternoon. Besides, I have some old files on a 1948 murder to dig up for a P.I. friend of mine. I'll walk you to the subway, it's on the way. So anyway," Kim said as they headed for the door, "how do they turn the light bulb on if there's nothing else in the room?"

◇◇◇

The man in the corner store was disappointed to see Doug and the unknown police officer exit The Stowaway bar since now he had to leave the air conditioned store and start walking. Although he grew up in Singapore, he never got used to the weather. It was always too damn hot, too damn sticky. The heat drained the life out of you, made you old before your time. Just look at old Chinese people and then look at old Europeans, especially those Scandinavians. The only difference is the weather. He kept the AC going full blast in his apartment, cold enough to hang meat, his friends said. Go ahead, make jokes, we'll see who lives longer.

He took a deep breath of the artificially perfect air and got ready. He watched as the two men walked down the street, back in the direction of the police station. He waited until they had reached the other side of the intersection before he pushed open the glass door and headed out into the heat. He hit the speed redial on his cellular and listened through the receptionist's long greeting before giving the room number. For the past two days, the phone had always picked up on the second ring and today it was no different. "They're heading back to the police station now," he said. The voice at the other end said fine and hung up, like always.

He slowed down. The two men weren't in a hurry, and he was sure he knew where they were going. He kept an eye on them but his attention was on the same math problem he'd done ten times that morning. One twenty a day, two days so far. Two hundred forty dollars. If this lasted a week more he could pull in over a grand. It paid a hell of a lot better than his security guard job, but it meant venturing out into the unhealthy heat and humidity of nature. The night with the alarms was interesting, but mostly this guy led a quiet life. And that was fine too. Easy money. But there was a promise of an extra five hundred if he had to beat the piss out of the guy. Man, he thought, that would be sweet. That would more than cover the cost of a new Daiwoo window-mounted AC for the bedroom.

He kept totaling various combinations of days and beatings, watching as the cop went back to his office and the man headed for the subway. Thank God. The trains were always cold.

Chapter 29

In daylight, Raffles lost its palatial feel and had to settle simply for grand. The sun echoed off the blindingly white walls, and the whole hotel seemed to stretch out with its feet up on the balustrade, a cold gin and tonic it its hand. Select shops lined two sides of an open courtyard, the other two sides strategically obscured by frilly gazebos and flowered trellises. Jazz, as light and sweet as the aroma of the tropical flowers, floated around the fountains and fishponds, mixing with offbeat beeps from the cash registers in the gift shops.

The main shop was filled with esoteric souvenirs, the one-of-a kind specialty items that would appeal to the aristocratic tastes of the Raffles guest, but more likely purchased by the budget tourist, pretending to be a Raffles guest. Walls of brass and dark wood, watercolor prints and etched glass. Doug wanted to buy his mom an ashtray to replace the one bought in Morocco and lost in Cairo, but the only ones the shop carried were Steuben crystal and more expensive than a week at the ZRZ Publishers/ Hotel. The keychains were blue-light special priced at eighty dollars, but he passed on those as well. My son went to Singapore and all I got was this hundred and twenty dollar Versace tee shirt. He decided he didn't see anything he really liked.

The other shops had more employees than items for sale. Two scarves and a handbag were attended by a sextuplet of sales associates, identically dressed in tailored LBDs, who floated around the glass table like priestesses in some high-fashion cult. And all nine employees watched him enter and exit the unnamed perfume store, protecting the sacred fragrances from his plebian nose.

The hotel's museum slipped in at the end of the shops, and the Zen-like austerity of post-modern retail gave way to the Victorian clutter of pre-war memorabilia. The walls were covered with framed prints and photographs, the display cases filled with odd travel mementos and hotel bric-a-brac, painstakingly arranged to appear randomly tossed together. Massive room keys, luggage tags from hotels in Istanbul, Shanghai, and Havana, whiskey flasks with well-worn leather cases, opera glasses, a receipt from the hotel's laundry dated 1921, handfuls of old photos showing mustached men in tuxedos and white military uniforms dancing with even whiter young women in low-necked gowns. On one shelf of an antique cabinet was the framed original of the newspaper clipping Doug had seen reproduced in the subway, again shouting that The Truth Must Be Told. A red arrow singled out the key line—"Let the traveler note: Eat at Raffles and Sleep at Raffles." And on the shelf just below, as if it had been set down so to sip some tea, *Sea to Sea* was laid open to the very page that mentioned Raffles by name. Doug had to stoop down to read the passage that said, "Providence led me to a place called Raffles Hotel, where the food is as excellent as the rooms are bad. Feed at Raffles and sleep at Hotel de l'Europe." So much for The Truth having to be Told.

Ngiam Tong Boon's recipe for a gin sling was there, just as the bartender had promised, as was the story behind the tiger that was shot under the billiards table. But that story went from adventurous to cruel when he read that it was just a cub. There were pictures of movie stars whose names Doug didn't recognize and when he did recognize a name, he couldn't figure out which face it matched in the picture. The display tended to show only old-time photographs, back in the days when travel meant steamships and trunks, not jumbo jets and backpacks. It was less a museum and more an advertisement for the whole Raffles experience. More than a hotel, it was a way of life, and the museum laid out, in black and white, just what that life should look like.

There were three rooms in the museum, making it smaller than the Rolex shop, but big enough to squeeze in several display cases of silver fountain pens and sherry decanters. The three ceiling fans, connected by wide leather belts, just like those in the Long Bar, barely added a ripple to the centrally controlled AC, and that hint of soft jazz that haunted the entire hotel crept its way around the cabinets and cases. Calculatingly hypnotic, the museum stirred a sense of envy and a strange desire to buy an Authorized Museum Reproduction.

Doug studied the photographs in the After the War—New Beginnings section, but there were no photos of Uncle Russ. One stunning woman in a crowded party scene might have been Edna, but he couldn't be sure. He was leaning against the wall, studying a staged group photo of a polo team, when a quiet cough came from the other room.

"Careful sir," the man said, smiling, "we wouldn't want you to soil your shirt on our dusty walls." His crisp British accent and even crisper Raffles sport coat didn't prevent the real message from coming through: Don't touch.

"Oh, sorry. I'm just trying to see if there's anyone here I know."

"If there is, you have aged well. That's the 1950 Polo team," the man said as he walked over to the photo, "captained by Geoffrey Harkness. Their undefeated season is slightly marred by the fact that there were no other teams on the island that year. Pity. They were quite good. The man second to the left, first row, is C. F. Holley. He lost his arm fighting in Burma and, I would wager, was the only semi-professional, one-armed polo player who also wrote limericks based on Bible stories in the entire South East Asian region."

"That's probably a safe bet."

"One would think so, sir, but Major Brooks—second row, just below the porch light—lost his arm in the war as well, gangrene I believe, and he, too, wrote limericks. Not quite biblical but inspirational, none the less."

"Do you know everybody here?" Doug asked, looking around the room.

"No, sir," he said, his Raffles smile firmly in place, "but I do my best."

"Well, I'm Doug Pearce. I don't play polo and I have both arms." He stuck out his right hand as proof.

"Archer, sir," the man said, not clarifying if it was a first name, last name or occupation. He had a firm, well-practiced handshake. "How are you at limericks?"

"There once was a man from Nantucket...."

"Ah, of the Brooks variety. His favorite location was Kho Phuk."

"I can see why. How come you know so much about the polo team? Part of the job?"

"Part of the job, yes sir, but I have been with Raffles," his head seemed to dip when he said the name, "for twenty years now and I suppose one could say that I have made it my hobby to know its history. All of the assistant managers spend some time each year as part-time curator of our museum. It is my favorite assignment. I learn something new each time."

"Maybe you can help me out then. My uncle stayed here back in 1948."

"Sir," Archer said, smiling even wider, "you don't assume that I know *every* guest, do you?"

"Oh no, of course not. This was different. My uncle stayed at this hotel and was murdered."

Archer drew in a breath and leaned back on his heels. "*Here,* sir?" He sounded both insulted and shocked.

"I don't know if it was here, I really doubt it, but he *was* staying here, that I do know."

"Staying here and murdered here are two *very* different things."

"Of course. I've got a, uh, friend over in the police department who's looking up the actual report."

"*Really,* sir. Involving the police at this late date?" Archer leaned even further back on his heels. His smile had drooped to a flat, pink line.

Doug sighed, took a deep breath and tried again. "There's this lady in Canada," he began and told Archer an abbreviated and sanitized version of the story he told Kim at The Stowaway. Archer kept his hands clasped behind his back but returned to his upright position as the story unfolded, the flat, pink line reforming into a standard Raffles smile.

"So anyway," Doug concluded, "I was hoping that you'd have something here, I don't know what, that could help me out. I guess I was being unrealistic."

Archer held up his hand, his forefinger tapping against his chin. "Something in your story sounds familiar. Not the photographs part, it's the name. Pearce. Let us check the cards and see what they say."

From a drawer in a roll top desk, Archer produced a wooden box that held index cards, like an old library catalog. He thumbed through the first box and halfway through a second before he slowed to read each card. After several minutes he looked up at Doug. "Russell Pearce?" His smile stretched again.

"It seems, sir," Archer said, removing the card, "that your uncle's account is in arrears."

"Where?"

"He owes us some money, sir. It seems he left without paying his bill."

"Well, he was sort of dead."

"Yes. And he 'sort of' charged quite a few drinks to his room before he died." Archer checked the card again. "It seems that his belongings were confiscated by the hotel manager and sold to clear the bill."

"You keep records on everyone who skips a check?"

"Personally, no. The hotel does. Your uncle's account information is here in the museum because we apparently have stored some of his sports equipment."

Doug looked around the room and glanced in the glass cases. "Do you know what it was? Where it is?" Doug asked.

"Of course, sir," Archer said with pride. "If you'll permit me…." Doug stepped back as Archer walked back into the main exhibit room, pushed on a wooden panel until a sharp click could be heard, and then swung a doorway that, until it was open, appeared invisible. He switched on a light in the hidden space, illuminating a short hallway lined with floor to ceiling shelves. The shelves held numbered file boxes and it was one of these that Archer removed and carried out into the exhibit area. He rechecked the card before opening the box and began removing wads of tissue paper. Next to the box he set the artifacts, each with a small label, attached by a string. A collection of noisemakers emblazoned with *Happy New Year 1950!*, a plastic transistor radio, a coconut carved to look like either Bob Hope or Richard Nixon, a tin of Half & Half tobacco that sounded like it was filled with change, and a streamlined chrome and glass hood ornament were all removed from the box before Archer said, "This must be it."

The glove had dried out to a pale tan, and it felt more like cardboard than leather. A scuffed baseball peeped out from the pocket, held closed by length of twine, tied in a bow. Archer checked the label before handing it to Doug. "Russell Pearce's baseball glove, sir."

Doug held the glove with both hands like it was actually a treasured artifact. He was surprised at how small and light it was, the padding either pounded down to nothing, or never there in the first place. The webbing showed signs of multiple repairs and there were shadows of letters printed on the glove but they wouldn't have been legible fifty years ago. The twine had worn thin grooves into the leather and it needed a good coat of oil, but other than that it looked ready to play. Doug started to undo the bow.

"Ah, careful, sir. Property of the hotel." Archer reached over and lifted the glove from Doug's hands.

"I thought you said that it was Russell Pearce's glove?"

"Oh it is, sir, or rather it was. As I said, your uncle's belongings were confiscated by the hotel in order to cover his outstanding bill." Archer began replacing the Hope/Nixon coconut and the noisemakers. "With the debt outstanding, the hotel retains possession of the guest's belongings and can do as it sees fit. Someone saw fit to put it in the museum." The way he said "someone" indicated that he would never have made such a foolish decision.

"Oh this is just great," Doug said, his hands out as if he was checking for rain. "I come halfway around the world and I finally find something and now I can't even touch it. I mean, come on, give a guy a break."

"There is that outstanding bill, sir," Archer said, rechecking his card.

"And?"

"And once the bill is paid, sir, the hotel would have no reason to hold onto the debtor's possessions." His smile was his own, now.

"And that would be…" Doug said.

"The bill is in pounds sterling, of course." He produced a fountain pen from his coat and removed its top and began jotting numbers on a piece of tissue paper. "Let us assume the current exchange rates for the pound, the United States dollar and the Singapore dollar. As I have always held usury in disdain…interest, sir. I will not apply interest. So, with the outstanding debt…." Archer's voice trailed off as he worked his calculations. He rechecked his numbers, of course.

"Sir, do you wish to settle the bill of your uncle, Mr. Russell Pearce?"

"Will I get the glove then?"

"When the bill is settled, yes of course, sir."

Doug took a deep breath. "Okay. How much?"

"The total bill comes to thirty-three dollars, and forty-six cents. Singapore dollars. About twenty-five dollars, U.S., sir. Given your family's history with the hotel," he said, his smile now a wide and open-mouthed grin, "I trust you'll understand that I must insist on cash." To his grin, Archer added a slight, dignified chuckle.

◇◇◇

It took a full two hours to formally settle the bill. Archer insisted that the entire management staff be present and the hotel's photographer arrived to record the moment the decades-old bill was finally paid. Doug had to retell the story a half dozen times and Archer selectively recorded the details in his notebook. "An old baseball glove and an outstanding debt are not the kinds of things we celebrate at the museum," a Mr. Fung Kee Fung told Doug, "but a dutiful nephew traveling thousands of miles to settle the account is." Doug tried to clarify the real reason why he visited the museum, but the managers were already massaging the story so that it added to the Raffles mystique. The Truth Must Be Told. There was an awkward moment when it was learned that Doug wasn't a guest at the hotel, but Doug helped them through by saying that he was staying with friends. A final round of photographs, handshakes, and re-enactments of the settling of the bill concluded with Doug being handed a gift certificate for dinner at a Raffles restaurant, a keychain, and a promise that the next time Doug visited Singapore, his photograph (black and white) would be hanging on these very walls.

On the subway, which was colder than the air-conditioned museum, Doug unraveled the twine, slipping his left hand in the glove and fishing out the ball with his thumb and first two fingers of his right hand. The glove felt awkward, bent out of shape by years of misalignment, and it was stiff and difficult to close. He pounded his fist into the pocket of the glove, trying to work out the leather cavity created by the ball. The ball itself was more gray than white and slightly misshapen, like it had been smacked out of the park a few too many times. The red stitching was loose and uneven but looked no different from the old American League balls on the wall at a Friday's. As the subway raced along the dark tunnels, Doug sat tossing the ball into the glove. He waited for some cosmic connection, some spiritual link to his long dead family member, but nothing came, just a sense that he was no closer to the solution than he was when he first looked in that cardboard box at Edna's, a million years ago.

Chapter 30

Two pink While You Were Out notes were taped to his hotel room door. ZRZ Publishing employees enjoyed both casual dress Fridays and a three p.m. start to the weekend, but someone had made sure his messages were delivered. The first let Doug know that Edna had called at eleven thirty a.m. Two checked boxes clarified that she was returning his call and that she wanted him to call back at his earliest convenience. In the space below was Edna's phone number, just in case he had forgotten, and an extra note stating that there was a twelve-hour time difference between Singapore and Toronto. Doug wondered if that gentle reminder was from the hotel staff or from Edna.

The second note was from Aisha. The first checked box noted that she had called, the second that she wanted to see him. The note said that she called at one p.m. and that she was staying in Room 120 at Raffles. There was nothing about death threats or stealthy assassins.

Doug lay on the bed, thinking about the two women in his life. He owed Edna more than an explanation of how he was spending her money. And he still had nothing to show for it. Yeah, it was her money and she could spend it any way she wanted, including sending an unemployed bottle filler on an old-fashioned snark hunt, but that part of him that was raised to work hard and do his best made him wish he'd have something important to say. Doug decided to wait to call her back until after he got the police report, just in case, by some act of God, something would jump out at him.

He had known since Morocco that he didn't really care about his uncle's murder; the guy was a thief, a killer, and who knows what else, and he ran with a rough crowd. Every job has its hazards. And he also knew he'd never find the diamond. Things like that don't just turn up. But he also knew he wanted to solve the mystery, not for Edna and certainly not for Uncle Russ. He wanted to solve it for himself. Before this summer he'd done nothing, seen nothing, accomplished nothing that a thousand other guys from Pottsville hadn't already done. After Singapore he'd go home, apologize to Edna, and within a month be back in the rut he climbed out of when he climbed aboard that first flight out of central Pennsylvania. This was it, and he knew it. Lose now—and that seemed all but guaranteed—it would set the pace for the rest of his life.

But there was always Aisha.

He reread the note and tried to read between lines that weren't even there. She must have gotten the message he was finally able to leave with the front desk, but she sure took her time calling back. What was it about her? She was self-absorbed, superficial, conceited, and condescending and she knew just what to say to make a guy feel like a complete idiot. What did he see in her, anyway?

That's a stupid question, he thought. He knew exactly what he saw in her.

The question was, what did she see in him?

Doug put the baseball glove on and tossed the ball up towards the blades of the ceiling fan. As always, he found his mind drifting off and within five minutes he was making the game-winning catch in game seven of the World Series, flat on his back in Three Rivers Stadium.

◇◇◇

Doug decided it was time to go when the Raffles staff started to ignore him.

At first they had jumped every time he approached the front desk, waiting for him to ask to use the house phone before nodding at the phones at the end of the counter. After the first half hour they merely smiled and after that, they did their best not to notice his pacing.

The note said she wanted to see him and gave a room number, and Doug assumed she'd be waiting for his call. He went from being anxious, to worried, to bored, to frustrated, to mad, to indifferent. He dialed 7-120 one last time, listened for the six rings and the click signifying the call was being transferred to the hotel's operator, before heading out of the hotel. The staff behind the desk watched him leave without raising their heads from their paperwork.

It was a hot and humid night and Doug felt beads of sweat rolling down his back as he walked towards the quay. Fifty years ago it was a nasty warren of warehouses, brothels, and opium dens where ships from around the world bellied up to its docks. Savvy entrepreneurs snapped up the real estate while it was still reasonable and converted it into a charming warren of theme bars, souvenir shops, and seafood restaurants. The crowds were larger now and less dangerous and businesses in the area made more money, but no one seemed to be having as much fun.

Doug grabbed a #54 from a mom and pop restaurant located near an arching footbridge, and flipped the pages of a *Singapore At Night!* magazine he found on the subway. He rested the frosted mug of his Singha beer against his forehead. The heat didn't seem to be bothering anyone else, he noticed, as they strolled through the crowds, snapping family photos and chewing on sno-cones. Some older men dabbed the back of their necks with handkerchiefs, and one younger guy a few tables over looked ready to keel over, but the average person seemed unfazed by the weather.

The guidebook had said that Singapore was a mix of several ethnic groups and that, from time to time, tensions ran high between the Chinese and Malay people of the island. He was smart enough not to admit it, but to Doug everybody looked alike. He was sure it was the same for them—seen one white guy, you've seen them all—but mandatory sensitivity training at the brewery had taught him that admitting this was a proven way to get yourself fired. He took a long pull on his beer and wondered if he had a counterpart at the Singha plant, an average Joe—or Chang—who plodded along, day after day, only to get fired for no known reason. Hopefully Chang had an Edna to bail him out.

Doug flipped through the magazine. It was a Friday night, he was a young single guy in a foreign country, he had a hundred U.S. worth of pink Singapore dollars in his wallet and the magazine showcased places to spend it. So what if he got stood up, it had happened before. A full-page ad for The Big Red Door promised an all-night party with drink specials. He was going out.

Chapter 31

The phone picked up on the second ring. "He's going into a nightclub. Alone." He wiped a wet bandana across his forehead, pushing the sweat back into his hair. The voice at the other end said fine, but added, "stay with him" before hanging up.

Oh great, he thought, The Big Red Door at eleven-thirty on a Friday night. There was the main entrance, the big, red door of the name, but there were three other doors as well. If the American had gone to The Lair or 2Loud, just down the street, he could have stayed outside and waited for the guy to come back out. And there was a nice breeze just picking up, too.

He let the American get inside before he crossed the street. He didn't worry about being spotted since he figured that, to the American, all Asian people looked alike. Hell, all white people looked alike to him, why wouldn't it be the same for that guy? It was hot inside, naturally, hotter and more humid than it was out front. The American had already worked his way to one of the bars.

He hated places like this. No dart board, no video games, a tiny pool table on a cramped loft where no-talent punks played eight ball and drunk chicks danced on the bar. It was smoky and they played a mix of European techno and Hong Kong pop, all at the same glass-rattling levels. The girls were underage, sarong party girls, breaking curfew, or office workers shouting TGIF. The guys were beefed-up wannabes, drooling over the sarong girls, or office geeks, still in their white shirts and solid color ties. And it was hot. It was already crowded and it would get more crowded and that meant it would get even hotter. He tried to find an open spot under an AC vent while keeping an eye on the American, the tallest, whitest guy in the place.

The American made his way up to the loft where he quickly won five games in a row. Even from this far away, he could tell that the American was an average player at best, but compared to the competition, he looked impressive. The American seemed to make friends easily, chatting with the guys in white shirts and the office girls like he'd known them for years. He was always amazed that someone could walk up and start talking with a total stranger. He couldn't do that. He knew the person would probably start asking all sorts of questions, like what do you do and where do you live and why are you sweating so much, and he just couldn't be bothered. The American ordered a couple of pitchers of Singha and teamed up with one of the office girls to play a game of doubles against more office geeks. The bouncers at the door kept letting more and more people in and the air conditioner, if it was ever on in the first place, wasn't even noticeable anymore.

Two hours later the American and the office girl were still dancing, but how anybody could dance in this fucking heat, he didn't know. And then the deejay puts on some song that *everybody* seemed to love and the next thing the whole place is bouncing up and down, trampling whatever cool air there was left in the building, and his beer was getting warm and *that* was a mistake since he knew better than to drink beer when it's this fucking hot, and, Jesus, he felt weak all of a sudden and why is that chick looking at him that way, yes, I know I'm sweaty, he wanted to yell but didn't and maybe the AC finally came on because he felt a cold chill race across his back and he looked up for the vent and saw the ceiling and then saw the wall, then saw that chick step away from him, holding her drink tight against her chest, then he saw the floor come towards him, and it was cooler there, just like he thought it would be. Between all the legs of the bouncing dancers, he watched as the American headed towards the exit, his arm around the short-haired office girl. Lucky bastard, he thought, as he closed his eyes.

Chapter 32

The first SMRT train from Queenstown didn't pull out until five forty-five a.m., so Doug had enough time to grab a cup of coffee and a doughnut from a twenty-four hour 7-Eleven. By all rights, he should have been exhausted, but the two-hour nap seemed to be enough. He didn't want to rush out, that was Jang's idea—"Trying to explain you to my roommate…" she said as she shook her head was all she offered as an explanation. It was a good line and Doug had used it before himself, but he would have preferred staying a bit longer.

"This is going to sound like bullshit, but I don't usually do things like this," she said when she invited him in for a drink.

"I mean it," she continued when Doug said nothing, "you're the first guy I've brought here since I moved in six months ago. Okay, second, but he doesn't count because...well…he just doesn't."

Doug complimented her on her decorating—1960s retro—her music selection—the Stones—and the wine—pink. He had already complimented her on her outfit—LBD—her haircut—short and spiky—and her perfume—"Christmas gift from Mom." She said thanks in all the right places as she lit an end table-full of candles. They talked about Singapore, travel, friends, and jobs.

"I never met anyone so interesting," she said. "Honest. Why are you laughing? That's why I wanted you to come up for a drink, you're different from the guys I know."

"You must know some real losers."

"Not really. They're all pretty successful, some even have their own homes, and in Singapore, that's saying a lot, but they're so, so..." she looked around the room for the word, finding it in among the candles, "*predictable*. They will live and die at the same jobs they got right out of university. Same handful of clubs, same drinks, same vacations, same everything. I dated a few of them and *believe me* they are *all* the same. Here you are, taking a summer off, traveling around the world. That's amazing." She grabbed the wine bottle on her way past the kitchen and plopped down on the couch, her legs across Doug's lap. "Now, tell me more about Egypt."

Doug hadn't said anything about being a detective on a case and knew if he added it in now she wouldn't believe him. He said that a friend of the family had wanted him to look up some old acquaintances here and there and that he had grown bored of the brewery anyway. It wasn't far from the truth, in fact it probably was the truth. In any case, Jang found him interesting just the way he was. And as he rode the first train towards the Geylang district, hiding his open cup of coffee under his shirt to avoid a five-hundred-dollar fine, he thought a lot about that.

◇◇◇

Chong Kim Siap was waiting at the door of ZRZ Publishers and Tourist Hotel, Ltd. when Doug walked up the street. He spotted Doug and half-jogged down the block to meet him. "That's a strange hotel you picked, but you guys probably like those out-of-the-way places."

"Out of the way? Isn't this the heart of town? How you doing, Kim?" he said as he shook the young man's hand.

"Late night on the case?" he said, pumping away on Doug's arm.

"In a way. I was out at The Big Red Door and I met this girl...."

"Say no more, say no more," he said, then added, "You guys. Geeze."

"You're here early. You find something important?"

"You tell me," he said, handing Doug a thin white envelope. Inside was a photocopy of a mimeographed form, the blanks completed in a slanting cursive.

"This is it?" Doug said, holding up the paper.

"That's it. They weren't as obsessed with paperwork back then."

Doug sighed and put the paper back into the envelope. "Thanks, Kim." He knew the kid wanted to watch him mine clues from the report but he didn't feel like play acting this early in the morning. "What do I owe ya?"

"Professional courtesy. Just do me a favor," he said, handing Doug a card. "If you get any breaks in the case, give me a call." *Chong Kim Siap* was neatly hand printed on the Singapore Police Department card, the whiteout barely visible under his name.

Chapter 33

Just as Edna was saying that she'd accept the collect call, the delivery truck began backing down the street, its warning beep echoing off the buildings as it inched its way past the phone booth.

"I'm sorry about the mix-up the other night," Doug was shouting into the phone. "I still don't get that time difference thing."

"It's only nine p.m. now, so I guess you have it right. How are you doing, Doug? You really should call more often. What have you found out?"

Doug looked up into the cab of the delivery truck. The driver was leaning forward to be closer to the lone mirror, his eyes wide open and his tongue working back and forth across his upper lip in time with the beeps. Doug forced his finger deeper into his ear and pushed the receiver tight against his head.

"I've been going over the police report," he said, holding up the photocopy for her to see, "and I have to tell you that, well, I don't see anything here."

"What does it say?" she said, just loud enough to be heard over the beeps.

"The report says that he, uh, Russell Pearce, was found in Room 302 of the New Phoenix Hotel, and they give a street address but it doesn't match anything on the street map I have. It looks like that whole area was torn down and built over since there are office buildings there now. Anyway, it says he was shot once in the neck and he bled to death in the room. They figure it happened close to midnight but nobody heard anything." From down the street came a dull thud as the backing truck bumped up against the front of a parked Toyota. The beeping stopped, replaced by the two-octave whine of the car alarm.

"They found the gun. It was a Russian pistol, a…" he double-checked the report, then sounded out the word, "a 'To-ka-rev,' model TT-33. 7.62."

"That would be the caliber," Edna said. "It's a common size."

Doug could barely hear the car alarm now, the police car's siren blotting out most of the noise on the street. He leaned into the corner of the phone booth, which, despite the laws, smelled of urine. "Edna, it was Charley Hodge's gun."

"No it wasn't."

"Yes it was. His initials were on it," Doug said, and under the police siren but still distinct, he could hear Edna drawing in a deep breath.

"It was not Charley's gun," she said, each word clipped off clean so there would be no mistake.

"Edna, I know that's not what you want to hear, but it looks like Charley and my uncle got into a fight over that damn diamond and Charley shot Uncle Russ. All the evidence points to it."

"What evidence, Douglas? You haven't found a thing."

"I've got the police report right here," he said, holding it up again. "It says, where does it say it, ah, here, it says 'Witnesses agree'—down below it lists these Raffles hotel people as wit-nesses—'that the victim was expecting one Charley Hodge the day of the murder.' And then they find the gun with his initials and the gun matches the bullet they find at the scene. Edna, come on, be realistic here."

"I know what I know, Douglas. Charley Hodge did not shoot your uncle." Her voice sounded different, a tone she had not used before, maybe the same tone Nasser Ashkanani heard in his shop all those years ago. "I know I don't have the proof, that's what I sent you there to find."

"Yes, Edna, I know," Doug shouted into the phone, just as the police siren stopped. The sudden silence and his own voice surprised him. He paused and started again. "I know why you sent me on this trip."

"Well if you know what to do, do it. Find the evidence that clears Charley and figure out who murdered your uncle."

"I've tried, really, I have tried, but I just can't do it. I'm not cut out for this."

"I have spent a small fortune flying you around the world…."

"I never asked you to. You insisted."

"…and now you're saying that you just feel like giving up…."

"I never said that." He was shouting again, but there was no police siren in the background.

"…and you haven't even tried to find out what happened…."

"What? I went to frickin' *jail*…."

"That's not my fault."

"Oh geeze," he said, resting his forehead against the phone booth door. A minute of static hissed in his ear before Edna spoke again.

"Can we start over?" she said, the sharp edge missing from her voice.

"Let's," he said, and for the next ten minutes they talked about the weather, shopping malls, jet-lag, and Raffles. It was Edna who said, "Tell me about the police report."

"Okay. There's only one page and it doesn't look like there was any follow-up. There's a line at the bottom that says Status but there's nothing written there. What I'm thinking is that the first guy took a report and that was it. They didn't even try to find any leads and just assumed that this drifter guy was killed by his friend." He didn't believe it as he said it, but when he was done saying it, it sounded plausible.

"I can't say I'd blame them. I'm sure there were a lot of unsolved crimes at that time and if some foreigner gets himself killed in a flophouse, that's his tough luck."

"Did my uncle write to you from Singapore? Any cables?"

"Yes, and I showed you that last note in Toronto, remember? It was that short letter he wrote on the Raffles stationery. Let me get it quick."

Doug listened to the steady hiss of the intercontinental static. Down the road the truck driver, the cop, and the car owner were exchanging paperwork in a quiet and orderly manner. Across the street a shop owner was hosing down his sidewalk, singing along to a Chinese rock band on the radio.

"Here's all that it says about the diamond," Edna said as she picked up the phone. "'Don't worry, I still have that third eye. It's not on me but I keep it within my reach.' The rest of the note is just pleasantries, things about the weather, how he misses people...."

"Anyone I know?"

Edna laughed. "Stop it Douglas, you know it wasn't like that between us. But yes, he did say he missed me. Now, here's what I'd like you to do," she said, as if she was asking him to cut the lawn. "You can't check his old room since you say the hotel's gone...."

"The whole neighborhood is gone."

"And you say that Raffles sold off all of his things to clear the debt...."

"*I* cleared the debt," he corrected.

"And all the police have is a report, and not a very good one at that."

"So?"

"So how are you set for money?"

He mentally went through his wallet. "I've got a couple hundred U.S. and I have hardly put a thing on my Visa card."

"Well, save your receipts. There's an outstanding zoo in Singapore and you already know about the shopping and the restaurants. Now, when you get a plane ticket, see if you can get one that flies via Vancouver and get a two-day layover...."

"That's it?" Doug said. "We're all done? What about the diamond? What about clearing Charley and finding the killer?"

"Douglas, you've been halfway around the world and we really don't have any more than when we started. It's time to admit defeat. That's alright, I knew this was a long shot before I even wrote to you in Putzville...."

"Pottsville."

"...and you did a fine job with the little you had to go on, but I guess there was nothing to find after all." And, after a sigh, added, "You did the best you could."

◇◇◇

Flat on his back in Three Rivers Stadium, Doug caught the last out of game four of the Pirates' sweep of the Yankees. It was the tenth series he had won in the past half hour and it was getting too easy.

Over the years, he'd won World Series, Superbowls, and Stanley Cups, dated pop stars and Playmates, run small countries, invented anti-gravity boots, traveled both back and forward in time, saved the world and bowled three hundred. Recently he had solved the case, found the diamond, married a beautiful woman, owned Raffles, and spoken Chinese. He was pretty good at imagining success, despite his total lack of experience.

Doug tried to time a toss so that the ball passed through the spinning blades of the ceiling fan, but they knocked the ball into the bathroom, just missing the open toilet. Next he tried to lob the ball safely onto one of the A-laden shelves over his head, this time avoiding the spinning blades. It took six tries but it finally found a spot. He stood on the bed to get the ball and, already bored with this new challenge, pulled down a copy of *Scolasticia Encyclopedia*, volume 1. He flipped to make sure that there was no entry for baseball, but volume 1 ended with Auvergne (a province in central France, pop. 1 million).

He checked to see what *Scolasticia* had to say about adobe and it fit the facts as he understood them. He skimmed past aerosol, looked at a map of Africa, read the short history of Alcatraz, completely skipped the section on algebra, checked the stats on Mohammad Ali, and stared at the chart on alphabets.

An hour later he knew much more about the letter A.

And he knew who killed Russell Pearce.

Chapter 34

In most places, as long as you have on shirt and shoes, you can expect service. But there are holdouts, none in Pottsville, but several in Singapore, that require a bit more formal attire. Raffles Grill was one of those places, even with a gift certificate signed by Mr. Fung Kee Fung. Fortunately Raffles housed several restaurants and Doc Cheng's, the hotel's trendy but less stuffy restaurant, offered a more casual dining experience. The fact that he was the only man without a tie attracted some attention but his date's scandalously short dress attracted much more. It didn't matter to Doug. He knew he was sitting across from the most attractive woman in the place.

"I'm glad you got my message," he said. "I was having a hard time getting in touch with you."

"I wasn't expecting you to call," Jang said as she dipped her steak-house style fries in a pile of catsup and hot sauce. "I'm just amazed that my roommate gave me the message. He's kinda protective."

"He's jealous, that's all."

"Please, he'd rather be out with you. You're his type—tall, good looking, sexy eyes…."

"Gee, I'll give him a call. Anyway," he said, "I'm glad you could make it."

"You kidding? This is the first time I've ever been in the building and I've lived here all my life. I wouldn't have missed it."

"Well that makes me feel special."

"Oh stop," she said, pointing a catsup-soaked fry at him. "If you were a jerk I wouldn't have shown up. Besides I figure I have to see as much of you as I can before you take off on some other wild adventure. So when do you leave?"

"I have some things to take care of here first. There's a woman staying at this hotel, I met her in Morocco back in June. We sort of had a business agreement but I have to let her know that I don't think it's gonna work out."

"Is she pretty?" Jang said.

"Stunning. Breathtaking actually." It was the truth.

"Oh," she said, and shifted her hamburger on her plate. "Why didn't you ask her to dinner tonight?"

"I wasn't thinking about her. I was busy trying to figure out how to get in touch with you." That was the truth, too.

"I'm glad you did," she said. "But I'm afraid this place is going to cost you a fortune."

"Actually, the hotel owes me a favor," Doug said. He told her about his uncle's brief stay at Raffles, about the glove and ball and how he had paid the fifty-year-old debt. He stayed close to the fiction that Mr. Fung Kee Fung dictated to the *Straight Times* reporter. The Truth Must Be Told, sort of. Besides she'd read about it in the morning paper. He had hoped to point the story out to her himself, maybe as they enjoyed a cup of coffee, snuggled tight on her single bed, but she had already mentioned that she was staying at her parents' house that night. "My mom's birthday," she said. "My dad and I and my kid sister are taking her to Sentosa Island for the day. It's really boring and we've been there a thousand times, but that's what she wants."

"Lucky her."

"Yeah," Jang said, "well I was hoping to get lucky myself tonight, so what say we skip dessert?"

"Lucky me."

◇◇◇

Andrew Chan watched as the American and his date—a local girl with short hair in a wonderfully short print dress—headed out of the lobby and asked one of the doormen to hail them a taxi. The man had good taste, Andrew thought as he smiled. He checked his appearance, reflected in the polished brass table lamp next to his podium, before he picked up and dialed the phone.

"This is Andrew Chan at the Outer-Lobby Desk.... Fine, thank you, sir.... No, sir, there's no problem," he said, but still looked down to re-check the crease in his pants. "I wanted you to know that the gentleman in the photograph has just dropped off a message for Room 120, sir. Shall I have it delivered? Yes, sir, immediately. Thank you, sir."

Andrew rang the small brass bell on the podium and watched one of the uniformed houseboys all but sprint toward him. His smile was so fixed that he unwittingly shared it with the errand boy. Plankton, he thought. Numerous, at the bottom of the hotel's food chain, but the base on which the entire hotel rested. "Never forget," Mr. Fung Kee Fung said, "the staff members below you are as important as the staff members above you."

"Deliver this to Room 120 immediately," he said as he handed the envelope to the houseboy. "Report back to me as soon as you are done."

Andrew knew what it was like to be plankton and he knew what it was like to move up the chain. One misstep and he'd be gobbled up from below. But as he watched the American and his date get in the taxi, he was certain that wouldn't happen to him.

Chapter 35

The ball didn't leap off the bat. First there was a mushy thump, like hitting a baked potato, and instead of arching gracefully across the park, it dropped, exhausted, after twenty yards and limped another two before stopping dead. A German Shepherd pup rushed over to sniff it.

"Thanks, kid," Doug said, handing back the cricket bat. Swinging it proved harder than it looked but he couldn't miss hitting the ball with the wide, flat blade. The kid resumed his bunched-up stance in front of the three plastic Coke bottles that served as a wicket and waited for his dad to bowl the tennis ball his way. Doug headed out to where the misshapen baseball recovered in the sun.

The park was near the quay, overlooking a wide harbor that was ringed with sleek, fifty-story, blue-glass and chrome office towers, and some turn-of-the-century government buildings, looking like the poor relatives of the Raffles complex. At the entrance of the harbor spouted the Merlion Fountain, the half fish, half lion symbol of Singapore that dated all the way back to the 1980s, an advertising agency's version of an ancient mythology. The park was well kept and filling up with divorced career men and their kids, the scheduled Sunday morning quality time. It was sunny, already warm, and Doug was feeling pretty damn good.

He had done it. He had solved a fifty-year-old murder. He had cleared Charley Hodge's name. He hadn't wasted Edna's money. He didn't fail, he didn't quit, and he didn't fuck up.

True, he didn't know what to do now, but he still felt good. His evidence wouldn't hold up in court, but he knew he was right, as right as Edna had been about Charley, and that's all that really mattered. He watched as the pup managed to get his mouth around the ball and trot off towards the benches that lined the walkway under the tall palm trees.

He wanted to call Edna but it would have to wait. He needed time to figure out how to tell her without getting all excited and sounding like an amateur. He had a professional responsibility to be cool. He practiced that cool as he walked over to the bench where a teenaged kid and the dog were playing tug-o-war with his ball.

"I'm afraid your dog ran off with my ball," Doug said.

"No he didn't," the kid said, not bothering to look up. "He found it in the field."

"He picked it up after I hit it with the cricket bat."

The kid held onto the ball, pulling the dog's head to the left and right, while the dog growled and wagged his tail harder. "This ain't a cricket ball," the kid said.

"I know," Doug said, struggling to stay professional and cool. "It's a baseball. An *old* baseball. And it's mine."

"Are you Mr. Reach?" the kid said, pulling the dog in a wide arc around the end of the bench.

"No."

"Well, this belongs to Mr. Reach. Says so right on the ball."

"That's not a person's name. That's the name of the company that made the ball. Like Spalding or Nike." He wanted to add "you little shit" but decided to be professional.

"Maybe, but he found it in the field so now it's mine." The kid looked up and brushed his thick black bangs out of his face. He had wrestled the ball free and leaned back on the bench like he was in his living room. The dog ran off, chasing a bird. The kid smiled at Doug and said, "Waddya gonna do, call the police?"

"No. An ambulance."

"An ambulance? Waddya gonna do, hit me?" The kid laughed.

"Yes," Doug said. He wasn't laughing but he did have a strange smile on his face.

The kid looked at Doug and thought before he said anything. Doug felt his smile grow wider and stranger. "Fuck it," the kid said, throwing the ball over his shoulder. "Thing's a piece of shit anyway." He ran off, as if he was chasing his dog.

Doug's smile shifted. Cool.

He walked over to the poor ball. It wasn't enough that it had been hauled around the world, stuffed in duffel bags with dirty socks, bounced off the bulkheads of tramp freighters, baked in desert suns, soaked in tropical monsoons, stuck in a box in a museum for half a century, chopped by a ceiling fan, and smacked with a cricket bat, now it had to endure a stringy coat of dog spit. The poor ball deserved a break.

Mr. Reach. How could anybody be so stupid, Doug thought. The letters were faded but it was obvious that it was machine-printed on the ball. The kid was just trying to be funny. "It's not my ball," Doug said, trying to capture the cocky Chinese-English tone in the kid's voice, "it belongs to Mr. Reach."

It's not on me.

Doug stopped and looked at the ball.

But I keep it within my reach.

Doug sat down in the open field.

The stitching was worn and frayed, and there were spots where it missed one of the holes in the gray-white cover. There was a slack, saggy feel to the ball, like the taut winding inside had slipped loose. Or had been replaced. There were two shades of red stitching and strange knots where there should have been smooth seams. The weight felt right but a bit off balance.

He used his hotel room key to cut through the stitching, which pried up off the ball and broke. He opened a seam a quarter way around the ball then pulled on the leather casing, ripping the seam along until a crudely wound ball of string dropped free.

It unwound rapidly, the string piling up in his lap, and revealed an oval wad of white cotton, held closed by a dry, hard rubber band that crumbled as he pulled the cotton apart.

It was about the size of a large grape and its facets caught the midday sun, bathing the cotton in a rich, red light.

Chapter 36

Doug walked between the potted palms and perfectly positioned fountains, weaving his way towards Raffles Grill. His new shoes clicked audibly on the tile floor. He could almost see his reflection in the highly polished tiles, but there were enough ornate framed mirrors hanging on the walls if he wanted to check his appearance. But unless things had changed since he left the men's department of Tang's Plaza, he knew he looked good. The suit was from a Japanese designer he'd never heard of, but then he had never heard of the American designers the squadron of sales clerks insisted he'd love. The jacket fit well right off the rack. The sales clerks called it a classic-cut, navy silk pinpoint. To Doug it was a blue suit. The pants needed hemming but that was taken care of before he and his assigned sales clerks had picked out shirt, tie, shoes, and socks to complete the outfit. The sales clerks were paid to tell him he looked good. The looks he got from the women on the subway only confirmed it.

After his late-morning stroll in the park, Doug had returned to the ZRZ Publishing Group/Hotel, showered, shaved, and spent a few hours thinking things through. Using Dexter Lee's office—which, he noticed, contained complete sets of encyclopedias—he made several phone calls, the last one to Aisha. He had expected her to be a bit more excited when he called.

"Really? That's great," she said when he told her he had found the diamond, but it was the way she said it, like he had just told her about finding a misplaced sock, that bothered him. She didn't ask where he had found it or what it looked like or how he was doing, she just asked for directions to his hotel.

"Actually I'd like to take you to dinner later. I noticed a nice place in your hotel, Raffles Grill."

"That's not a nice place, Doug," she said. "That's a phenomenal place. I think you'd be a lot more comfortable if we just grabbed a pizza and ate in your room."

Doug had to insist three times until she sighed, saying, "I guess that'll be alright."

"Your note said that you figured out who killed your uncle," she added, referring to the message he had left for her the night before. "You're on a roll."

The *maitre d'* nodded when Doug gave him his name and led him to a smaller table, as far from the other diners as possible. Even by the hotel's own standards, Raffles Grill was impressive. Given the name, Doug had expected dark woods and brass fixtures, but soaring, ivory-white walls and delicate silver chandeliers gave the room an elegance that made royal families jealous. Fine-turned, high-backed chairs ringed china-laden tables, the silver cutlery glowing on the starched and pressed white tablecloths. The white theme continued with sheer curtains that swept down from the high arched windows and doorways, and with the legions of white-coated waiters that shimmered around the room. Adding dramatic contrast, Aisha sat at the table, her black hair up, showing off her long neck and the low neckline of what Doug was sure was a little black dress.

"You certainly clean up nicely," she said after the first wave of waiters had taken their drink orders.

"Oh this old thing?" he said. "You look beautiful, but I'm sure you know that."

"Modesty is an overrated virtue. Besides, I wanted this evening to be special. After all, you've had such an eventful stay in Singapore. Speaking of which, now that you've solved everything, what comes next for Doug Pearce?"

"That's why I invited you here tonight. I figured I could explain best over an expensive meal."

"Well you picked the right place," Aisha said, looking past Doug as she spoke. "I hope you don't mind but I asked an old friend to join us."

"Hello, Douglas," Sergei said as he pulled out the last chair and sat down. "You look good." He was wearing a light tan suit with an ice-blue shirt and matching tie. He looked tan, fit, and happy.

"Hello, Sergei," Doug said. "Or should I call you Sasha?"

"Let's keep it Sergei. I'm too old to be a Sasha anymore. Ah, just in time," Sergei said as the waiter returned with Aisha's martini and Doug's whiskey. "I'll have a gin and tonic," he said to the waiter. "The quinine in the tonic has kept me free of malaria most of my life," he added as the waiter turned to leave.

"You killed Russell Pearce," Doug said, sipping his whiskey.

"You know I was quite impressed when Aisha told me that you had figured it out. What was it that tipped you off?"

"CH. The initials on the gun."

"Ah, now, Douglas," Sergei said. "Don't they incriminate your uncle's friend, Charley Hodge?"

"It was a Russian gun. The initials were from the Russian alphabet."

"It's called Cyrillic, but go on."

"In Russian, C has the same sound as S in English, and the H is the Russian for N. So even though the initials on the gun are CH it's like saying SN in English. Sergei Nikolaisen. It was your gun."

"Bravo, Douglas, I am impressed. Really I am. At the time no one even considered any other possibility. Maybe you'll make a detective yet."

"You killed him."

Sergei took a deep breath. "Yes, yes I did. I'd like you to believe that it was an accident, that I didn't mean to do it."

"That's kind of hard to do since you shot him twice."

"I fired three times, I only hit him twice," Sergei said. "We were in my hotel room, talking, when he suddenly became angry. He wanted to sell the diamond right away, I had other plans. He charged at me and I panicked. I just kept shooting till he stopped." Sergei paused and looked across the table to Doug, the slight smile disappearing from his face. "He was a violent man, a dangerous man. He would have killed me, I'm sure of it. Still, it's not an easy thing to live with. It's not something I'm proud of."

"You had no trouble killing the guards when you stole the diamond."

"Douglas, we both know who killed the guards. In my plan, there was to be no shooting at all."

"That's what Mr. Ahmed said this morning when I called him in Morocco," Doug said. "The man has a great memory and once you get him started he loves to reminisce."

Sergei rolled his eyes and shook his head. "That is precisely why I didn't want him talking to you." He sighed and continued. "So, *monsieur* detective, what inspired you to call Mr. Ahmed?"

"Once I figured out it was your gun, I assumed that much of what happened to me was your doing, starting with Mr. Ahmed."

"I told him you were a reporter snooping into my private life and we came up with the hit-and-run idea to send you away," Sergei said. "He told his staff you were a hired killer. I heard that you put quite a scare into them. How did you get him to talk to you?"

"Simple," Doug said. "I told him the truth."

"Clever. But I don't suggest you make a habit of it. It's generally not a good policy."

"Oh I love *requin au four*," Aisha said, reading the menu. "What would go best with that?"

"I'm partial to Number 47," Doug said. "Tastes just like a Number 18." He turned back to Sergei. "So how long have you been following me?"

"I received word you were in Casa on your first day. After searching your room—oh, don't look so surprised, the poor man at the hotel gets paid next to nothing—I determined that you might have some information about the diamond that I hadn't been able to uncover."

"Same here," Aisha said. She was thumbing through the desserts. "When you came asking questions I figured you were hiding something. I didn't buy the dumb hick act, by the way."

"Yeah, I figured you were in this together." Doug tried not to look disappointed.

"Not at first," Sergei said. "For years each of us had kept an eye out for the diamond, myself much longer than Miss Al-Kady here has been alive. After I retired from the museum—this would be five years ago—I moved to Morocco. I had always liked the weather there and, as I said, I do have many friends in Casa. Thanks to her grandfather, Miss Al-Kady and I have known each other for years. Casa is like a small town and we share some similar interests." Aisha looked over and flashed her eyebrows up and down suggestively. "We became partners when we realized we needed to move you along. You seemed to take a rather long time making decisions and, since we were both confident that the diamond was not in Morocco, we prodded you a bit."

"That makes sense, but why all the warnings about dangerous killers out there? For a while it seemed as if you wanted me to quit."

Sergei and Aisha smiled at each other. "We disagreed on how best to motivate you," Sergei said. "You see, I didn't think the—what did you call it Aisha? The 'hick act'?—I didn't think that was an affectation. A naïve young man like you, I sensed you would be best motivated by the idea of danger and suspense… never letting you out of sight, of course. With the help of some friends of mine, I think we created a believable scenario."

"Captain Yehia, for one," Doug said.

"Yes, and the altercation in the back alley. Without the threat of violence, there really is no sense of danger."

"Cruising the red light district, Doug?" Aisha said with smile. "Tsk-tsk-tsk."

"You insisted that you were going to Cairo even though Miss Al-Kady and I were absolutely certain that the diamond was not there either. Remember, we've been looking for some time now. We wanted you in Singapore and assumed that's where you would be heading eventually. We needed time, something to delay your arrival in Cairo while we orchestrated a series of events that we felt would fit both Miss Al-Kady's and my approach to keeping you motivated."

"So you planted cocaine in my flight bag," Doug said, watching Aisha flip through the wine list.

"I'm innocent and pure," she said without looking up.

"That was not cocaine, Douglas, it was baking powder. We assumed you wouldn't be able to tell the difference. And I'm afraid it was I who slipped it in your carry-on bag while you were sleeping."

"So you paid off someone to have me arrested and thrown in jail, where I conveniently met Abe."

"An old flame of Miss Al-Kady's. There are surprisingly few opportunities for a character actor who does impressions in Egypt, even with the movie industry there. I feel he did a fine job."

"He said to say hi," Aisha said. "Oh and you're supposed to rent the movie *Aladdin*—he did some of the voices."

"You kept me locked up long enough to put together your little charade," Doug said. "So no one was shooting at us, no one fell off a building…."

"They were shooting," Aisha said, "they *insisted* they get to shoot. But no, no one fell off the building."

"Former boyfriends?" Doug said, trying not to sound sarcastic.

"Cousins," she said.

"Well it worked," Doug said and sipped his drink. "You got me moving. But the car crash in the desert wasn't necessary."

"Oh that was Abe's idea," Aisha said. "He and his buddies worked on that for hours." She started to laugh. "He says you were going to shoot out his back window, but that would have given it all away since there were blanks in the gun. That's Abe." Despite everything, Doug still found her laugh sexy and encouraging. "He said he worked really hard on the dramatic 'there was no crash' scene, but on the tape it sounds *way* over the top."

"He taped it?" Doug said. "You're kidding."

"For his portfolio. He wants to show he can do serious parts as well."

"You caused us some difficulties when you disappeared in Bahrain. We thought for sure you had run home to Pennsylvania," Sergei said.

"Not me," Aisha said, closing the menu. "I figured you got wise to us and just slipped loose. I mean after I heard Abe overdo it on that tape...." She shook her head, a strategically placed strand of hair bouncing lightly.

"When you managed to eliminate the man we had following you here in Singapore, we realized that you were ready to pick up the diamond and flee the country. We assume the woman you had dinner with last night was your contact here but, and this is truly embarrassing, my cab driver lost you when you left Raffles."

"We were just lucky you called. We thought for sure we had missed our last chance." Aisha poked at the fat olive in her martini, skewering it on the third try. She used her teeth to slide it off her fork, careful not to smudge her lipstick.

Doug was looking down at his drink, trying to remember eliminating anybody.

"You shouldn't feel bad, Douglas," Sergei said. "You've had the adventure of a lifetime. This one just ended a bit differently than you would have liked. Remember, it's not the destination, it's the journey that counts." He smiled at Doug. "It has been quite a time, hasn't it?"

"What makes you think it's over?"

Sergei laughed. "Because I know you, Douglas. I know the kind of man you are, what you are capable of and what, frankly, is beyond you. Look," he said, leaning forward, "I'll tell you what you'd have to do. First you'd have to get out of Singapore with the diamond."

"That should be easy."

"Ha," Aisha said. "You think I'm just going to let you waltz out on me? Hardly. Believe it or not, I can get rather demanding."

Doug looked at Sergei, who gave a slight shrug and continued. "Miss Al-Kady is right, of course. We would work to ensure that, if you did leave Singapore, it would be without the diamond."

"I take it you'd kill me. You had no problem killing my uncle."

"As I said, that was not my plan. I regret it and I would also regret seeing you hurt. But yes, we would see to it. But let's assume by some minor miracle you do end up with the diamond."

"*Major* miracle," Aisha said.

"Flying out of Singapore is easy, just don't get caught smuggling any stolen diamonds. This time jail would be for real, and for keeps. You might have to go through Malaysia or Thailand. All this would be the easy part."

"It gets harder?" Doug said.

"Let's say you get back to the States and you and this woman who put you up to this trip actually have the diamond in front of you. Would you know what to do with it? Do you know any international jewelry brokers who would be able to handle such a legendary diamond? You certainly can't walk into a jewelry store in the mall to try to sell it, nor can you take out an ad in the paper. I'm afraid you'd be stuck with an extremely valuable souvenir. But sooner or later the temptation would be too great and you'd try to sell it to someone and the FBI or Interpol would get wind of it and I'm afraid that would bring on the start of a different adventure altogether."

"I have connections," Doug said.

"No you don't, Douglas, don't be silly. You live in Pottsville, Pennsylvania. You count bottles for a living. You're kind, you're honest, you're a gentleman in a blue-collar sort of way. You're just not the sort of man that outwits murdering jewel thieves.

Not many people are. The truth is you're a nice guy, Douglas, and that's not a bad thing to be."

"And you look good in a suit," Aisha said, holding her hand out. "Well?" she added.

For almost a minute Doug didn't move, then, with a deep sigh, he reached into his coat pocket and took out a small wad of tissues. He placed it in Aisha's palm.

Aisha peeled back the layers of tissue to reveal the grape-sized red diamond. She plucked it out and held it between her thumb and forefinger.

"Oh my God, it's so beautiful," she said as she held it up to the light. Doug watched her as she stared at the diamond, her eyes wide and soft. He wondered what she saw as she looked into the dark red facets. She stared a moment longer, blinked twice, and the look was gone. "It's worth more than I thought," she said.

"May I?" Sergei said, reaching across the table. From his pocket he removed a jeweler's loupe and a small white box. He placed the loupe to his right eye and examined the diamond. "It's not flawless, but it's close. And as for its value, you're not alone Miss Al-Kady, it's worth more than I dared speculate." Sergei opened the box and set the diamond inside on a bed of white satin. "Thank you, Douglas," he said as he closed the lid and returned the box and the loupe to his pocket.

Sergei smiled at Aisha as he opened his menu. "Enjoy your meal, Douglas," he said. "I'm sure you see it our way. You really have no other choice. As for you, Miss Al-Kady, I suggest either the *risotto* or the *carpaccio de Beouf.* Both are marvelous."

"Sorry, Doug," Aisha said, laughing, "no hamburgers."

Doug left his menu closed on the table and cleared his throat. "Actually, I have another idea."

"For dinner?" Aisha said. "It's a little late now."

"No, it's about the diamond," Doug said. Sergei and Aisha looked up from their menus.

"You don't seriously think we're going to let go of the diamond now, do you?" Aisha said. "Deal with it, Doug. We win, you lose."

"Now Aisha, no need to be less than gracious. So, Douglas," Sergei said, setting his menu down and folding his hands in front of him. "After all I explained to you and after hearing Miss Al-Kady's rather firm declarations, you still have an alternative plan for the diamond. Interesting. And what, may I ask, would that plan be?"

"Well," Doug said, "it goes something like this."

Doug raised his hand and caught the eye of the *maitre d'*, who in turn caught the eye of Mr. Fung Kee Fung, who only had to raise his finger slightly to get the attention of Andrew Chan, who, smiling, led a swarm of Raffles security guards and TV camera crews towards the lone table in the corner of the room.

"What's going on?" Aisha said, her voice anxious and less confident.

"Don't do this, Douglas," Sergei said as uniformed guards and the bright lights of shoulder-mounted video cameras surrounded their table.

"Mr. Pearce, it is so very good to see you again." Mr. Fung Kee Fung extended his arm and cameras clicked as Doug stood and shook his hand. "Your adventures are certainly adding to the storied reputation of our little hotel."

A crowd three deep ringed the table but they stepped back far enough to allow Doug space to speak. "Thank you Mr. Fung Kee Fung, but it's this remarkable hotel that adds to my little adventures." Flashes from a dozen cameras accompanied Mr. Fung Kee Fung's humble chuckle. Sergei and Aisha sat quietly, swirling their drinks and staring at the ornate ceiling.

"Fifty years ago, *Al Ainab*, one of the most beautiful and legendary diamonds in the world, was stolen," Doug said, addressing the bank of television cameras and newspaper reporters. "Several people were killed in the process, including my uncle, Russell Pearce. He was murdered in this city and his killer was never found. This man here," Doug said, turning to face Sergei, "is the educator, museum director, and author Dr. Sergei Nikolaisen." Sergei stared at a chandelier, took a deep breath and raised his chin slightly.

"Thanks to evidence that has recently come to light, I can say with confidence that it was *this* man," Doug continued, pointing at Sergei, "who made the recovery of *Al Ainab* possible."

The news cameras shifted to Sergei as a dozen reporters scribbled approximations of his name in their notebooks. Sergei's shoulders relaxed and he turned to look up at Doug. "Thanks to his expertise, his wisdom, and his incredible patience, we were able to recover this legendary diamond."

"And this is Miss Aisha Al-Kady," Doug continued. The cameras shifted and zoomed in on Aisha while reporters, security guards and hotel management committed her name to memory. Aisha held a flat, hard smile as she stared at Doug. "It was Miss Al-Kady's brilliant research that enabled us to track the diamond to Singapore." As if on cue, Aisha tilted her head and smiled while lowering her eyes modestly. For a moment that corner of Raffles Grill lit up like noon from a barrage of camera flashes.

"Thanks to the knowledge and dedication of these two scholars, it was easy for us to locate the diamond, hidden among my late uncle's belongings, held in trust by the fine staff of this hotel. With Mr. Archer's assistance," a few cameras turned away from Aisha to get a shot of the museum curator bowing, "and the help of Chong Kim Siap of the Singapore Police Department," Kim winked and gave Doug a thumbs-up, "I'm pleased to say that the mystery of *Al Ainab* has been solved. Now," Doug said, turning to Sergei, "if Dr. Nikolaisen would be so kind…."

Sergei glared at Doug as the reporters and guards looked on. Then suddenly he smiled and stood up next to Doug.

Doug turned and offered his hand to Aisha. She gave Doug a cold smile as she took his hand. The cameras clicked to capture the group photo.

Sergei reached into his pocket and retrieved the small white box. "It's been our great honor to play a small role in the history of *Al Aniab*." He lifted the lid and held the box so that the camera crews could zoom in on the red glow.

Chapter 37

Edna Bowers signed her name with a flourish and handed the check to Doug.

"This should cover all these expenses," she said, referring to the pile of receipts on the glass-topped coffee table in front of them. It had taken over a month for the last charges to appear on his Visa statement and Edna had insisted that he wait until it was updated. "I added a little something extra, sort of a bonus. I don't want to hear any nonsense about you not earning it."

Her townhouse looked as it did in early June. The plants were a bit fuller after the summer sun and there was a stack of new books next to her chair, but not much had changed. Edna still looked far younger than her age and her slight tan indicated she had benefited from some time in the sun as well.

Doug's pickup truck had been stolen in early July. The neighbors couldn't recall a specific date they first noticed it missing, but it was insured and the money allowed him to rent the bubble-shaped sedan parked out front. Doug wore one of the shirts Sergei had bought him in Cairo and a pair of pants he had bought the night before in Buffalo. He hadn't put back on the weight he had lost that summer, but his tropical tan had faded away.

"So have you found any work yet?" she said, leaning back in her chair.

"Funny thing about that," Doug said. "A week after I'm back I get a call from the brewery. They want me back with a bit of a pay raise and a better position." He sipped his glass of red wine. "You wouldn't have anything to do with that, would you?"

"It's only fair," she said, "seeing as I'm the one that had you fired in the first place."

"When Mr. Odenbach offered me the new position he mumbled something about a foreign investor making staffing decisions for him. Didn't sound too happy, by the way."

"He'll get over it. Anyway, I needed you more than they did. When I learned that Sergei was still alive I had to put something together quickly. He's not as young as he looks, you know. I always thought that he knew something about the whereabouts of that diamond and I just knew that if a long-lost relative of Russell Pearce was asking questions, he'd assume that you knew more than he did and move things along for me."

"Let's see then," he said, "you get me fired from the only job I ever had, toss me in the path of a known murderer...."

"I wasn't certain he had killed Russ," Edna said.

"But you were pretty sure. You let me get led halfway around the world on the hope that something would pop up."

"Now that's not fair. Yes, I did send you to Morocco and yes, I knew Sergei would be involved and, yes, I did encourage you to go to Cairo since that's where *I* thought it would be, but I didn't have anything to do with all those things that happened to you. Next thing I know, you're in Singapore. That came as a surprise."

"You were kind of loaded when I called," he reminded her.

"Well it was quite a surprise the next afternoon, I can tell you. In any case, you proved that Charley didn't kill Russ. That makes it all worth it, it's all I ever really wanted. I knew that Charley was innocent all along."

"Of course you did, Charley," Doug said. He took another sip of his wine. "This is good. Cabernet, right?"

Edna sat quietly for a minute. Her index finger tapped the rim of her glass as she looked across at Doug, a smile slowly forming on her face. "Was that a guess or did you know?"

"A guess," Doug said. "But now I know. You were there in Cairo, I saw your picture, but the notes you sent me made it sound as if you learned about it all second-hand. That got me thinking. That and the pronoun."

"The pronoun?"

"Lack of, actually. It was always 'Charley this' and 'Charley that.' You never said 'he.' After a while it sounded funny."

"I stopped being Charley Hodge that week in Singapore. I assumed that if I told you I was the chief suspect in your uncle's murder, you would have never gone."

"So all those comments about Charley's wild encounters with beautiful women were just to throw me off the track?"

"No, those were real. There are some parts of my life I'm not afraid to admit. That doesn't mean I want to discuss them with you."

"And that's fine with me." He remembered Nasser Ashkanani's photograph with Uncle Russ and a young Edna Bowers, and he remembered the old man saying how the woman was too wild for Cairo. And he remembered how the old man said she was the mastermind behind it all.

"When I first heard Russ had been killed I felt so horribly guilty. We had had a little argument in Egypt over a young lady. We patched things up before he sailed but I was still angry. I was so young at the time," Edna said, shaking her head, still a beautiful woman. "I got drunk one night and told Sergei that Russ was taking the diamond to Singapore."

"Sergei is a resourceful man," Doug said. "He would have found him without your help."

"When I think it through, I know I'm not responsible for Russ' death. Years would go by and I wouldn't think about it." She closed her eyes for a moment and Doug could just make out a soft sigh. "Recently, however, I've been looking back a lot. The guilt, as irrational as it is, was getting to me. I needed to know what happened." She looked across to Doug. "Thank you."

"Anything for a friend of the family," Doug said as he checked his watch. "Geeze, I got to get moving. I'm meeting a friend at the Toronto airport. It's her first international flight. She's arriving from Singapore."

"That's wonderful. You going to show her Pottsville?"

"No, we're gonna swing down to New York City for a few days. And I want to stop in Cooperstown, see if I can pick up a ball to replace this one." He held up the gutted remains of the old Reach. "After that? We'll see what happens."

Edna nodded her head and smiled. Doug had seen that smile before. His dad smiled like that when he came to watch Doug play ball. His mom smiled like that no matter what he did. And he'd seen that same smile on Sergei's face when Doug told him how he had solved the murder.

"I saw in *The New Yorker* that Sergei accepted a position with the museum in Brussels," Edna said. "And there's a flattering if somewhat risqué profile on Miss Al-Kady in the European edition of *Vogue*. And as for me, well, you know I'll always be grateful. But it seems, Douglas, that everyone got what they wanted but you."

"Actually I found what I was looking for," Doug said and smiled, "inside a pyramid."